Relentless

Enjoy!

Jordan

Skye xo

SKYE JORDAN

NEW YORK TIMES BESTSELLING AUTHOR

Relentless

A RENEGADES NOVEL

Dedication

For Marina Adair and Joya Ryan
Thank you girls for helping me plot out
this fabulous story of love, loss, and the
powerful magic of second chances.
You ROCK!

One

The smokin'-hot, triple-D gave Troy Jacobs another one of those wicked I'm-gonna-fuck-you-until-your-eyes-cross grins from across the Venetian's concierge suite. Her attention should have excited him. Should have knocked him out of this damn funk. Should have guided his feet her direction.

But Lifehouse hung in the background singing "From Where You Are," layering Troy's melancholy mood with an edge that felt more bitter than sweet tonight. He glanced at his watch and muttered a curse under his breath. He needed to stay and schmooze at least another twenty minutes to make the director happy.

So as the lead singer spoke of distance, wishes, loneliness, and regrets, Troy lowered his gaze to the whiskey in his crystal lowball, resisting the urge to glance out the window for the hundredth time since he'd walked into the suite. A suite with a perfect view of Giselle's gorgeous face splashed across a billboard crowning the Vegas skyline. He worked to repress the familiar blend of frustration and hurt that created anger. Anger that ate at his soul.

"Got somewhere to be?" Zahara Ellis, a member of Troy's stunt crew, strolled to his side with that loose, sexy sway of hers and set her glass of red wine on the window ledge. The scrape she'd earned on the set earlier in the day looked raw against her creamy skin.

"Anywhere but here," he said. "How's that cheek? As soon as you bit the dirt, I knew it was going to leave a mark. It's bruising. You've got a very pretty blue halo going."

She lifted her wineglass and pressed it against the scrape. "Feels better with something cold on it."

Lifehouse's subdued tune transitioned into a fun, sexy riff from Nickelback's newest album, "No Fixed Address," which helped Troy pull his mind from the topic that had been dragging him down for almost a month.

"Was worth it," he told her.

"Easy for you to say."

He grinned, thinking back to the clips they'd come here to watch after a sixteen-hour day. "The dailies rocked."

"Thanks." She grinned, but then winced and let the smile fade. Zahara wasn't an official Renegade, but she contracted with the group when they needed a quality all-around stuntwoman. "You're doing great work with Channing. I know you want to be the one doing the stunts, but you're teaching him a lot."

Troy's gaze skipped to Channing Tatum where he was talking with the producer and director across the suite. "He doesn't need much coaching. He's the kind of actor who could put me out of a job."

"Never." She lowered the glass. "Casey's going to have to work magic with the makeup tomorrow. And speaking of Casey, I feel obligated to give you a heads-up. I overheard her and Becca talking. They've all but got you tied to the bed in your suite, taking turns until none of you can walk in the morning."

He rested his hip against the windowsill and lifted his drink to suck down half the Kentucky Mule floating there, then scanned for the brunette again. Casey had been joined by another dark-haired woman, a production assistant Troy recognized from the set, and now they were both giving him the same look.

"Oh yeah?" he asked, trying to cover for the dive in his mood.

"Oh yeah." The words dripped innuendo, along with a hint of disgust. "Hey, you deserve to play a little. I haven't seen you with a chick since you got here almost a month ago. But the murky depths of those women's minds scare me."

"Thought nothing scared you."

She hummed around a sip of wine. "It's tough to rattle me, but when they started doling out responsibility for the sexual paraphernalia-lube, cuffs, vibrators, anal beads, nipple clamps, cock cages-I have to admit, it turned dicey. I'm more than a little nervous for you. I think you ought to put 9-1-1 on speed dial in case you need to call in the cavalry." Her hazel eyes focused on him. "And, dude, I'm only half kidding."

He purposely tried to engage himself in the idea of a no-strings threesome with the bombshells. Z was right, Troy's schedule had been brutal, but not just for that month. He'd been traveling from gig to gig for going on fifteen weeks. He was in desperate need of extracurricular activity, but he was having trouble working up the interest. And the fact that he was still letting Giselle get to him seven years later seriously pissed him off.

"They must not have seen what kind of day we had." Troy tossed back the rest of his bourbon. "Please tell me you're as sore as I am."

"Hell, yes." Her soft smile revealed perfect teeth that reflected the strip's glow. "I'm going to make one more round of small talk here, then I'm headed to the hot tub, the masseuse, and bed, in that order."

"Damn, that sounds good." He imagined hot water and skilled hands easing his aches and pains. "Why didn't I think of that?"

"Probably because you're too busy thinking about what you've been trying to forget since you got here."

He pulled his gaze from his fellow Renegades stuntmen, Keaton and Duke, where they chatted up a couple of blonde production assistants, and refocused on Zahara. "If that's a riddle, I give up."

Her gaze returned to the window, her focus directly across the strip. She lifted her drink toward the Mirage. "She's really beautiful. So...country fresh, you know? And her voice..." Z shook her head and sighed. "There really are no words. She's absolutely amazing."

Troy's heart took a free fall straight to his stomach. His hands clenched around his glass.

He scanned the people in the room, searching for the leak to his past. Giselle had been long gone by the time Troy had hooked up with the Renegades. Then his mind came around to Rachel, Renegades' former secretary turned location scout, who now lived in Virginia with Nathan Ryker, Troy's best friend since childhood and the closest thing he had to a brother. Which meant...

"Fucking Ryker." he rasped. "This is worse than a family with everyone tattling on each other."

"She just wanted me to know so I could watch your back, make sure your head was two-hundred percent into the stunts. Would you rather she told one of the guys?"

"I'd rather she talked to me about it."

"She was going to, but you've been so busy, you two have been playing phone tag. She thought with the demands of the film, an outside perspective might be better. We all need that sometimes."

"That doesn't make it okay." Nothing about his situation with Giselle was okay with him. Not the way they'd broken up. Not the way she'd ignored his calls the first few months after. Sure as hell not the way she still talked to Ryker but not to him. Never to him. Not one damn word since she'd bailed for the bright lights seven goddamned years ago. And he *really* hated the way Ryker seemed to think Troy was still so fucked up that he might junk a stunt just because he'd seen her picture. "In fact, it's damned insulting."

"Did you know she had the title song for this film before you came?" Zahara asked.

"No." Not that it would have made any difference in his role here, but it would have been nice to know that her face would be splattered over every inch of the strip advertising her *Take Me Home* tour. "Overheard it on set. Ryker could at least have told me."

"I saw her in concert once," Zahara said, "when I was filming in Nashville. She's an incredible performer. Blew the crowd away."

Pride clashed with residual anger and tangled Troy's chest tight. Where Giselle was concerned, his emotions were as complicated as nuclear physics, as touchy as nitroglycerin, and as potent as TNT.

"Her voice is extraordinary, that's for damn sure," he admitted, his own voice edged with a bitterness he hated but couldn't seem to overcome.

"She's really changing up her image. Transitioning from country to pop. They're calling her the next Taylor Swift."

"Fuck that." Troy laughed at the ludicrous understatement. "They aren't even in the same hemisphere talent-wise. Giselle may sing in the country genre, but her voice would rock rhythm and blues, alternative, soul, jazz, contemporary. She's got the vocal dynamics of Mariah Carey and the technical ability of Celine Dion. She's always had a strong voice, but over the years, she's honed it into a fucking powerhouse. And her control…" He shook his head. "It's just unbelievable. She's got Beyonce's dexterity, flexibility, can lift it to be light and airy or push it to be solid, rich, and dark. She's even got a spunky, come-to-Jesus gospel flare she whips out once in a while. It all blends with the emotion she puts into every song and marks her work as something really, *really* special. So, no"-he shook his head, his gaze locked on the carpet-"Giselle is not the next Taylor Swift. She is already *way* beyond any level Swift will ever reach."

Troy forced himself to stop. To shut his mouth even though he could go on and on about Giselle's voice and the individual singing and performing talents that made her truly one of a kind. He lifted his glass toward a man in a black uniform and maroon half apron, who nodded in acknowledgment of his silent request.

When he glanced at Z, her mouth had edged up into a sly little grin. "If you say so, Kanye."

"Ha."

"Where'd a white girl like Giselle get a flare of gospel?"

"One of her foster homes. The mother sang in a Baptist choir and heard Giselle singing while she was folding laundry. Hauled her to church and signed her up. Giselle said she never did another chore because she spent all her time at choir practice. She would have broken out a lot sooner if her biological mother had left her the hell alone."

"Where'd you grow up?"

"Memphis." The bartender delivered his drink. Troy took the glass, held his hand up in a silent request for him to wait, and downed the whiskey in one swallow. Grimacing against the burn, he set the glass on the tray with a rough "Another, please."

Zahara waited until the server was out of earshot before she asked, "All the charity she does is for foster care. Is that how you two met?"

He nodded. "Ryker and I were seventeen when she came to our home."

Z made a soft sound in her throat. "Man, you two got a rough start."

"Rougher for her, a beautiful little white girl raised by addict trash in the armpit of Tennessee." Giselle had been fourteen at the time, with more scars than any one person should carry in a lifetime. "She's lucky the state took her away before her mother got a chance to sell her for a fix. That's where it was headed."

Z shook her head. "How long were you together?"

Troy took the third drink from the waiter and thanked him, then sipped. "Best friends for two years, lovers for three."

"Wow, long time. And so young. What happened?"

"Nashville." *And my own stupidity.* The memories knifed him in the gut. "Nashville happened."

Z waited for more, but when silence thickened between them, she asked, "And you haven't talked to her since?"

"Nope."

"Long time to be carrying a torch. Why don't you contact her? You know, reconnect? The film is the perfect excuse to start a dialogue."

"I'm not carrying a torch," he lied, scowling at Z. He just hadn't realized how hot it still burned until he'd gotten here. "How would you like it if your ex was plastered all over Vegas while you were trying to work?"

She lifted a shoulder, her gaze going distant. "Mmm, don't know. I've never been that much in love."

"Well, take it from me, no one needs that kind of heartache more than once in a lifetime. Besides, she wouldn't recognize me if we passed on the street. I'm a completely different person now-inside and out."

"Really." Z crossed her arms and narrowed her eyes with a sassy smile, lightening the mood a little. "I was under the impression you were *born* a bad boy."

"Bad, yes. But I was white-trash bad. Not bad-ass bad. And our worlds are light years apart now." He gestured out the window. "Look at her, splashed across the fucking *Mirage*, for God's sake." He shook his head and smiled despite the stab of loss. "Man. She really made it."

"So have you," Z said with a little scolding in her voice. "Not too many people can say they've got stupid-ass selfies with just about every Hollywood blockbuster star. Or that their phone numbers are programmed into the speed dial of every big producer in Hollywood in case of a freak problem with rigging on a set. You're equally as famous, just in a lower-profile way."

Troy laughed. "There's an oxymoron for you."

"You're not that different," she insisted, serious again. "You're both in entertainment. You're both here. You're both involved in the same movie." She tipped her head with a devilish glint in her eye and lowered her voice. "Don't you wish she could see who and what you've become?"

Only every fucking day.

"Nope. Like I said, rejection isn't my thing." He sought out Becca and Casey and found them watching his conversation with Z. With a single nod, they sauntered toward him. And even the sight of two twelves on a scale of one to ten coming at his beck and call left him lukewarm. "*That* is my thing now."

"Oh. My. God." Z's hazel eyes rolled. "You really are so bad."

He shot Z a grin. "With absolutely no plans of ever changing. I believe the present is the best way to keep one's mind off the past. And these two lovely ladies," he said, smiling at each as they slid into position on either side of him beneath his outstretched arms, "fit my current needs to absolute perfection. Catch you tomorrow, Z."

Troy guided the women toward the door of the suite, forcing his thoughts off Giselle, off the pain eating at his gut like acid, and redirecting his mind toward the thought of relief through sexual oblivion.

By the time he reached the street with Becca and Casey, the alcohol had softened a few of his rough edges, and the women's attentions temporarily numbed the hurt he'd been living with from his very first sighting of Giselle's photo.

The cool, dry June night air layered a thin film of comfort over him after a very long day working in the caves out in Red Rock Canyon west of town. He didn't even look up at her image as they passed the Mirage, headed toward Troy's favorite sex club in Vegas-an elite, members-only place, offering top-shelf pleasure. He'd scored the membership when his boss and former mega Hollywood star, Jax Chamberlin, had gone and fallen in love. A few tugs on a couple of powerful strings had arranged a transfer of Jax's membership to Troy. He would never have been able to meet the who's-who qualification otherwise.

Tonight was free-sex Friday, which meant the main salon would host live sex on-stage. How that differed from the live sex happening everywhere else in the club he didn't know. But it didn't matter because he was way more interested in the whips and chains residing in the Dungeon anyway. Beyond drinking away his angst over Giselle, Troy couldn't think of any other immediate fix for this desolate ache than fucking it away in the roughest manner imaginable. Booze would hinder his performance on set tomorrow. Sex wouldn't. And, lucky for him, the women at his sides had some hard-core predilections for domination and pain with their pleasure. Or so they'd said. Tonight, he'd see for himself.

They slowed as a limo crept along a driveway leading from the back of the Mirage to the street, cutting off the sidewalk path as it waited to turn onto Las Vegas Boulevard.

"Who do you think's in there?" Casey asked.

Becca glanced up to the top of the Mirage. "Ooo, maybe it's Giselle Diamond. She's headlining here."

"Troy," Casey said, her tone hushing as if someone might hear them. "Go knock on the window and ask for an autograph."

He barely resisted rolling his eyes. "You two are around movie stars all goddamned day, and you still need autographs?"

"She's not a movie star, she's a musician. A singer. My *favorite* singer." Becca turned her pleading brown eyes up to his. "*Please.*"

"She won't open the window for another woman," Casey said, "but she'd open it for a sexy thing like you. Just tell her you're working on the set-"

"No." He didn't mean to bark. He was just so god-damned sick of the way Giselle had been haunting him every goddamned minute of every goddamned day. She was plastered everywhere-billboards, buses, taxis, elevators. She was always in his head, she crept into his dreams...

One of the limo's rear windows slid down. Casey and Becca gasped in stereo, and Troy's gut burned with apprehension.

The rowdy shriek of several women from inside the car pierced Troy's bubble of unease. Three of the limo's occupants popped their heads out the sunroof, one of whom held a champagne flute and wore a plastic tiara adorned with fake jewels.

"Hey, handsome," one of the beauties called from the roof. "We've got a bachelorette party going on here. Want to be the beautiful bride's last hoorah?"

Laughter bubbled from the limo, and Troy's mouth curved. To his surprise, his mood lightened. Maybe a night hanging with a bunch of happy, drunk, celebrating chicks was more what he needed after all. He wasn't lecherous enough to touch the bride-to-be, but there were a handful of other hotties in there.

Before he had a chance to say anything, Becca tugged him toward the rear of the vehicle so they could pass. "Sorry, ladies, we found him first."

They fell into step with the crowd again. "Sure you don't want me to check closer?" Troy teased. "Diamond might be hiding in there among all those women somewhere."

"You're too handsome for your own good," Becca said with a half pout, "you know that?"

He just chuckled. In fact, he did know, but only because he hadn't been all that attractive in his youth. He'd been skinny, struggled with acne, and worn the male equivalent of a perpetual bitch face. So the frequency of women's attentions over the last four or five years continued to surprise, flatter, and amuse him. And for the last few weeks, he'd have to take any flicker of amusement he could get. Now, he found solace in the fact that his role in the film was almost over. He could move on to the next project, where Giselle wouldn't push her way into his every waking moment.

A woman emerged from the shadows of the alley, turned toward the strip, and fell into step with the crowd. The fact that she was alone in a sea of couples and groups caught Troy's attention first, but her hair was what held it—a spill of fat golden curls to the middle of her back. A deep, shiny gold. Not blonde, not wheat, not red. A true, rich gold. The rare but natural color of Giselle's hair.

The woman was alone, dressed in black, wearing a felt hat, and walking with purpose. She'd come from the direction of the Mirage's rear entrance, where all the loading docks and backstage doors lived.

He cut off the little *"Is that...?"* floating through his mind before it could invade his common sense, and tried to smother the tingle of awareness burning in his belly by reminding himself he would *not* run into Giselle on the strip in a city of over half a million people. The color of the woman's hair probably had more to do with the Vegas lights than reality. Besides, she'd never go anywhere in this insane city alone. She was too famous, too recognizable, and her show that night had ended barely an hour before. She'd be soothing her strained vocal cords with a steam bath in one of the Mirage's penthouses right about now, with a staff of thirty to fulfill her every need. Probably had a handful of boy toys fanning her with fucking palm leaves.

The sidewalks were packed. People moved in two main swarms, one in each direction, a standard crowd for a Vegas Friday night. But Troy couldn't let his gaze pull from those curls bouncing gently against the woman's back...

Stop.

This was becoming a real goddamned problem.

Troy purposely slowed his step, letting Goldilocks drift into the sea of people ahead and disappear. And without that little spark of hope, his chest went dark again.

Casey and Becca paused in front of the Bellagio to watch the water show, but Troy couldn't stand still, so he paced along the edge of the crowd.

When he found himself at the alley leading to the club, he peered down the dark, quiet walk. The unmarked purple door was illuminated by a single light and guarded by one big man in a simple tan suit.

The promise of oblivion made Troy's mouth water like a Pavlovian dog.

He turned, searching the crowd for Becca and Casey, but the body count was too high. So he continued toward the club, head down, wondering just what it would take to get Giselle out of his head. Out of his heart. When would he finally be able to put her behind him?

He paused at the discreet entrance and displayed his ID.

"Welcome, sir." The man pulled a royal blue satin half mask from his pocket. "Enjoy your night."

"I have two guests," Troy said, taking the mask. "They stopped for the water show next door. Brunettes. Their names are Becca and Casey."

"I understand." He gave a single nod. "Please, stay near the lobby so you can identify them when they arrive."

Troy agreed, secured the mask, and entered Rendezvous. He lingered in the lobby, waiting for the ladies. The seating areas of the main salon were crowded but not full. From where he stood, he couldn't see any more than various corridors leading to other areas of the club, spaces designed to suit a variety of fetishes and fantasies.

Rihanna's voice pumped out "S&M," and the rich sounds pulsed through Troy's body, releasing a little stress. He wandered into the large room holding the main stage and took in the act playing out there, a live display of erotic dominance. But his gaze glazed over the edgy scene of a woman on her knees, the man standing behind her gripping the end of a leather strap looped around the woman's throat.

He wondered if Z was right. If seeing Giselle now might help him finally let go. Maybe seeing how she'd changed, seeing how completely she'd sold out for fame, would kill his romantic memories. Maybe showing her how well he'd done for himself despite her abandonment would give him that elusive power to cut the last lingering tie she held on his heart.

Getting ahold of her would be tricky, not to mention awkward...

The smack of leather against flesh sizzled through Troy's body and focused his gaze on the stage again. Intricately placed spotlights cast the performing couple in dramatic, almost artistic, shadows. The man brandished a crop in his free hand and brought it down for a swift crack on the woman's bare ass. Her cry of pained pleasure flooded Troy's groin with heat. He was already half-hard.

Lil Wayne's "Pussy Monster" rocked the room as Troy let his gaze roam the woman's body, curvy and luscious and partially naked. Some type of costume that had been pulled down to expose her tits and pushed up to show her ass. Another set of roving lights titillated the audience with flashes of the performers' bodies and gleamed off her spiked heels.

He scanned the space, filled mostly by couples and groups lounging to watch or engage in foreplay before they took their activities into another room. The sight of attractive couples, semi-naked, touching and kissing added blood to Troy's cock, turning it rock hard. He was definitely overdue for a night of mindless, rabid fucking.

"Sir," the bouncer whispered to him from the door. "Your guests are here."

Troy returned to the front, where he vouched for the women, who had donned purple masks, marking them as guests, not members.

"Where should we start?" Becca asked, giddy.

"Let's see what's going on in the other rooms before we decide," Casey said.

When she tugged on Troy's arm, he stayed put. "You two check it out and report back. I'll be…"

His words evaporated as two women emerged from a corridor that led to Champagne Court, an upper-crust sex playroom with plush lounges, soft lighting, and pretty much anything pleasurable that money could buy-from toys to drugs to sexual services.

Goldilocks. The woman from the street strolled out beside one of the club's guides, someone who gave newcomers a tour and explained the rules and prices that accompanied special services. Goldie wore a crimson mask, the color of a prospective member, which meant she'd passed the rich-and-famous requirement. Troy's mind immediately twisted back to Giselle, and nerve endings sizzled in his belly.

And *goddammit,* he hated how this relentless hope of seeing Giselle kept tipping his brain off axis.

"Hel-lo…" Becca waved a hand in front of his face. "Are you with us?"

"Sure." He refocused on the women. "Go ahead. I'll be right here."

They shrugged and disappeared down the hallway leading to the Dungeon.

Troy scanned Goldilocks from the tips of her shiny black rhinestoned spikes to the top of her golden head. She wore a trendy black leather trench that hit her just above the knees, and now held her hat in the tight curl of one creamy fist. And damn those masks. They did an excellent job of hiding a person's identity. It covered her face from her hairline to her nose, curving down to hide most of her cheek. There was really nothing but the woman's hair color to link her to Giselle. Well, that and her size, a smallish five foot three, maybe one hundred and ten pounds. Yet her mere presence made Troy's gut turn somersaults.

His mind spiraled and spiraled, first convincing himself the woman was Giselle, then assuring him she wasn't. Couldn't be. Giselle wouldn't be caught dead in a sex club. And never alone.

The guide tucked one hand intimately into the crook of Goldie's arm, head bent close to speak quietly. As the women inched closer to Troy on their way toward the main salon, the guide said something that pulled Goldie's gaze from the partial view of the stage through the arched opening. The action there now drew deep moans and pleasure-drenched mewls. Goldie glanced toward the guide with a little smile on her lips, but instead of meeting the guide's eyes, her gaze slid past the other woman to Troy. And locked on.

He felt the punch of excitement at the center of his body. Tingles spiraled through his torso, raced down his spine. His mind toggled like a pendulum.

Yes, it's her.

No, it's not.

With her eyes on his, her smile grew. A tentative, nervous smile. And a tiny dimple created a sweet little divot just outside her lips on the left.

Everything inside Troy froze and heated, stalled and raced-his heart, his lungs, his mind.

That dimple confirmed it-this was Giselle.

Every muscle in his body pulled taut, poised to act-to do what, he had no idea, because for the first time in over half a decade, since he'd pulled his shit together after she'd walked away, Troy didn't know what to do or say or think. He couldn't make sense of her presence, still half questioning his own sanity.

The instant recognition he'd expected to see in her eyes never came. She scanned his face, curious, maybe intrigued, then let her gaze slide down his body in a slow search, as if she were trying to place him. But when her attention returned to his face, her expression had shifted in a way Troy could only label as...distant? Disappointed? Aloof? He didn't know. All he knew was she didn't recognize him. All he knew was she turned away.

The grip on his heart tightened.

Yes, he'd changed. Yes, between his mask and his beard, his face was pretty much fully covered. But that didn't stem the pain. It didn't keep the knife from driving into his heart or the irrational insecurity from the past rushing back. In fact, those torturous months of transition at the end of their relationship, when Giselle had risen from unknown wannabe to golden child, flooded back into Troy's head and heart as if it had been seven days ago, not seven years. And he felt the pain of his humiliation at the hands of her new groupies with the strength of a sledgehammer. He'd been downgraded from her best friend to a leech, from her lover to her lesser half, from her strongest supporter for years to her greatest weakness in a matter of months. He'd turned from her everything into absolutely nothing.

And now, even she didn't recognize him.

The guide settled Giselle into a small table toward the back of the room along the far edge of the stage. She faced the door but didn't look at Troy again, and his insides smoldered with irrational hurt and anger. All his issues, issues he'd fought to put behind him, resurfaced, instantly transforming him from a strong, capable, grown man to an angry, abandoned asshole.

The guide exited the salon, and Troy stepped into her path but kept his voice soft when he asked, "Is she alone?"

Her wide dark eyes appraised him before answering. "She is, but she's observing tonight. Prefers to get the feel before she jumps in."

"Thank you." He refocused on Giselle and found her watching him. Their gazes clicked, and fireworks lit off in his gut. But her gaze cut toward the stage, as if she didn't want to get caught looking. Which begged the question-*did* she recognize him after all?

She sat straight, legs neatly crossed, hands resting in her lap. In the midst of a relaxed, sexually open crowd, she looked uptight and out of place. Troy's mind spun and spun, trying to figure out why she'd be in a place like this if she didn't want to be. Or why she was so tense if she wanted to be here. And why in the hell had she come alone? A beauty like her in a place like this... alone? That was just a traumatic experience waiting to happen. One more scar a woman like Giselle didn't need.

He caught his train of thought. What in the hell did he care? She was not his concern. She didn't even deserve his concern. For all he knew, this was some sexual fantasy she was playing out with a guy already here in the club. Or she was waiting for someone to come in. Or...*shit, it didn't matter.*

A man approached her, lowered to a crouch, smiled, shook her hand. She responded in a perfectly appropriate way-with a smile, a shake, small talk. And a rejection. All very tense, uptight, and rigid.

Troy rubbed a hand across his mouth and turned his back on the salon. He wasn't going to be able to stay now. He wasn't going to be able to engage with anyone else tonight. Maybe not for weeks. Or months. And goddammit, that just sucked. He was *still* so seriously screwed up.

Becca and Casey returned and, in the process of wrapping their arms around him and rubbing their bodies along his, turned him partially toward the salon again.

"Ready to get it on, handsome?" Casey purred.

"Let's head straight to Ecstasy," was Becca's suggestion, referencing one of the free-for-all sex rooms where one could purchase the drug of the same name.

Troy glanced at Giselle again. He caught her watching him just before she cut her gaze away, then scraped her bottom lip between her teeth.

The very real possibility that she recognized him and was ignoring him snapped his very last thread of human decency. If he were normal, if he were mature, if he were everything he should be, he'd simply confront her. But he wasn't. He never had been. And even though his logical mind knew he should walk away, even though his logical mind knew nothing could come of watching her here but pain, bad feelings, and disappointment, his heart...or his emotions...or his psyche...*something*...was festering deep inside. It was as if seeing her had tripped a self-destructive switch inside him. As if it was just a matter of time before the fuse burned out, reaching the explosive, and Troy imploded.

And in some sick and screwed-up way, Troy looked forward to it. He relished the anticipation of submerging in the pain that was all he had left of Giselle.

Swinging both arms around the girls' shoulders, he sauntered toward the salon. "Let's warm up in here first."

Two

Giselle had been at the club only twenty minutes, and she was already coming out of her skin with unease. She didn't like the mask color coding. Didn't like being marked as a newcomer. But, if she were being realistic-probably not the best mindset for this environment-she was sure everyone here could tell she was new at this with one glance her way.

She was well into her first glass of wine-wine she shouldn't be drinking-when her cell vibrated. She drew it out of her purse to find exactly what she'd expected-a text from Chad: *Everything okay?*

Giselle tapped out a quick *I'm here and I'm fine,* barely resisting the *leave me alone for a change* that tingled on her fingertips. He was only doing what a good manager did-trying to take care of her.

She was about to stuff her phone away when another text came through. This one from Brook: *So? Is it as bad as you thought?*

Giselle smiled at her personal assistant's question and texted: *Wild. Will call when I get back. Turning my phone off.*

She zipped her silenced phone inside her clutch, then sighed as she picked up the glass and finished off the chardonnay. She'd have to hydrate well tomorrow to counteract the drying effects of the alcohol on her vocal cords.

Letting her eyes fall closed, she tried to collect her scattered thoughts and winging emotions, but the sounds of sex and rap music filled her ears-a female's moans and the slap of sweaty flesh to the beat of raunchy lyrics, only half of which she understood.

It had been so long since she'd felt a man's hands on her body, she'd been both electrified and unnerved by the club's tour alone. The sight of others engaged in hedonistic sex excited and disturbed her in the most… provocative way. And this raw spotlight on sex only amplified the pressure building between her legs. Now, not only were her panties wet, but she felt every pump of her heart, every brush of her skin. She was hot and damp and light-headed.

She opened her eyes and focused on the stage, where a very fit, very intense, very naked man shoved his partner back on the settee center stage. She was as curvy as he was muscular, and threw her arms overhead with the type of abandon Giselle craved but was never allowed. Everything in her life was scheduled, planned, measured, and calculated. Normally, that gave her a sense of security. Until she saw these wildly unscripted pleasure, and she realized what she was missing. What she'd been missing for so very long. And the years of restriction seemed to pile up all at once, giving her a deep and urgent need for abandon and raw connection.

That's not why you're here.

Giselle refocused on the stage. The man dropped to his knees, shoved his partner's thighs wide, and dove between them, ravaging her pussy with his mouth.

The woman's cry coincided with Giselle's sharp gasp of surprise. Lights brightened and faded and swept over their bodies like a sensual touch. The woman's hands reached for the back of the lounge, fingers digging into the shiny fabric as her hips lunged rhythmically against the man's face.

Giselle's sex throbbed. She switched the cross of her legs to ease the ache, but she still felt split in two, half of her wanting what the woman on stage had found while also wanting to bail on this whole idea.

But she couldn't leave yet. Not until she got what she needed.

She let her gaze travel over the spectators. When she heard the term "sex club," she'd always envisioned skeezy, which was what Brook had been referring to in her text, but there wasn't one skeezy inch at Rendezvous. The club definitely catered to the elite. From what she could see, the membership was attractive, well dressed, heavily bejeweled, and on the younger side, between twenty-five and forty-five. The rooms she'd seen on the tour, while wildly varying in theme, were all exquisitely appointed with granite, slate, glass, and stainless steel. A guide monitored every room at all times, keeping it stocked and clean in the most unobtrusive manner she'd ever seen. Of course, the patrons were too busy to notice much of what was going on around them, but the guides, just like the waitresses, were hardly more than shadows.

A middle-aged man with a clean-shaven jaw, an expensive suit, and a royal blue half mask approached her-the third man to approach since she'd taken a seat. The blue mask indicated that he was a member, which meant he was elite and wealthy, possibly famous in some way. His hair was dark, but graying handsomely at the temples. He held a drink in one hand and offered her his other in greeting. "What do you think so far?"

She'd been using her red mask and her newbie status as her out tonight, since she had no intention of getting involved in the activities.

"Little too soon to tell." She shook his hand-quickly, firmly-then deliberately pulled hers away. "I'm not ready to jump into the game just yet. But thank you for the greeting."

His grin widened, and he chuckled. "Don't think I've ever heard such a polite 'fuck off.'"

"I didn't mean it that way." She held his gaze and softened her smile. No one liked to be rejected. "I'm truly just trying to acclimate."

"I understand. Hope to see you again."

"Thank you."

As he moved on, Giselle let out a long, slow exhale of relief, hoping her disinterest in three different men would translate clearly to the other patrons.

Movement near the door drew her gaze, and she glanced that direction as the devilishly hot stranger from the lobby strolled in. His mask was also blue, but his girls were visitors, if Giselle remembered the color-coding correctly. While his face was covered with either mask or heavy scruff, she could still get a feel for his strong, handsome features. And there was just no hiding that body. He wore black slacks and a white button-down, both fitted to all his lean muscle. He had each strong arm curved around a beautiful, built brunette, but his gaze was directly, purposefully, on Giselle as he entered.

Her heart took an extra hard beat. Her breath hitched. And Giselle looked away again. But now she found herself caught between the live, erotic, passionate sex onstage and the stranger who made her think of Troy.

Troy.

Her heart constricted with a bittersweet squeeze. She let her eyes glaze over the empty wineglass in her hand as the pain vibrated through her body like a plucked chord, then slowly stilled, leaving a familiar ache. She'd met men who'd reminded her of Troy over the years-a smile, a voice, a laugh-but none quite as much as this man, yet she hadn't even met him.

And she *really* didn't want to think about Troy tonight. Not here.

Music thumped in her ears, something techno and sexual. The sounds drifting from the stage grew in frequency and intensity. Giselle glanced around for a shadow server. She met the woman's eyes and instantly knew her silent request would be filled.

The level of nonverbal communication here awed her, and curiosity pulled her gaze back to the devil and his demons. He'd taken up residence on a small love seat on the opposite side of the seating area, but instead of watching the rising passion on stage or engaging in foreplay with his two beauties, his heavy-lidded dark eyes watched her.

Giselle held his stare for an extended moment with a strange mix of fear and attraction melding into angst. The thought that he recognized her made alarm burn across her neck. She didn't care what the guide had told her about their strict confidentiality rules, didn't care how Chad had assured her that Rendezvous was secure. She still grew nervous she'd be identified and outed. And had to deliberately remind herself all publicity at this stage of her career was good publicity.

She forced the tension from her shoulders and broke the devil's gaze as a shadow server set Giselle's second glass of wine on the table. She nodded a thank-you and drank deep as dual moans exploded on stage. When she looked up, she found the man banging his partner in a frenzy of hard, quick thrusts.

Like watching a train wreck, Giselle couldn't look away. The open, expressive carnality infused her with an intense craving. The raw, rough sexual acts made something elemental claw at her gut.

God. It had been so damn long since Giselle had been handled like that, she'd forgotten what it felt like. But the sights and sounds brought back memories. Only, the memories were attached to Troy. He'd known how to fuck like the worst of the bad boys, how to make love so sweetly it brought tears to her eyes, and every combination in between.

Giselle took another deep drink and glanced toward the devil, searching for the qualities that reminded her of her first love. Their gazes clicked with an explosive connection, a match to propane. Heat rattled her core and spread outward.

She knew she needed to look away. But something about his gaze challenged her to watch as the women rubbed all over him. One kissed his neck and combed her hand through his long, dark waves. The other knelt between his spread thighs, unbuttoning his shirt, and following the open path with her mouth.

And they did it all while *he* watched *Giselle*.

Why did she find that so...electrifying?

She finished her second glass of wine and spoke to the shadow server when she returned with a third. "Can I get something else, please?"

"Of course." She crouched to Giselle's level and smiled, instantly turning from an elusive slave-like figure to a real woman. The sight helped Giselle relax. "What would you like?"

"A snakebite?" She was ridiculously off the wagon, but if there was ever a time she needed a little Dutch courage, tonight was the night. "Guinness and cider?"

"Absolutely," she said softly. "One of my favorites."

"Thank you."

The woman moved gracefully around the guests and out of the salon. And when Giselle's gaze paused in the devil's vicinity, she found him pushing from his seat, his long muscled body stretching to its glorious full height-his gaze purposefully on hers.

Her stomach grew wings and fluttered, making her a little nauseated. What would she say if he approached her? What if he recognized her?

But her distress was wasted. He simply wrapped his arms around the women he was with and led them toward the lobby...and the various themed sex rooms beyond.

A mixture of disappointment and relief expanded in her gut. This was really for the best because Giselle wasn't just out of her league here, she was out of her sport. Normally, she was ultraconfident. Her childhood hopscotching through foster homes had forced her to speak up for herself. Her adulthood living her life in front of fans and cameras had honed her independence into a buoyant persona that had served her well in her career.

But after Troy, sex became one of those neglected areas of her life. The one she never had time for. The one that nobody tempted her to explore. And one that carried a certain amount of risk as her success grew. Now, sitting at the center of a hedonistic jungle, that self-assured woman dissipated into someone who was more nervous than in control.

So she did what she always did when she found herself in an uncomfortable position-she pretended, something every neglected child excelled at.

She returned her attention to the stage where the male performer flipped the woman onto her belly, guided his cock between her legs, and pounded her from behind. Giselle watched the full length of his impressive cock slam into the woman over and over, each thrust eliciting dual cries of ecstasy.

Her belly squeezed into a ball of desire. But this was a dark desire. A needier, greedier desire she rarely experienced. One that turned her on in a very unique way. And, dammit, she wasn't here to get turned on. She was here to learn how to perform so that others got turned on when *they* watched *her.*

She forced her gaze to the audience, searching for reactions, for…something…that would give her help figuring out how to turn people on from the stage. Which was ironic considering how much of her life she currently spent on stage entertaining thousands. But she only found clusters of people mauling each other. The open display of foreplay en masse short-circuited her sexual connections. Her body experienced overload-overload with no outlet.

This had been a lousy idea on Chad's part. She should have gone to a strip club. There she could at least watch the way women danced to please the customers. But she couldn't very well just stroll into one of those. Maybe she'd rent a few videos. But, what kind of videos would give her what she needed? What she really needed was practice. And just how in the hell would she manage that?

With another shift of her crossed legs, she let out a breath and glanced to her right, searching for the waitress. She was done here. She'd just pound her snakebite, wander back to her suite and pass out.

"Your drink." The smooth, deep male voice came from her left, and Giselle startled, cutting her gaze that direction. Only to find herself eye to eye with the devil. Her belly quaked, then floated.

"Oh shit." She laughed the words, covering her heart with her hand. "You scared me."

"Sorry."

He didn't smile, but the thin lines at the corners of his eyes crinkled with humor, and close up he reminded her less of Troy. His eyes were the same rich color of gooey-just-baked-brownies, but his hair was darker, his lips fuller, his jaw squarer. And his body was much thicker and stronger, carrying at least forty more pounds of muscle. Still, there was something…

"I commandeered your drink from the bartender," he said. "Mind if I sit?"

His voice was deeper than Troy's too. Smoother than Troy's.

And why in the hell was she still thinking about Troy?

"I, um…" she stammered, forcing herself to speak loud enough to be heard over the music, "I'm only here to watch."

"That works for me. You watch them; I'll watch you."

And he was way, way, *way* more confident than Troy.

His moves were swift and smooth as he dragged the other chair closer to hers and slid into it, still managing that casual, I'm-so-hot slouch in a chair far too small for his size. The position made his unbuttoned shirt fall open, showing a muscled chest, ripped abs, and ink on one of his pecs that disappeared beneath the fabric. Giselle's mouth watered without her consent. But she was also annoyed.

"What if I don't want you watching me?"

His mouth tipped up, a little more on the right. "Then you shouldn't have come to a swingers club, angel."

Angel.

The generic pet name plucked that chord beneath her ribs again. Troy had called her angel.

The devil's gaze scoured her face, slid down her neck, and wandered over her chest showing in the deep vee of her dress, making her whole body tingle. She'd decided on a middle-of-the-road, simple, black lace cocktail dress in the hope of melting into the crowd, something she hadn't been able to do since her second album went platinum. But the way the devil was looking at her told her she'd failed again, only this time, it seemed she was interesting for a whole different reason.

"And…" He let the word hang in the air as his gaze slid back up her body and settled on hers. "It would have helped if you hadn't been born so fucking beautiful."

Surprise zinged across her skin. What in the hell did a woman say to *that*?

She picked up her drink and let the velvet Guinness slide down her throat as she pretended to watch the stage, but moving her head and refocusing her eyes made her realize just how quickly the alcohol had hit her.

"Look," she said, glancing his way again, only to find those dark eyes fixed on her face. "I appreciate you bringing the drink, but I'm not here to hook up. Sorry."

"Meeting someone?"

"No. And I don't want to meet anyone either."

"That's easy to do here since we don't use names. You can meet someone without really meeting them." He grinned, oh so full of himself. "Like you're not meeting me now."

She frowned. "You're hurting my brain."

33

He laughed, the sound low and easy and light, then hit her with a very pointed "If you're not interested, why have you been watching me?"

"No, no, no." She wasn't going to let him turn this conversation around. "*You're* watching *me.*"

"You wouldn't know I was watching unless you were watching back."

She couldn't stem the embarrassed grin that lifted her mouth. The alcohol was definitely helping her relax. She shrugged one shoulder and looked away. "You sort of remind me of someone."

"Do I?" he asked with too much intensity, leaning closer. "Who's that?"

"I'd rather not say."

"Is that reminder a good thing or a bad thing?"

She thought of Troy, and for the millionth time since she'd walked away , Giselle wondered where he was now. When she spoke with Nathan, he always assured her Troy was fine, but she never asked for more and Nathan never offered. It was better that way.

"A good thing. A very good thing." Then her mind drifted to the end of their relationship, to the anger, the hurt, the disappointment, and her smile faded. "Mostly, anyway."

"I'll stick with 'a very good thing.'"

She met his gaze again, and deliberately put her past out of her mind. Instead, she scanned her memory for where she might have met *this* man-a party, a concert, backstage...? She met so many people. "Do you...I mean, have we met?"

His expression softened a little, and those brown eyes slid to her mouth as he answered. "Oh, I'd never forget you, angel. Maybe we met in another life...if you believe in that sort of thing."

If she was ever going to believe in such things, tonight would be the night.

"If you're not here to hook up," he said, resting his chin in his hand, "what brought you in? Are you indulging a voyeuristic fetish tonight?"

She wasn't sure what to say to that, because she wasn't interested in either answering or not answering. She really just wanted to enjoy looking at him, listening to his voice, feeling his presence. And he encouraged her to stare with an open, intent, unwavering gaze, as if she were the only woman in the room. As if raw, live sex wasn't pumping on a stage just yards away.

She exhaled slowly and glanced over her shoulder. "Where are your demons, Mr. Devil? Surely you want to go play with them in the dungeon, or purgatory, or some other equally evil room in the back."

Another one of his sexy chuckles brushed the air. "This devil sent his demons away to play on their own. I've got a sudden taste for something more...heavenly... tonight."

His voice was low and smooth and controlled. He was sophisticated, but not in an old-money, corporate, politician kind of way. She would peg him as more independent, clever, off-the-cuff. More...venture capital-like. Someone who ran his own show. A self-made man with money and power, earned from time in the trenches.

And his intelligence seemed more street savvy than intellectual. She liked all that. It meshed with who she was. Maybe that was why she felt drawn to him.

"What do you think of the show?" he asked without looking away.

When she glanced toward the stage, she found the woman on her knees, sucking the guy as if she were ravenous for his cock. The man had one hand tangled in her hair, the other hanging loose at his side. His head dropped back, mouth open on a guttural growl that shook through Giselle.

"Do you like sucking cock, angel?" His voice dropped to a secretive hum and shivered over her skin, lifting gooseflesh. The direct and shocking question sizzled through her body like an open current.

She laughed out, "What kind of question is that?"

"The kind people ask in sex clubs. Is this the first one you've *ever* been in or is this just your first time here?"

Her face flushed with heat, and she was wishing she'd used her common sense and told Chad this idea was ridiculous. "Ever. You must not be a regular here, or you'd know that."

"Mmm, no. I'm from out of town."

"This is Las Vegas. Everyone is from out of town."

His lips kicked up on one side. "True. Where are you from?"

"Good question. Sort of…everywhere, I guess. You?"

"LA."

"And do you frequent these clubs in LA? Is this your lifestyle of choice?"

His smile faded. He pulled in a slow deep breath and let it out with a heavy "No."

She lifted one brow in disbelief. "No?"

"No. This is the only club I belong to, and I don't come often." He returned his gaze to hers, his eyes direct, his expression so serious, he looked almost grim. "I come here when the darkness closes in. I come for distraction. For oblivion. So, no. This isn't the lifestyle I prefer, but one I occasionally need to stay sane."

The pain in his words resonated with Giselle. She hummed in empathy. "I guess we all have scars." When he didn't respond, Giselle returned her gaze to the stage and let her eyes blur over the rising pleasure there as she shored up her barriers for the devil's inevitable departure. Once he'd moved on, maybe she could get out of here without feeling like she was running away like a scared puppy.

Instead of standing, the devil slid his forearm over the table, easing close enough for his scent to touch her nose-an electric balance of musk, spice, and man that made Giselle's bones melt. "Bet you like the power of pulling a man's control right out of his body just like that."

Her head barely moved in a shake to deny it. Her lips parted on a breath to tell him he was wrong.

"Look at him," he said before she could speak. He took her chin between his fingers and gently eased her head back toward the stage. Her skin tingled beneath his touch. His voice lowered to a conspiratorial hum. "Look at how she's controlling him. Controlling his pleasure.

Giving enough to make him want more, then taking it away until he's willing to do anything to feel her hot, wet mouth squeeze and suck and stroke until he comes."

Her pussy surged at his words. His dirty talk was seriously hot. She ached and throbbed. Her breasts swelled tight, and her nipples stood on end, so sensitive even the brush of her dress's silky fabric shot a tingling sensation deep between her legs.

Giselle cleared her throat softly, trying to find a response with a brain that was suddenly soaked in a combination of alcohol and need. Her heart beat in her ears. Her breath came quick and shallow.

"Bet you like controlling a man like that. Like teasing and playing until he's begging you to suck him off." His fingers feathered over her jaw, around the shell of her ear, down her neck, leaving a blinding trail of heat. "Bet you like the salty taste of a man when he fills your mouth. The powerful sensation of his release deep in your throat."

Giselle pulled her gaze from the excitement on the stage, her eyes narrowed on his face, and she gave in to the irresistible urge to lick her lips. His full mouth kicked up in a knowing smile, showing a small crescent of absolutely perfect teeth-sparkling white and completely straight. Which only made her think of the way Troy's had overlapped a tiny bit.

Then he slid his thumb slowly along her still-wet lower lip, his eyes following, and Troy slipped out of her mind again.

"That mouth of yours was created to suck cock," the stranger murmured. "Full lips, strong jaw...Bet your mouth wrapped around a cock would take a man directly to heaven." He paused and barely whispered, "Want to go to heaven with me, angel?"

Yes.

Absolutely.

"No." The word came out weak and hesitant, so she said it again. "No. I'm just here to-"

"Maybe you'd rather get sucked." The backs of his fingers traveled up and down the side of her neck, flooding her with heat and tightening her breasts. "Do you want my hot mouth on your pussy? Tasting you? Licking you? Fucking you with my tongue? Fingering you open until I find your clit, then taking it between my lips and sucking...sucking...sucking...? Oh, so good. I can almost taste you."

"Please stop." Her skin had become so sensitive, she couldn't take the slide of his fingers on her neck and covered his hand with hers, pulling it away. "I'm just here for a little research. I'm not interested in participating, as inviting as it may be. I'm sorry."

He'd twisted their fingers around until his big hand covered hers, but he held it lightly. The calluses scratching her skin confirmed her theory of him being a self-made man. And that piece of information, more than any other single thing she'd learned, was a huge turn-on.

"Research," he said, his voice entertained, possibly a little condescending. "Looking for some ideas to spice up the bedroom at home?"

"It's for work." She picked up her glass and drank. She should have stopped at two glasses of wine so she had more control over her barriers. This intimate pressure from a stranger made her want to run. And it was too soon to run. If she left now, she'd walk away feeling stupid and weak and ashamed.

"What kind of work do you do?" he asked.

The fact that he didn't recognize her eased a sliver of stress. "I'm in entertainment."

"Ah," he said, sitting back, his hand still lying over hers, his fingers stroking absently. "You work at a club like this, then?"

She laughed, relaxing a little. "No."

"Stripper?" he asked with a teasing edge now. "Escort?"

She laughed harder. "No, look-"

On stage, dual climaxes hit, the performers' vocal enjoyment drowning Giselle's brush-off and shooting what was left of her nerves to hell. She was officially fried.

"I'm in entertainment too," the devil said, drawing her attention back to him once the moans and groans died down.

"What?" she asked, unable to follow the conversation in such a bizarre setting. The overstimulation dragged her mind in five different directions, the dim lighting cast shadows over everything and everyone, and the alcohol was starting to mess with her head. She focused on his grin. A hot, teasing, I'm-so-messing-with-you grin that sparked her impish tendencies. "Entertainment, huh? Do you work at a place like this?"

He chuckled, and the warm sound tingled through her belly. "No."

"Stripper, then? Escort, maybe?"

"No." He laughed the word, then grew a little more serious. "I'm in movies."

"Oh." She drew out the word as if everything made sense now. She grinned and pointed at him with a lazy gesture. "Porn. I could totally see that."

He dropped his head back and laughed. The sound was so deep, so rich, so absolutely buoyant it turned just about every head in the room and made Giselle smile. And, yes, once again, she heard a little of Troy in his laugh.

"Oh damn," he said, his voice light and happy. "That was good."

The sizzle in her belly told her it was time to leave. This was the kind of man who could get her in big trouble.

She picked up her purse. "Look, it was nice talking to you, but I'm about done here."

"Already? You could have gotten that"-he swung a loose gesture toward the stage-"on the Internet and saved yourself fifty bucks in drinks."

He was right. "Well, I tried." She stood. "It just didn't turn out to be what I needed."

"Why don't you tell me what you're looking for? If I can't give it to you, I promise to point you in the right direction."

She shook her head and reached for the glass, grabbing a sip for the road. "I don't think you can help me."

She'd gotten two steps toward the door when he said, "Hope you find what you're looking for, angel. The experience makes the performer."

Her feet stopped, his last sentence resonating in her head. In her heart. An expression she'd heard while filming her music videos. "What?" She turned to face him. "What does that mean?"

One shoulder rose in a lazy shrug. "That's why you're here, right? To gain the experience of a swingers club so you can accurately portray it…somewhere else?"

"I'm not an actress."

He laughed softly, but the sound wasn't nearly as happy as it had been moments ago. One finger rose to slide around the rim of her half-finished snakebite, his gaze following the motion as if drifting in thought. "We're all actors to some degree, aren't we?"

That was an insightful statement. And if he was in movies, he had to know more about acting than she did-because she knew a thimbleful in an ocean of information. She didn't even act onstage in concert. While she rehearsed with a choreographer for flow and audience engagement, everything she did was natural. Everything she did was what she'd do anyway, maybe just in a different order or from a different location onstage.

This devil could easily be full of shit-they were in Las Vegas, after all, and everything here was one type of façade or another-but he also had to be someone to have a membership. Which meant he might be a great source of information.

She strolled back to stand in front of him and crossed her arms. "Go on."

"It sounds like you're looking for the same input method actors use-drawing on an experience to research a role, gaining the emotional, psychological, physical, sensory information they need to transfer into the character they're portraying."

When he paused, she said, "Maybe I am."

His smile flashed, then instantly faded. "So, why don't you tell me what kind of role you're going for? If you can't find the experience here, there are several other clubs in the city that might work for you."

She glanced away. "I can't go to those other clubs."

The curtains reopened, and a new couple wandered onto the stage. She didn't think she could handle another show like the last. Not without coming apart at the seams.

She heaved the air from her lungs and faced the devil, but she stared at the ink disappearing beneath his shirt, wondering what he'd depicted so permanently on his skin.

"It's…just a part in a music video," she said, "which includes simulated sex. There will be cameras and lights and costumes and makeup and crew and…"

Her throat grew so tight with the admission, she had to pause to deliberately draw air. She licked her lips. He was staring again, those dark eyes so intense, it felt like he was digging around in her soul.

"Anyway," she said, growing uncomfortable, "I'll figure something out."

"So," he said, catching her just as she turned for the door again. She turned back to find her half-empty drink in his hand. "Why didn't you just bring your man and get it on in one of the rooms? Most guys would jump at that opportunity"-his gaze slid along her body again-"especially with a woman as gorgeous as you."

"I don't have a man in my life at the moment."

He laughed. "Bullshit. A woman like you always has a man-or five-in her life."

"Actually, I do have five, but they're my coworkers... or, more like employees...not my lovers. My career is all-consuming."

"That's...a serious injustice to all of mankind."

She laughed. "Just a tad overstated, but thank you." She glanced toward the stage, where a man was hooking a woman to a metal screen with cuffs at all four corners. "Ugh. This is too much. I'll figure something else out."

"I have the perfect solution."

She met his gaze. "Unless it's a solution that *doesn't* include screwing you, I'm not interested."

His eyes narrowed thoughtfully. "If that's your line in the sand, I'll respect it. And I'll still give you the experience you need." With his eyes on hers, he finished off the snakebite and set the glass down. "If you want to nail that part, angel, I'm exactly the man you need."

Three

This was *so* not what Giselle had planned for her excursion tonight. And as the devil pulled open the door to a room called Indulgence, he also kept what felt like a possessive grip on her waist. A grip that created opposing sensations in her body and mind.

You've gone too far, a little voice whispered in her head. *What are you thinking?*

Inside, the room was illuminated by hundreds of candles and subtle cove lighting. It smelled of exotic flowers and soft spices. Giselle fumbled for something to do with her hands since she'd stopped at the front desk and left all her belongings in a locker. The guide hadn't shown Giselle this space, probably because it wasn't one of the most popular. While the dungeon had been filled with dozens of couples and several groups, Indulgence held four other couples and one threesome, each in various stages of undress, some engaging in full-on sex, others performing oral sex, and still others toying with foreplay. The music was far more sedate, quieter and sexier while still edgy.

The existence of clothing gave Giselle a little room to breathe. When she'd taken the tour, the guide had explained that clothing was only allowed in the main salon and two other rooms in the club. All other areas required partial or full nudity to enter. But even without being forced to strip, her chest felt as if it were wrapped in steel.

She still wasn't sure exactly how this man had charmed her just enough and in just the right way to get her back here, but her sex ached, and all she wanted to do was turn into him and lose herself, yet she wasn't ready to make the first move. And wasn't that just a big fat laughable irony? The woman who was considered borderline animalistic in her single-minded ambition to hone her craft and build her career didn't have enough self-confidence to take the first step with a guy.

The devil's hand slid up her back and beneath her hair, where he took a gentle but possessive hold on her neck. Giselle curled her fingers into fists and dug her nails into her palms to quell her jittering nerves.

One wall of the room held platforms with mattresses and ornate chairs. Mirrors were scattered throughout the space, reflecting darkness and debauchery. A few private rooms had been tucked into corners, where drapes were gathered to one side in a pretty swag. The sultry duo, Krewella, floated on the air.

The most eye-catching elements of the room were three thick poles stretching from floor to ceiling, each spearing a lighted glass platform. One of the mini stages had been raised off the floor twenty feet or so, where a woman rode her partner bronco style.

"You are wound wire tight, angel," he murmured, as they strolled around the edges of the room.

His hand massaged her neck, and she wanted to touch him, but she wasn't sure how, didn't understand the rules or the etiquette in this strange new land, not to mention one of the reasons she'd come in the first place-that it had been so long since she'd had physical contact with a man, she feared she'd forgotten what to do and how to do it.

"You'll be uncomfortable during the video shoot too," he said. "And you probably won't have as much alcohol in you as you've got tonight."

They passed bodies writhing and rocking. Groans filled the air, making Giselle's hands fist. A string of pleasurable mewls made her sex clench.

"I want you to take that little voyeuristic streak of yours," he said quietly, "and soak in the material. Let the anxiety build. Let it grow and expand until you feel like you're going to pop. Until it becomes bigger than you are. Then, you'll focus your mind on whatever purpose you choose and drive all the potential energy from that anxiety into your target."

They paused beside one of the glass platforms at floor level. A purple-blue neon light framed the base, and a clear wall created a safe border. He turned toward her, cupped her face in both hands, and stroked her cheeks with his thumbs. His eyes were warm and rich, rimmed in sooty black lashes, his gaze so completely intent and focused and compassionate.

"Now, put theory to practice. Stop fighting the anxiety and use it. Give in to it, harness it, and let it drive."

He paused, watching her, waiting for her to follow his instructions.

Giselle took in a deep breath, relishing his masculine scent, and let it out slowly, purposefully releasing the tension knotting her shoulders. She gathered all the anxiety and stress and fear scattered throughout her body, drawing it in and focusing on him the way she would focus on whoever the producers cast as her lover for the music video.

"Good." The single word drew her gaze to his lips, and they moved slowly with, "Now where does it take you?"

Almost without thought, she lifted her hands and pressed them against his abdomen. She shivered at the first intimate skin-to-skin contact. He was as firm and supple and hot as he looked, and Giselle sighed in utter appreciation. She slid her hands beneath his open shirt, then stepped close and let her hands wander. And, *God*, he felt more amazing than her altered senses could fully appreciate.

"Very good." His lids grew heavy, eyes hot with lust. "As you've so perfectly demonstrated, giving in to the fear is the fastest way to regain control. Let's take the next step."

He slipped one finger beneath the strap of her dress and lifted it off her shoulder. Then lifted his opposite hand to the other strap. Giselle sipped a breath and covered his hand with hers. If that fabric fell over her shoulder, the dress would slide to her feet.

By the spark of challenge brightening his eyes and the dare edging his smile, he already knew that. "This is the next step, angel. Unless that simulated sex scene is going to take place clothed…"

Damn. Her eyes slid closed.

She took a breath.

Bit the inside of her lip.

And released his hand.

But he didn't move.

"Open your eyes," he said quietly. "Are you in control or is your anxiety? Choose yes or choose no, but *own* your decision."

Anger and fear blended. Her mind hyperfocused on where she was and what she was doing. Then she channeled her options-moving forward or backing out. Backing out left her right where she was when she'd come in. That was unacceptable.

She opened her eyes and met his directly.

He took a second to scan them, read them, then gifted her with a full, gorgeous smile. "I knew you had it in you."

And flicked the other strap off her shoulder.

Her dress eased down her breasts, her belly, slowed as it glided over her hips, then vanished into a pool of darkness at her feet.

And the devil's hot gaze followed every inch of its retreat.

Giselle forced her eyes to stay open when they wanted to close, but let them blur in the distance. And her mind raced.

What am I doing?

What in the hell am I doing?

Air hissed through his teeth, and Giselle forced her eyes to focus. But he was still scanning her body, his hungry gaze stroking her like a touch and kicking up heat.

"Fucking beautiful." The raw sincerity in his voice pushed a thrill through her veins. Then he offered his hand and gestured to the glass platform. "Are you ready to take your stage?"

Panic trilled along every nerve. She glanced sideways, found a couple along the edge of the room watching them, then looked around, and found everyone watching. She swallowed, met his eyes again, and admitted, "I don't know if I can do this."

He lowered his hand. His voice was patient, but his gaze was direct. "If you can't do it now, here, in the dark with a stranger you'll never see again, around a bunch of other strangers you'll never see again, you can kiss that video role good-bye. Because when you shoot that simulated sex scene, there will be lights, cameras, and action with two dozen stagehands and cameramen looking on."

Giselle cut her gaze to the floor and swallowed again. Her throat was dry, her stomach felt raw. This wasn't all that different from the extreme butterflies she used to get-sometimes still got-before a performance. And if she wanted to take the next step in her career, she had to get past this.

Bigger deals and bigger venues went to bigger names. She'd maxed out the leverage on her talent. She was considered one of the strongest voices in the business, one of the freshest songwriters of the decade. But that only sold so many tickets. Following sold more. Lots more. And Giselle needed a bigger following.

Sexy sold. And as Chad liked to tell her, over and over and over again, she had to be the woman other women wanted to be, the woman men dreamed of. That would give her the following she needed to break out.

"Your call, angel," the devil said, sweeping one hand through her hair. "What's it going to be?"

She should tell him to go find a real woman, someone who could fulfill the animalistic urges he'd come here to satisfy. But in her gut, she knew that woman resided in her somewhere. She'd just been buried for a long time. For whatever reason, he'd given up on two sure things to spend time with her, and he'd already given her some of what she'd come here to find. She wanted to give back. Even if he was a stranger she'd never see again, she wanted to give him a little taste of success for his efforts.

She lifted her eyes to his with an overwhelming sensation of vulnerability, but some of the apprehension had softened beneath the alcohol's effect. "Can you lead?"

His smile flashed white-hot, and this time, it was edged with arrogance. An arrogance Giselle was pretty sure he'd earned. "I was born to lead."

Stretching his arm out to her, he offered his hand a second time. "Let the show begin."

Troy was going straight to hell.

He'd suspected as much for a long time. But as Giselle laid her fingertips in his, Troy knew he was going straight to the very *bowels* of hell.

She was scared, way out of her element, and she needed him-needed him to show her how to get into her role for this video. Needed him to make her feel safe. Needed him to satiate the lust making those ocean-blue eyes shine. The sight gave him an unholy thrill that vibrated through his body. And the fact that she didn't recognize him only added a wicked kick to his excitement.

Oh yes. There was no doubt about it. Troy would be seated at Satan's side for eternity.

Might as well enjoy life while he could.

He turned and drew her toward one of two unclaimed frosted-glass platforms. He'd never been in this room before, but by the light and shadows pouring over the couple still rocking another glass shelf above, the sight was undeniably provocative. Perfect for a show.

The glass shelf was deep and wide with plenty of space for a couple to maneuver safely. Still, when he pressed the controls, he only lifted the glass five feet, roughly eye level for the spectators on their own stationary platforms circling the room.

Coldplay's "Magic" filled the space as the floor moved smoothly and slowly beneath their feet. Troy faced Giselle, threaded their fingers and lifted their joined hands overhead, stretching her beautiful body for everyone to see. And as they turned a slow circle, he scanned her for the first time in seven long years, taking in every sexy curve and taut plane.

Simply stunning. Small and utterly feminine, she'd turned from a girl into a woman over the years with a luscious fullness to her breasts, a deeper roundness to her hips. He could see the work she'd put into her voice with a strong core in her tight waist and flat abs. He could see she was still a girly-girl by the pink satin thong and bra lined with a heavy helping of sexy black lace.

The mere act of sliding his gaze over her beautiful body made a distant but consuming ache build deep in his body, one that encompassed every part of him-body and soul.

The pain sparked anger. A complex, self-protective, brooding anger. He'd spent seven years feeling helpless when it came to his lingering feelings for Giselle. Seven years feeling out of control and tossed aside and worthless whenever he thought of her.

All he wanted was release from that haunting grip. Giving Giselle what she was looking for tonight might just end up giving him what he needed most as well-closure. She wouldn't feel or taste as good as he remembered. She wouldn't fill the emptiness in his soul as she once had. He'd give her the experience she needed to succeed. He'd have one last chance to feel her again. Just feel her and release her. Feel her, release her, and move on.

It all seemed like a pretty fair deal.

He stopped with Giselle on the outside of the platform, closest to the audience. Her gaze cut toward the cluster of couples gathering for the show. Even the pair on the higher platform moved lower for a better view.

He lowered her arms and released one hand to take her chin between his fingers, bringing her gaze back to his. For someone who breezily captivated thousands of fans per concert, her discomfort both surprised and pleased him. Here in this moment, she still needed him-for support, for guidance, for security. At one time, being needed by Giselle had been his life's sole purpose. Now, it gave his otherwise full life a spark that had been missing since she walked away.

"Look at me." He cupped her cheek, holding her gaze to his. "From this point forward, it's just you and me, and our job is to put on a show. We are performers. Those people are our audience. And you will deliver, because you're a professional. Right?"

She pressed her lips together, but her gaze focused, her mind's eye homing in on the goal. "Right."

"Good girl." He slid his hands to her waist. "Face the people you're here to entertain."

She pulled her lower lip between her teeth. The sight made him ravenous, but he planned on getting out of here tonight without ever tasting her again. Because that might be the one thing that could drag him under.

When she didn't move, he said, "Take control of that anxiety, and turn."

When she obeyed. Troy circled her wrists, dragged her hands to the edge of the clear railing, and curved her fingers over the slim edge. "They're all here to see you, Goldilocks," he murmured at her ear and fitted his rigid cock to the low curve of her spine.

The perfect fit made his chest cave a little. Her scent filled his head, the soft floral tease of a perfume called *Forever.* The perfume Troy bought for her. The first perfume she'd ever worn. The fact that she still wore it tore at something deep inside him.

"Let's give them what they came for." He started by stroking every inch of her body.

His hands roamed up her arms, over her shoulders, and down her back. By the time he'd wrapped his arms around her waist, she was writhing to his touch and in time to the music...just like he remembered. Her soft moans electrified his skin and flooded his cock...just like he remembered. And when he slid his hands to her tits, cupping and squeezing the perfect mounds beneath the silk, her nipples puckered, her back arched, and her ass rubbed his cock...just like he *fucking* remembered.

I'm so screwed.

He forced the thought away. He was in control here. He knew this would be over as quickly as it began. And he would be the one to walk away this time.

Lowering his hands to her hips, he stroked her tight, perfect ass. Let his hands fall down the backs of her thighs, then whisper up the front. The heat of her pussy touched his hands long before he reached that sweet spot, and when he stroked her lightly, her hips rocked into the touch.

The movement consumed Troy's gut with fire and made him hungry. Starved. Greedy in a way he hadn't been in years. Controlling this was going to be harder than he thought.

"Let your mind go," he whispered and dropped a kiss to her shoulder. "Focus on the feeling in your body."

He lifted her arms overhead again, but pulled them back to circle his neck. As she moved with the position, her ass rubbed his cock. Heat washed his lower body, and he moaned into her ear. "Rock me, baby," he said with a gentle thrust against her. "Lose yourself in the music. Lose yourself in the show."

Her fingers dug deep into his hair, and she swayed against his groin. Troy's air released on a growl of deep satisfaction, and he let his teeth settle into the flesh at the base of her neck. Her gasp confirmed that bite of pain still excited her.

Her head dropped back against his shoulder, and her body rocked and retreated. Again. And again. And again. The thrill swamped Troy's brain with a burst of white light.

"Oh yeah, give me more." He slid his hands down her arms, her sides, stroked the swell of her breasts, then roamed her taut abdomen. She was perfect. So fucking perfect. Smooth, warm, tight, sweet. And this wasn't enough. Not nearly enough. Dammit. *Dammit.* "I want it all. Give me all you've got. Feel me. Smell me. See me in your mind's eye. Imagine watching us grind from the floor. Commit it all to memory."

Her soft sound of heightened pleasure clawed at his gut. He lowered his lips to her shoulder and opened his eyes, watching her gorgeous body writhe beneath his hands. The sight of his rough, calloused hands stroking her smooth, perfect skin was so erotic. The toned curves of her backside massaged his cock, caged in his slacks. What he would give to strip her naked and take her long and hard right here, on the glass, in front of all these eyes. Witnesses to his heart's release.

Giselle turned her head and kissed his neck. Troy's brow tightened with the sweetness of it, the warmth of her mouth, the stroke of her tongue against his skin. That was good. It was all so good. He could feel the tangled knots in his heart loosen, freeing him. Finally.

Fucking finally.

He lifted his head, opened his eyes, and saw them reflected in a mirror across the small space. The sight shocked him for a long moment. She looked like a goddess, her hips rocking and rubbing, her hands in his hair, her mouth on his neck.

"Look," he said, leaning back to break the suction she had on his pulse point. One that made him more than a little crazy. "Look across the room."

But instead of doing as he asked, she fisted one of the hands in his hair and pulled his head down, dragging his mouth to hers. He tried to pull back for all of three seconds, until the feel of her lips registered, and he melted.

Giselle's lips on his.

How many times had he dreamed of this over the last seven years? Thousands? Hundreds of thousands? The sweetest ache he'd ever known swamped his chest. His brain cleared completely, and he just floated in the moment. A moment he never wanted to end, even while knowing it had to end. Soon. Because he felt himself slipping...

Then she pressed her tongue into his mouth and hungrily searched for his. When they touched and swirled, when she sighed into his mouth and softened against him, everything inside Troy softened too. Which was when he knew he was *seriously* fucked.

This stupid stunt had backfired.

And while his mind spiraled for a Plan B, Giselle ate at his mouth in hungry licks and bites, condensing his mind to mush.

She broke the kiss with a breathless "You kiss like a *god.*"

Troy lost it. He just snapped. Too much denial buried too deep. Too much pressure for too long. It had to come out sometime.

He gripped her jaw, pulled her head back, and covered her mouth again. Tasting her with all the hunger in his starved soul. Knowing he'd never taste her again, never touch her again, he took and took and took. But it wasn't enough. He couldn't get enough. And this was why he couldn't ever let go, because he couldn't ever get enough. He always needed more.

She turned her head to escape his mouth and took deep gulps of air. "Can't breathe."

He couldn't breathe either, but it was because his stupidity was choking him to death.

Just like he had then, he was smothering her now because he couldn't fill this goddamned hole inside unless she was his. All his. Two hundred percent *his.*

Searching for control, he slipped his fingers between her breasts and popped the latch of her bra. Back to business.

She stiffened and released his head, her hands lowering to cover herself. But his arms were in the way.

"Let them see," he said. "You're gorgeous. Share it. With them. With me. Let me touch you. They want to watch me touch you. You need to feel me touch you."

Her body softened again, and he replaced her arms behind his head. Molding his hands to her ribs, he slowly slid upward, until he pushed the bra cups out of the way and her breasts were in his hands. He leaned his head against hers. "Perfect. So perfect."

So soft, so plush, so taut. Her nipples puckered into knots beneath his palms. And as he brushed his fingers across the hard flesh, she hissed in a gasp.

"Open your eyes. Look at what you're doing to the others." He kept his touch featherlight, something that used to drive her crazy. "Look at how they can't take their eyes off you. Feel their eyes on your skin. Imagine their gazes creating this feeling on your nipples."

She whimpered and rubbed her ass against his erection. Lust hit so hard and so fast, his whole body tightened. His fingers clamped down on her nipples, and Giselle cried out. *"Yes."*

The spike of pleasure dug deeper, the bodies around them writhed faster, echoing Giselle's pleasure. And driving Troy's.

He pressed his forehead to her shoulder. Forced his mind to clear. And found a sliver of control just as she tried to turn in his arms.

Troy held her still out of desperation. If she turned into him, wrapped him in her arms and loved him, he'd break.

He needed to bring this to an end.

Reaching behind him, he hit the controls, and the glass lowered as slowly as it had risen. By the time it touched down, Troy was ready to run.

But when he released her to exit the platform, she turned into him. Her arms snaked around his body, slid underneath his shirt. Then all Troy could focus on was her perfect curves and warm bare skin pressed against his. A desire he hadn't felt in years welled up inside him and flooded over.

As if she meant to snap his one thread of resistance, she looked up at him with those big blue eyes, all smoky with desire-the way he'd dreamed she'd look at him again for seven fucking years, and said what he'd dreamed she'd say to him again for seven fucking years. "More. I want more."

Desperation gnawed a hole through his heart. He gripped her arms, closing his fingers tight, and met her gaze deliberately. "You don't want more of me, angel. We're from different worlds."

He pushed her back, but even the relief of getting all that skin off him didn't help, because now she was on full, gorgeous display in nothing but a thong and heels, and she wasn't grappling for her clothes.

He reached for the bra he'd dropped on the stage and the dress at her feet, but she was still standing there with that hot gaze on him when he straightened.

"I'm willing to give you what you need-"

He wrapped one hand around the back of her neck and fisted her hair, fighting to hold his voice down. "You have no fucking idea who I am or what I need."

She pulled in a sharp breath but looked more confused than scared. "Then tell me."

He needed to get her the hell away from him before he took exactly what he wanted, exactly the way he wanted it.

"The way I need to fuck you is not nice. It's not slow or sweet. I need to fuck you hard and dirty. I need to hear you scream and beg. I need to fuck you by my rules, cuffed and tied. I need to hear the sound of leather smack your bare ass, need to see red welts rise on your tits."

Her eyes were wide. Her lower lip disappeared between her teeth. He was finally reaching her. But she wasn't running yet, so he lied some more.

"I need to fuck you anywhere you can take it, and I need you to do exactly what I say, exactly where I say, exactly when I say." He paused, let it all sink in, while all he could think about was what he really needed: her perfect body on a featherbed, somewhere quiet and extremely private. Where he could kiss and touch her and make her writhe with pleasure, not pain. "Am I making myself clear?"

"Yes. And, yes, I still think you're exactly what I need."

He shook her, angry she didn't run from him. "How would you know?"

"Because I'm dripping wet."

Fire flared through his body, licking his cock, filling his balls, rising through his belly. "Then why are you shaking?"

"I'm excited."

"You're scared."

"A little," she admitted. "But I'm channeling my anxiety into exactly what I want-you."

The hell of this was, she *didn't* want *him*. She wanted the stranger she thought he was. And that hurt. It hurt on top of all the other hurt. Which helped Troy gain perspective.

This was no fantasy. This was no reunion. This was… nothing. Absolutely nothing. Just like every other fuck he had here. Every other fuck he'd had over the last seven years.

Nothing.

The only thing he could do with this opportunity was turn it into what he'd hoped for in the beginning, a chance to put Giselle behind him once and for all.

"I don't play games." His gut felt as heavy as concrete. "There are no safe words. No means no. Stop means stop. If you use either of those words, whatever's happening will instantly end. I'll walk out. It will be over. Do you understand me?"

"Yes." Her eyes were wide, flooded with a mixture of relief, trepidation, and excitement, which made him crazy. "Yes, I understand."

Fine. He had an out. Because based on what he knew of Giselle, she might talk big, but she wouldn't be able to handle the kind of sex delivered at a sex club.

Four

Giselle forced herself not to drag her dress from his hand to cover up for the short walk to a cozy corner room. At least it looked cozy at first glance, but as the devil let the single drape fall closed over the opening, Giselle darted a look around.

Her gaze passed over a strangely shaped lounge, mirrors, hooks on the wall holding...

"Choose a collar," he ordered behind her, making her jump. "A wide one."

She was shivering with nerves, with lust, with a dark streak of the unknown. But he had already pushed her past every boundary she'd never believed herself capable of hurdling. In their short time together, he'd taught her a simple but powerful lesson on harnessing anxiety and putting it to use in powerful ways. And she believed he had a lot more to offer-more wisdom, more insight, more pleasure.

More everything.

But as she stroked her fingers over the leather collars, she was intensely aware of the huge gap between wanting something and getting it.

So she did exactly what he'd taught her to do-she balled up all the anxiety thrumming through her body and drove it into choosing a thick black leather collar. Hardly more than a crazy necklace, right?

He took it from her hand. "Turn around."

She obeyed, and her whole body strained with tension as he fastened it around her neck. The mirror's reflection hit her hard and made her mind slide sideways. She watched as he ratcheted the leather tightly. Her body looked sleek and so intensely sexual in her sweet little thong and spiked heels, with the blood-red mask covering most of her small face. She had the strange sensation of watching it all happen to someone else. Could almost have made herself believe it if her body wasn't exploding with sexual need.

The lusty music mixing with the sounds of sex beyond the curtain made her body ache, made her sex full and wet, made her shift on her feet. And as he fastened the buckles on the collar, her vision faded at the edges, her neck muscles strained, and her breaths came quicker.

This was definitely not some crazy necklace.

She lifted her hand, sliding her fingers between the leather and her skin.

"Claustrophobic?" he asked.

Shallow wisps of air made the tension in her body ratchet higher. "Yes."

"Good," he said, his voice rough and knowing. He let the heavy mass of her hair tumble down again and stroked all ten fingers through the strands, his gaze following the motion. "It will get worse before it gets better."

A sharp strike of panic cut through her, lightening her head and making her sway. He slipped one arm around her waist from behind, steadying her. He had the strangest way of reading her. Of knowing what she needed when she needed it. Of knowing when to push her and when to ease off.

And when she'd steadied, his hands slid slowly up her body, feeling all the curves in her waist, all the ridges in her abdomen before cupping her breasts. He didn't rush into sex, as she'd expected. He lingered, touching her as if they had all night. The way he so expertly squeezed and pinched and brushed her breasts and nipples until she had to rub her thighs together to ease the desire building between her legs made her wonder if there were some men in the world who were so experienced they knew every hot button on a woman.

Giselle had never imagined being attracted to a man like that, a man to whom she was nothing but another lay, but tonight, that wasn't even on her problem radar. She had all kinds of time for regret later.

Once the panic eased, she grew used to the pressure around her throat-as used to such a thing as she could-and her breaths came easier. But the angst burning in her belly persisted, and the heat from that fire sank deep between her legs, making her desperate for counterpressure.

He turned her toward him, hooked a finger through the ring at the front of the collar, and slowly drew her to him until her lips pressed his. He stroked his tongue over her lips, then pulled back, leaving her hungry.

Her whimper of disappointment made heat spark in his eyes. "This"-he tugged on the collar-"means I own you. For the time we're in this room, you're mine to do with as I choose, with the exception of 'no' or 'stop.'"

A fury of emotions whipped up in her belly. She was shaky, her anxiety like a cliff edge where she balanced on one foot in high wind. For the tenth time since she'd solicited him, she wondered if she'd made a big mistake.

Huge mistake.

Monumental.

Life changing.

Yet her body quaked with the need for sexual release. Wild sexual release. The kind that would relieve the anxiety and build her confidence. And she was certain he could give that to her.

He used the ring to pull her toward the lounge. There, he stepped behind her again and gently turned her head to the left, showing her a different mirror reflecting their image now, one that displayed their full bodies in profile.

"This is the best kind of voyeurism," he murmured in her ear, his gaze on hers in the mirror. "The kind where you get to watch *and* experience at the same time."

His big, warm hand stroked down her spine. The other joined in as he cupped and squeezed her ass. Want curled between her legs, hot and wet. Then he lifted one hand, fisted her hair, and pulled her head back. Giselle drew a sharp breath and met his gaze in the mirror directly ahead as he licked her shoulder, then rasped, "You are so beautiful."

A fine tremble had built in her body, one she couldn't control.

"I love the way you shiver," he said against her neck. The dark thrill in his rough voice made her sex clench. "I want to make you shiver *hard*. Do you want that?"

"Yes." She focused, pushed all her fear and anxiety into the thought of feeling him, of that intense, luscious release that was so very different with a man than by her own means. "I want that."

"Good girl." The satisfaction in his voice washed dark desire through her body. He pressed a hand to the small of her back, guiding her toward the lounge until her lower body was pressed against the cool leather-like material. "Bend over." He pressed the front of his body to the back of hers and circled her waist with one strong arm. Pressing a kiss to her shoulder, he patted the chair's highest curve. "Belly here." He pointed to the lowest curve. "Head there."

When she glanced over her shoulder at him, he kissed her in that all-consuming way that made her forget everything but him. He added pressure to her back, bending her forward. Crowding her. Easing her into a position where her ass was high, her head low.

She drove her anxiety into the kiss, into lusciously stroking his tongue and biting his lip. He growled with approval but drew away when she was bent completely over the chair, her upper body against the downward curve. He slid his hands down her arms, closing his fingers at her wrists. The cuffs there clicked closed before she realized they were even on her arms.

Reflexively, she pulled back and met resistance. Panic struck at the center of her heart. Suddenly, all she could focus on was the chair holding her in position, the collar tight on her throat, her hands immobile.

Trapped. She was trapped.

Her breath quickened. Blood rushed to her head. She gripped the chair for support.

"Perfect," he said at her shoulder. "You're perfect."

No. She wasn't perfect. Not even close to perfect. Every part of her throbbed. Her mind pinged in a hundred different directions.

He must have seen or sensed her panic, because he paused, looked directly into her eyes, and said, "Do you want to tell me something?"

No.

Stop.

The words rang in her head. But her body needed his touch.

Breathe. Breathe.

"Nothing," she whispered.

"Very good." He eased away, his hands stroking her ass. His thumbs hooked into her thong and dragged it down her thighs.

Oh God.

She squeezed her eyes closed, turned her wrists in the cuffs. She felt the same way she had when she'd first walked into Indulgence, like she couldn't do this. But she thought of the alternative-leaving unfulfilled-and couldn't make herself tell him to stop. She was just...in a whole different place than she ever believed she could be. And wasn't that what this whole escapade was about?

When she tried to look at him over her shoulder, she caught the movement in the side mirror. God, the mirror. Her dim reflection shocked her. She saw herself naked, bent over the lounge with her ass in the air, wrists cuffed, throat ringed in black leather, light hair spilling across the dark curves of the lounge. And he stood behind her, his gaze devouring her, his hands stroking.

For a split second, she had another one of those bizarre out-of-body experiences, as if she were looking at someone else. Someone wickedly hot and wildly abandoned. Someone so secure with her sexuality, she could release all control. But Giselle knew better. She knew what was on the inside. Someone so completely opposite from the woman in the mirror. Another burst of panic exploded in her belly, and a whimper of alarm ebbed from her throat.

"No one knows what's happening on the inside but you," he said, as if he knew what she was thinking. His warm hand stroked her back, following her spine in a slow, tantalizing sweep, dropping kisses along the same path. "All anyone else sees is the gorgeous, strong woman in the mirror. Performance is about letting go of what you know. About getting into a character's skin. It's about relaxing and enjoying the experience of being someone else or, in this case, being the best version of yourself. It's about learning you can let go without fear."

He kissed his way down her spine, his mouth warm on her body. Giselle memorized his words. Soaked them in. Made them her own. And her muscles loosened. Her mind quieted.

Then his tongue touched the tail of her spine and continued between her cheeks, and everything fired to life again. His hands gripped her cheeks and parted them so his tongue could continue along the crevice, and circle the pucker hidden there.

Giselle gasped and stiffened, her hands digging into the chair. "Oh *God*."

But as quickly as he'd sought out that erotic spot, he moved away. In the mirror, Giselle watched him kneel behind her. Felt his hand behind one knee, pushing it to a padded ledge alongside the lounge. Then the other. Opening her. Exposing her completely. The air licked at her wet skin, shooting sensation all through her pussy.

And as quickly as cuffs clasped around her wrists, they closed around her ankles. Cuffs she hadn't seen. She lifted her head, testing her restraints. And found she had very little room to move.

She was trapped. Spread. Vulnerable. Exposed.

"Hold on, hold on." Giselle's eyes squeezed closed. Panic invaded her brain, cell by cell. "Give me a second."

"I only understand 'no' or 'stop.' Beyond that, how fast or slow we go is up to me." The warmth of his tongue slipped along her inner thigh, stopping just before he reached the spot where she needed his mouth most. "Your shivering is the hottest thing I've ever seen. Are you letting go? Giving me control?"

"Yes." Her answer was immediate. She needed relief. Needed his touch. Needed his mouth. Needed, needed, *needed.*

"Good girl."

How could two simple words pump such a thrill through her body? She bit her lip to keep from asking him to get on with it. That wasn't letting go or giving him control.

"You have no idea how much pleasure it gives me just to look at you like this."

She heaved a whimper.

"Oh, I like that sound." His fingertips touched her shoulders, slid down her ribs, traced her waist, her hips, then disappeared. She groaned and shifted against the lounge.

His hot chuckle streaked over her skin like fire. "Angel, you are the wickedest temptation ever."

In the mirror, she saw him lower his head and anticipated the touch of his lips on her skin. Instead, his tongue swept over her pussy in one hot, wet wave. Pressure, heat, and moisture seared through her sex, followed by the scrape of his beard.

She gasped and her spine bowed on a cry of surprise and pleasure. Her voice echoed off the walls, joined by the rattle of metal as she jerked against the cuffs. And, God, that was just…so…wrong. So…wickedly, decadently wrong.

"Mmm," he hummed. "Delicious."

In the mirror, she saw his head dip and braced for more. But when the wet warmth slid over her sex again, she still bucked against the restraints, electric currents arcing through her body.

"Oh my God." She was dizzy. Couldn't think. Could only feel all the sensation coursing and pulsing across her skin, deep into her sex, clouding her brain. "Oh my-"

He licked her, again.

And again.

Full strokes with that wide, flat tongue, smoothing away the prickling scratch of his beard and making her cry out with pleasure. Waves and waves of electric heat and pressure massaging her clit, her opening, her ass. The sight of him dipping his head before each stroke, the way he licked his lips after and met her eyes in the mirror just before he went down on her again, heightened anticipation and peaked pleasure.

She was trembling violently by the time he settled his mouth over her with constant pressure. She pushed against the lounge with her knees, rocking her sex toward him. He hummed, acknowledging her efforts, but showed no sign of quickening the slow plunge and retreat of his tongue into her pussy or the swirl of his tongue across her entrance or the purposeful scrape of his beard over her folds.

He lifted his head and blew on her wet skin. Exquisite tingles of torture raced across her sex. Her folds opened like a flower, reaching for his mouth. She whimpered and finally begged, *"Please."*

"Angel," he said, his voice low and raspy, "I thought you'd never ask."

Then he closed his mouth over her pussy again, but this time with purpose. He ate at her with his lips and tongue, scraping with his teeth and beard, holding her on the razor edge between release and insanity.

"Please," she cried. "Please, *please.* Yes."

With a soul-shattering orgasm spiraling straight at her, she rocked back and into his mouth. She needed more pressure, and she needed it faster. His fingers dug into her thighs, and he growled. But he didn't touch her clit, which kept the orgasm just out of reach. "Please let me come," she whimpered. "I want to come."

He pulled his mouth off her with a pop of suction. "Then come."

He lifted a hand and smacked her ass. Hard.

She jerked and cried out, more in shock than pain, but the sting radiated across her ass, into her sex, and pushed her closer to the edge. She bit her lip against the absurd burst of emotion, but the laugh still broke through. He'd spanked her, and it had brought her *pleasure*. This was all so *insane*.

But her laughter died instantly when he dropped his mouth back to her pussy, and his flat hand back to her ass. The slap ricocheted against the walls. The combination of pleasure and pain shot her out of her skin with tangled sensations but didn't allow her to climax.

He switched hands and smacked her other cheek, and the sting sang through her body. God, that was good. So good. And so wrong on some level. A level she'd think about later.

She opened her mouth to scream for more when he finally, finally, *finally* stroked her clit with his tongue, then spanked her again. Stroked her clit, spanked. Stroked, spanked. Stroked, spanked...right into the stratosphere.

She let out a scream at the orgasm's first wave, but it crashed hard, cutting off her air and contorting her body with ecstasy. The excitement pushed through and crashed, pushed, crashed, pushed, crashed. Leaving her quaking, shivering, spasming, and limp.

Her chest heaved. Her muscles quivered. Her hands ached where her fingers were fisted so hard, her nails had left a pattern of half-moons in her palms.

The sound of Disclosure's "You & Me" drifted to her ears, along with more sounds of sex in the room beyond. Her head was spinning so hard, she couldn't lift it from the lounge. She opened her eyes and found her hair spilled across her face.

The heavy strands cleared in one swoop, and the devil's brown eyes smiled into hers. Before she could ask him to let her go, he kissed her, his mouth hungry and hot.

"Wild," he rasped pulling out of the kiss. "You're incredible."

"Up," she said, voice rough. "Can I...get up? I feel... so dizzy."

"That's the head-rush effect," he said, releasing the cuffs on her ankles. "Makes the orgasm more intense."

Probably had a little to do with how much she'd drunk too.

He released the cuffs on her hands and slipped a strong arm around her waist-thank God. If he hadn't, she'd have melted to the floor. That orgasm had left her too weak to stand.

He turned her to face him and kissed her long and deep and hot, sending a clear message that this was far from over.

Carrying her around the lounge, he straddled the chair and sank into the lowest curve and stretched her out in front of him. She rested her head on his thigh, her belly on the lounge, her legs stretched out on the floor. And just floated there until the clink of metal touched her ear. She lifted her head, searching for the source, and found him unfastening his belt.

With a surge of energy, she pushed his hands away and unfastened his pants, then stroked the thick erection beneath his cotton boxers. *This.* She'd missed this. A long, thick, hard cock to fill her.

He combed her hair off her face, gripped her upper arms, and dragged her into the vee of his thighs, positioning her perfectly to take him into her mouth.

"Show me how much you like to suck cock, angel."

He waited, his eyes hyperfocused, as she took his cock from his slacks. He was as thick and long as he'd felt against her, veins snaking around the shaft, as wickedly thrilling as the man. His fingers curled beneath the edge of her collar and used it to drag her mouth to his cock.

Instead of taking him the way she knew he wanted-filling her mouth in one stroke-she licked the wide, wet tip, then pulled the thick head between her lips and sucked lightly before releasing him.

His growl was deep and hot and frustrated. And made Giselle smile.

"I knew it," he said, his voice edgy with need. "You love having control."

"I love savoring. There's a difference." And she loved his cock a little more, stroking the shaft with her tongue, her hands, her lips. He was burning hot, musky, salty. So raw. So supremely male. Such a turn-on.

He slid his fingers toward the back of the collar. "Suck me the way I know you want to."

She let him control her head so he pumped into her mouth the way he wanted. And she sucked him the way she loved to suck. And, oh, she had definitely stayed away from this too long.

"Fuck, yes," he growled, pulling her down, quick and shallow, then deep and slow, then finally releasing the collar to slide his hands down her back and over her ass while she took him deep. "Feels sooooo good, angel."

He let his hands roam up her back and held her head in place as he pumped his hips and plunged into her mouth. The guttural sounds of raw pleasure rolling from his throat lit Giselle on fire.

He abruptly dropped his ass deep into the curve of the lounge, and his cock pulled from her mouth. Giselle eased back, licking her lips, but made a sound of disappointment. One that was cut off when he reached out, gripped her waist and hauled her into his lap.

He pulled a condom from his pocket, ripped it open with his teeth, and covered himself in seconds. Then his head was stroking her entrance, then pushing inside...

"Oh *God*..." She bit out the words from behind clenched teeth before her throat closed, cutting off everything but the guttural sound of pleasure. He felt even bigger than he looked, and the sensation of him stretching her was mind-bending bliss.

"So...fucking tight," he rasped, pulling back, then working himself another inch deeper, and doing it all over again and again with unending patience. He didn't ask if she was okay, didn't rush it, didn't back off, just expertly maneuvered their bodies until he was balls-deep and Giselle swore she felt him in the back of her throat. She was trembling, panting, her fingers digging into the shirt at his shoulders.

The sensation was delicious. Decadent. Intense. Extreme.

Breathing hard, he released her hips, closed his fingers around her wrists, and pulled them behind her back. The pressure on her shoulders made her sit straighter, which also pushed him deeper.

A growl rolled through him just before he rocked his hips back, then thrust hard. The pressure spread through her in the most delicious way. Her head fell back, her mouth dropped open, and a wild sound of pleasure rolled from her throat.

This is insane.

She would have said the words aloud, but he was deep, deep, so deep. All she could do was use her legs to lift her body and meet his thrusts. They immediately fell into a slow, perfect rhythm, the kind of rhythm she'd never found with anyone but Troy. And the thrill pulsing through her with each thrust gave her a glimmer of hope that this kind of fulfillment was still out there. That maybe she wasn't destined for a life of wanting something she couldn't have. That if she'd found it with this stranger, surely she could find it with someone else, someone she could build a life with.

That realization alone had been worth the trip here.

"Watch me fuck you," he said, growing breathless.

She opened her eyes to the sight of their perfect grind. His shirt had fallen open at his waist, and his abs rippled with each thrust. The sight had to be the hottest thing she'd ever seen.

"Watch how you move," he said, "match it with... how you feel, so you can...find the rhythm again...when you need it."

He transferred both her wrists into one big hand, pulling tight. But the stress was forgotten when his free hand cupped her breast and his head came forward, his mouth covering her nipple.

Heat and suction filled her breast and pumped straight to her pussy. She dropped her head back, deepening the curve of her spine and forcing him deeper. So damn deep his cock hit some hot button of pleasure with every stroke. Her mouth dropped open on a cry, their rhythm picked up speed, and a deep, full-body orgasm spiraled toward her.

And it was beautiful.

Absolutely. Goddamn. Beautiful.

"Ah *God*," she cried.

"Bring it, angel," he rasped, and increased both his speed and the power of his thrust. "Bring it."

"Oh my G-" the intensity coalesced, her orgasm cutting off her cry as it peaked.

She broke, splintering into heat and light and pleasure, rocked by wave after wave of wicked ecstasy that wiped her mind of everything but the intense fulfillment infusing every cell of her body.

Only when the thrill quieted did he release her hands, grip her hips, and ride her to his own completion, first shouting pleasure, then pressing his face to the hollow between her neck and shoulder and growling like a deeply sated animal.

Giselle let her fingers slide through his hair until their breathing regulated, and when her devil finally stirred, Giselle's mind floated back from fluffy clouds and white light and blissful perfection to her far harsher immediate reality, one she'd now have to find a way to live with-she'd just screwed a total stranger.

Yet Troy continued to drift into her mind. To the way he'd called her angel. To the way he'd said, "Bring it, angel" during sex. To the way he'd loved to press his face to her neck and breathe her in after he'd come.

A sudden and intense wave of profound sadness came out of nowhere, swamping Giselle with loss and regret, filling her mind with Troy while another man still filled her body.

The wrongness of that only deepened Giselle's confusion. And the hope she'd experienced just moments before dimmed. It wouldn't matter if she found another man she could enjoy if she couldn't find a way to put Troy behind her.

And when the devil finally leaned away, he dropped his head back against the lounge, flopped a forearm over his eyes, and muttered something that sounded a lot like, "Satan, here I come."

Five

Troy hung midair in the largest cave at Red Rock Canyon just outside Las Vegas. Light from the crews above had faded soon after he descended into this cavern, and if it weren't for the headlamp on his helmet, he would be surrounded by a setting that mirrored the state of his soul-utter darkness.

Now, his lamp illuminated the rusty hue of rock as sweat slid down this neck, his chest, and soaked into his tee. To think the caves were a dozen or more degrees cooler than the desert floor outside made him grateful, even if he did feel like he was basting in a giant oven.

Voices and movement from the crew above echoed down to him. Lifehouse's *Smoke & Mirrors* album bounced through the cavern. Normally, the music would have layered a light atmosphere to the set, but again, he wasn't in a normal state of mind. And as Jason Wade sang "All That I'm Asking For," Troy felt the lyrics heavily in his heart. Wishing, more than anything, for the chance to go back in time and do things over with Giselle all those years ago. But based on what he'd done only two nights ago with her, he knew nothing would change, because, where that woman was concerned, he always seemed to make the shittiest decisions.

Raucous laughter overhead forced Troy's mind back to the job. Keaton and Duke had been in rare form on this trip. And Zahara's famed pranks had been instigating one hilarious incident after another, often to the detriment of filming. No one could act when they were laughing their asses off, and this movie had more retakes than any he'd ever been involved in.

Every movie had a feel of its own. An atmosphere, a cohesiveness, a personality that developed from the combination of cast, crew, and location. Under normal circumstances, this film would go down in Troy's book as one of his top ten favorites, but from the moment he'd stepped off the plane to Giselle's face on a billboard, he'd been a flaming pile of shit.

He pulled a bottle of water from his harness, downing half. Then pulled out the radio and asked the engineer on the other end, "How deep is this thing?"

"Looks like…" Paper rustled over the line as Ed Miller turned pages of the map graphing the cave. "Sixty feet."

"Nope. I'm at sixty now." He tilted his lamp to shine below him where the shaft narrowed like an ice-cream cone. But the bottom of this thing dropped out of sight. "Doesn't matter. I'm going to take some measurements."

He traded his radio for his tape measure, stretching it toward the wall, but the space was too wide and the metal bent, falling away. He reeled it back to try again.

He could guess at the distance, but he wasn't the estimator type. He was a perfectionist. He had to get all the numbers out on paper, had to do the math, then put that math through the app Rubi, the genius girlfriend of another Renegade, created for the same purpose-to keep them all safe.

Too bad he didn't plan out all his decisions this carefully. If he did, he wouldn't have a knife of guilt through his gut now.

Easing the tape toward the wall again, he rehearsed an explanation for his impulsive and degenerate behavior at the club with Giselle. Only no excuse he'd created over the last two days justified the way he'd pushed her. And pushed her. And pushed her.

None other than the fact that he'd been expecting her to break and back out.

But that wouldn't go over well with Giselle when he faced her.

If he faced her.

The tape snapped down again. Troy swore and reeled it in. This was a shitty measuring method, but it was all he had. So he started over. He wished he had Josh on the job. Unfortunately, Renegades' risk assessment manager of choice, was on his honeymoon. But if Troy couldn't shore up some of the structural issues he was finding in this cave related to the stunt the filmmakers wanted, he might just interrupt the couple's blissful retreat. Because Troy didn't trust the engineer Paramount was using to assist in the stunts as far as Troy could throw him. And Troy preferred safety over regret.

At least in stunts.

Obviously, when it came to Giselle, he just couldn't keep himself from fucking up.

His self-disgust deepened, making his gut ache. He should have listened to Zahara and contacted Giselle like a normal person. But he'd never been normal. Nothing about his life had ever been normal. Which was exactly why he was hanging in a cave trying to measure the diameter of a cavern so he could dive into it head-first at full speed.

Evidently, some people could overcome their screwed-up beginnings. Giselle and Ryker had both broken out of the self-destructive mold. Giselle had made her deepest dream of becoming a country music star a reality. Ryker had decades of success in the army, and a great relationship with an awesome girl.

Sure, Troy had found success. At twenty-nine, Troy had more money than he'd ever believed he'd see in a lifetime, and more work than he could handle. He'd even extended his stunt work into successful bit acting parts when the need arose. And he had a hell of a lot of fun looking invincible, skilled, talented, sexy, bad-ass, and fearless with his stunts.

But deep down, he was a coward, plain and simple. His personal life was nothing but meaningless hookups, and his close friends included only a handful of people. Because, while he might freely risk life and limb professionally, personally he couldn't face any risk. Not after losing Giselle. The truth was, he was just enough of a coward to find a way to get out of facing Giselle, because he hated what he'd done with her at the club. Loved it and hated it. That depraved behavior was reserved for strangers who sought it out for their own dark purposes-purposes Troy didn't want to know about-not for some-one like Giselle. Someone he'd cared about. Someone he would always care about.

He'd tried to soothe his conscience by telling him-self he hadn't come anywhere close to demonstrating the debauchery a club like Rendezvous had to offer, but that wasn't helping. Even what little he'd done had been too much. He'd lost control. He'd taken advantage. And he hated himself for it.

The familiar whir of cable sounded overhead, signal-ing incoming company just as Troy's tape touched the wall.

He glanced at the measurement and doubled the distance since he was positioned at the center of the shaft, then winced.

Whoever had come down came to a slow stop ten feet to his right. "How does it look, boss?"

The eerie, smooth, radio-crackled voice just feet away startled Troy, and he jerked his head that direction. Instead of one of his fellow stunt people, he faced the goddamned stunt dummy they'd collectively named Skip.

"Holy *fuck*." Troy's body released the sudden ten-sion, but his heart still hammered beneath his ribs, and the tape measure fumbled in his grip. He tilted his head back and yelled, "You *assholes!*"

A chorus of cackles, laughter, shouts, and high fives resonated above, where the entire crew lined the lip of the shaft, watching. Troy couldn't help but smile. He shook his head, laughing with relief, then cued his mic. "Laugh while you can. Payback's a bitch on crack."

Grinning, Troy looked over the stunt dummy. The guys had made Skip themselves from various movie props. He had the head and torso of a CPR dummy, the legs, arms, hands, and feet from a mishmash of soft mannequins from a long-ago zombie movie. Today, they'd dressed him in a Grateful Dead T-shirt, ripped jeans, and, of all things, a cowboy hat.

"Dude," he told Skip as he reeled in the tape. "You scared me."

"Sir," Skip's "voice," courtesy of Keaton impersonating an English butler, came from the radio duct-taped to one of the dummy's hands. "I must say, we are collectively a tad worried about you. You seem unusually blue this trip. Worse over the past few days. I'm not sure if the others have mentioned it, but I did earn my psychology degree at Yale, sir. If I can be of any assistance, I'd be happy to lend an ear."

Troy cued his mic. "I don't want to offend you or anything, Skip, but...you don't have ears."

"Oh dear." Pause. "Oh my." Pause. "That's quite beastly, isn't it? All right, then. I'll see what I can do about that. As far as the cave goes, how may I be of assistance, oh great one?"

"You can give me about five more feet of mobility in here."

"I'm afraid I can't accommodate you there, sir. Seems as you have a nasty little problem on your hands."

Troy had more than one nasty little problem. "You're incredibly unhelpful today, Skip."

"Hold on, I may have a jolly good idea, sir."

"Since you have more brains than my collective coworkers, lay it on me."

"Indeed. What might you say to allowing me to attempt the stunt prior to your swift and elegant descent into this dirty little shaft, sir? I believe I may be able to save you…well…an intense headache, as it were."

"Very gracious of you, Skip. But you're too valuable to lose. You and I both know Keaton is our true stunt dummy."

More laughter echoed above.

"Ed," Troy said into the radio, "Skip and I are ready to come up."

"You got it," Ed said, laughter in his voice. "Coming up."

Above, the whir of machinery sounded. Skip ascended first, solidifying Troy's intention to get creative with payback for his stunt comrades. Once they'd pulled Skip over the edge, Troy slowly rose through the shaft.

Feeling a little lighter, he dragged his phone from his pocket to check for missed calls or messages-the service down here was spotty but surprisingly decent if he caught a signal just right-but found neither. He was both relieved and frustrated that Ryker hadn't called him back yet. On the one hand, Troy wasn't looking forward to the lecture he'd get from his best friend when he asked for Giselle's cell number. On the other, he wanted this guilt monkey off his back, and he'd already tried a dozen different ways to get ahold of Giselle at the Mirage. The woman had remarkable security.

Security who'd let her go unescorted to a sex club.

What the hell was that about?

By the time he reached the lip of the cavern and climbed out, the guys had Breaking Benjamin's "The Diary of Jane" playing at one hundred decibels. Keaton, the doof, held Skip like a human female, twirling around the dingy cave as if it were a dance floor. Duke and Zahara danced alongside, all three of them singing along with Ben. The crew looked on, laughing.

Troy chuckled, relieving another sliver of stress. "You guys are idiots."

"We're practicing for tonight," Duke called back before he dipped Zahara, who squealed and laughed, her dark hair brushing the cave floor.

Troy turned down the music and pulled a fresh water bottle from the cooler. "What's tonight?"

Duke pulled Z upright, only to have Keaton dip Skip, then pretend to make out with him.

Troy sat on the cooler and uncapped the water with a roll of his eyes. "I knew you were off, dude, but not that off."

Keaton pulled Skip upright and danced cheek to cheek. "Don't listen to him, darling. He's just jealous." Obviously in a dramatic mood, Keaton caressed Skip's bald head. "We'll be the cat's meow on the dance floor tonight, you and me."

Duke pushed Z's shoulder, and she made a triple spin, ending with a flourish only to spin back to Duke and pick up the tango, imitating Keaton and Skip.

"Good Lord, did someone leave the catnip out again?" Troy drank the rest of his water. "What the hell is tonight?"

The song ended, and both Duke and Keaton finished out the dance by dramatically dipping their partners.

"The mixer," Keaton said, back to his normal self as he sat Skip in a row of chairs, then crossed the dummy's legs and laid one arm over the back of the neighboring seat. "The one they told us about- Oh." He looked at Duke and Zahara. "He wasn't here." Then to Troy. "While you were out picking up cable, Karen from publicity came by, said there's a title song mixer tonight. You know, a swanky-dank, meet-the-singer-type gig. It's in one of the small banquet rooms at the Mirage."

The sting of something like fear streaked down his spine. It could have been excitement. It could have been shock. It could have been all of them combined, because this meant he could meet Giselle face-to-face without the need to utilize any middleman.

Keaton took the seat next to Skip. "They even invited us stunt grunts-go figure." He looked at Skip. "We're coming up in the world, buddy. Bet there will be some fine ass there tonight, maybe even a mannequin or two. Okay." He sat back and spoke to the crew. "What's for lunch today? I vote Cabo Wabo."

"We went there yesterday," Brianna, one of the crew, complained.

"And we should go again," Keaton said, "because it's just that good."

As the others argued over a lunch spot, Zahara bumped Troy's hip with hers. "Scoot over."

He moved and lowered his head. "You didn't think to tell me this?"

"I forgot all about it until these guys started messing around," she said, keeping her voice low. "It might be a good opportunity to reconnect with her."

Oh no. They'd already reconnected-on the most intimate level.

Yet, they hadn't.

What a mess.

He wiped sweat from his brow with a shrug of his shoulder. A huge part of him considered ignorance bliss in this situation. Over the past two days, he'd been having a tug-of-war with his conscience, one side sure it would be better to let her go on thinking she'd fucked a stranger, the other...

God, he didn't know if it was a good thing or a bad thing, but he had an overwhelming need to confess. Something he'd never experienced before. And he still couldn't tell if it was the right thing to do or not.

Z's hand covered his forearm, her hold firm. "I know you probably don't want to talk about it, but just let me say one thing, and I'll drop it. You're a guy who goes after what you want. I've known you for three years, and you've always gone all out for every part, always been there for every friend. You live your life balls to the wall. And all I keep thinking is, why stop now?

"The reality is, the chances of you two ending up in the same place at the same time again with the opportunity to talk to each other is pretty damn slim. Even if there's no chance of getting back together, I think you should at least take this chance to show her your face, say hello, and put yourself back on her radar. At best, sparks will fly. At worst, you got the chance to say, 'Hey, look. I didn't crumble to dust when you left.'

"I really think you'll regret it later if you don't."

Troy nodded, because Z was right. He would spend the rest of his life hating himself for doing what he'd done at the club without telling her it had been him. Because if he knew Giselle like he thought he knew her-and based on what he'd learned of her from that night, he believed he still knew enough-he was pretty sure she'd be at least a little wigged over the way she'd gotten caught up in the night and what she'd allowed herself to do with someone she'd considered a complete stranger.

"Thanks, Z. I'll think about it."

But as Zahara stood and started gathering gear before they took their lunchtime break, Troy continued to waffle over whether or not he should poke the sleeping bear or simply let it lie.

Giselle's hand whipped a signature across the photograph. She capped the pen as she grinned up at the director of the film, Jeff Michel. "Tell your daughter I said hello."

He chuckled and slipped the image into an envelope. "I'll have to put in earplugs first. Thank you so much."

"My pleasure." She twirled a strand of her hair around her finger and pulled it forward, laying it purposely over the mark on her neck, a bite from the devil she'd been struggling to hide for two days.

Her mind instantly drifted back to the moment he'd created it, and desire flared through her body. In some ways, it still seemed like a fantasy. Like it hadn't really happened. Like she'd only imagined it. Then she'd see some mark the interlude had left on her body, like a line on her wrist from the cuffs or this welt from his teeth, and the reality that she'd been so taken with a stranger she'd met him and had sex with him in public all within an hour would come rushing back at her with frightening speed.

She pressed a hand to her stomach as acid rushed in. Not for the first time, she considered going back to therapy. A one-time thing was bad enough, but she couldn't stop thinking about him. A man whose name she didn't even know. A man who'd probably already forgotten he'd even touched her. Really, how could she have done that? She'd never even had a one-night stand before. Talk about radical behavior. And when she thought about it too long, it truly scared her. What had spurred it? How did she keep it from happening again? What if she couldn't control it?

Brook came up beside Giselle with a fresh drink. She was wearing a beautiful midnight-blue cocktail dress that made her eyes pop even more than they normally did. Her black hair was wrapped into a fun little spring of curls on the back of her head, and her makeup was sexy, yet natural.

"So sorry to interrupt," Brook said, then to Giselle, "Gloria would like to have a few minutes with you."

"Not a problem." Jeff nodded at both women. "Thanks again."

As the director wandered back to chat with other guests, Giselle turned to Brook and took the drink. She'd been Giselle's first assistant on the road. They'd become instant friends, bonding over Giselle's heartbreak over Troy. And while her agents, managers, tour coordinators, and sponsors had wielded the power to hire and fire her band members and backup singers for bigger and better as Giselle had grown, she'd always kept Brook as her personal assistant.

"Thank you." She drained half the tonic water and lime, sighing at the feel of the bubbles on her throat. "God, that's heavenly."

She paused a moment to glance around the small banquet room Chad had booked for the mixer, wishing she could grab a drink from the bar. Wishing she'd picked up a Xanax on her way out of her room.

The setting was nice. A quaint space the perfect size for a gathering of a hundred or so. The lighting intimate, the room decorated in rich navy and gold. A bar sat against one wall, tables and booths dotted another area, a small dance floor filled one corner. Everyone seemed comfortable and engaged. Everyone except her band and her backup singers.

"I don't understand them," Giselle said. "It pisses me off that they're so worried about what they might not get that they can't enjoy what they have. They've all made minimal effort tonight when it would only benefit them in every way to use this opportunity to both show that they're team players and to put out feelers for other work.

"They're all so damn talented, but every time one of these big mixers comes up, everyone gets tense, and all the gloves go on. The guys start bickering among themselves; they start asking me a million questions there's no way I could answer. Helen and Simone get quiet, start lurking and eavesdropping. God, I hate that. I swear someday one of them will stab me in my sleep."

She hooked a thumb toward herself. "I'm the singer. I'm the one who's supposed to be temperamental."

Brook burst out laughing. "I guess you didn't get the memo."

Giselle sighed, and Brook's laugh made her smile.

"I think they're making up for your even-tempered good nature," Brook said.

Giselle made a growling sound, turned her back on her band, and drank her bubbly water. "Whatever." She glanced around the room. "Is this a friendlier group than normal, or," she was going to say *is that my imagination*, but smirked and said, "am I just comparing them to my band?"

More laughter bubbled from Brook. "They're definitely a friendly group. They say it's just the ambience of a film crew. Everyone's casual and fun, sort of like a family."

Giselle sighed. "Wouldn't that be nice?"

"No kidding."

"Think they'll adopt us?"

"Bet we could persuade them. You could be their entertainment, and I could keep them organized."

"We're a pretty good team."

Brook lifted her brows. "I've also got my eye on one of the stunt guys. Man, talk about hot…"

"Show me."

"Last stool at the bar," Brook said, "Black hair. Looks like he's got a little Asian in him, or maybe Spanish or something. His bone structure makes my mouth water, and the way he fills out his clothes…Mmm. I bet he's modeled."

"Oh yeah," Giselle said. "Wow, what a smile."

"Lights up the freaking room."

"Have you made contact yet?"

Brook sighed. "No. What's the point? I mean, sure I could do a one-nighter with him but…" She shrugged and turned away. "I'm kinda getting tired of saying good-bye, you know?"

"I do know." Giselle's heart grew heavy. "And I'm sorry."

"Hey, not your fault. I have a choice. I keep following you, don't I?" Brook squeezed her arm. "I think we're almost done here. You've hit all the major players. But Gloria really does want to talk to you. She's not happy."

Giselle took another sip of her drink, glancing around the crowd for her agent. "I can't remember the last time I saw Gloria happy."

"Can't say I blame her. Chad's a diligent gatekeeper. If I were her, I'd be frustrated too. I know Chad's trying to take care of you, but sometimes he's extremely selective about what gets through to you."

That news made her shoulders drop two inches. "To be honest, their little battles are getting on my nerves."

If she were *really* honest, everyone around her was testing her patience except Brook, and all the tension only added to her sense of isolation. From the outside, it looked to all the world as if she had a tight-knit band who loved each other like a family, and support staff who came together to collectively lift Giselle to the peak of success.

She'd never imagined success could bring such loneliness.

"Let's just get through this last big push," Brook said. "Then you can reevaluate. If they can't get along, maybe one of them has to go. Or maybe both. Not a bad thing, just a change. You need people who will grow with you." Brook circled her shoulders with one arm and squeezed. "Hang in there. Something's going to pop soon."

"Yeah." She laughed. "Me."

Brook had just joined her in the laugh when a strong male voice interrupted. "You've been avoiding me."

Tyrone Gleason approached, and their laughter died. He was a handsome thirty-five-year-old music executive who'd company-hopped like crazy to advance his career. He also woman-hopped and thrived on the drama of his lovers fighting over him. Giselle had told him more than once he belonged on a reality television show.

"Oh, Tyrone," Giselle said, leaning in to kiss his cheek. "It's not all about you, I promise."

His arm snaked around her waist, holding her close, and Giselle rolled her eyes in Brook's direction.

Her friend plucked Giselle's empty glass from her hand and gave Tyrone a stern look. "You can have her for five minutes. I'll be back to move her on to greener pastures in *five* minutes."

"Ten," he countered with a grin. "We have something important to talk about."

Giselle leaned against a high-backed chair at one of the tables in the bar area and lazily twirled her finger into a curl, pulling it forward again. "You look good, as always."

"You look better, as always."

She grinned. "What's this important thing?"

He darted a look around the room, a hot grin edging his full mouth. "I assume you've heard the rumor they're adding a Grammy category this year."

Tyrone had been on the Grammy's Producer's and Engineer's Wing Steering Committee until he took an executive position with Bose six months before.

"I've heard that rumor, but I haven't seen any official word."

"It's happening. And there's more than just one." His dark eyes caressed her cleavage. "They'll be announcing it at the same time they announce nominees in a few months."

When he didn't go on, she reached out and lifted his chin with one finger until his gaze met hers. "Are you going to tell me what the categories are?"

He grinned, a charming, lopsided grin. "I was thinking we could talk about it in your room."

"Then I guess I'll find out in December with everyone else."

He exhaled and gave her one of those heavy-lidded, I'm-losing-my-patience looks. "You'd have broken out a lot faster if you slept around."

A bitter laugh scraped her throat. "Tell me something I don't know."

"The categories are Best Voice of the Year and Best Songwriter of the Year."

A twinkle of excitement sparked deep inside her, but Giselle knew better than to get her hopes up. "Nice."

He lifted his brows and slid his finger along the strap of her dress, then over her shoulder. "Your name has been bouncing around the membership like a ping-pong ball."

She continued to smother that spark. Oh, what a Grammy nomination would do for her career. Not to mention a win. "Oh yeah?"

"Mmm-hmm." His finger traveled down her arm. "And Bose is looking to put money behind someone just like you."

"I heard Bose was turning away from sponsoring musicians and focusing on sports figures."

When he reached her hand, he threaded their fingers and met her eyes with a sultry, seductive look that did nothing for her. Absolutely nothing. Her mind only drifted to the devil, and just the thought of his smoldering gaze created pressure between her legs.

"That was based on a butt-load of money given out to newbies who wasted it on partying. We're always looking for hardworking, multifaceted artists who've shown they can handle themselves and their money. Bose is taking fewer gambles and investing in winners like you-artists who invest in their craft, continue to grow, improve, reinvest in themselves. You've got multiple talents, you're a darling in the press, an angel to your fans, and you just keep getting better every year."

"And this..." He gestured to one of the screens where a clip from the video trial she'd filmed the day before ran along with various other clips from music videos and concerts. "Girl, this puts the icing on the cake. Sexy sells, sweetheart."

He eased closer, invading her space and pressing his hand to her shoulder, then sliding it to her neck. He was really pushing his limits, and Giselle was going to have to put on the brakes very soon. Something that would inevitably rub him wrong. The man had a huge ego. And she was giving him a lot of leeway because he was also highly influential in the industry.

"And you are *extremely sexy*," he murmured.

"Thank you." She smiled and covered his hand with hers. "Tyrone, you know-"

"Here's that drink," Brook said, cutting into Giselle's gentle letdown and pulling the plug on the stress that had knotted in the pit of her stomach. Relationships in this industry were so fragile. Maneuvering them often exhausted her. "Your ten minutes are up, Ty. I've got half a dozen other people waiting to talk to her."

Giselle took the drink from Brook and smiled at Tyrone, pretending not to notice his scowl of irritation.

"I'm very interested in talking more about opportunities with Bose. We'd make great business partners."

Giselle let Brook walk her through the space.

"Oh man," Giselle said on an exhale. "I owe you big-time for that."

"He makes my skin crawl."

"Okay, who's next?"

"No one," Brook said. "I just couldn't stand the way he kept touching you." She stopped and faced Giselle, fussing with a curl, then the strap Tyrone had touched as if she was trying to rid her of him. "I just wanted to give you a break. Gloria's tied up with Dennis from American Express. What did Tyrone want?"

Giselle was about to tell her the news about the Grammy's new categories, when a dark-haired woman who'd been seated with the film crew approached.

She held her hand out to Giselle. "Hi, I'm Zahara." She shook both Giselle's and Brook's hands. "I just wanted to come by and say hello. I've seen you in concert and, wow, I was absolutely blown away."

The woman was warm and authentic and well-spoken. Giselle immediately connected with her and could easily have seen herself wanting to get to know her under different circumstances. Circumstances that allowed her to have a life.

"Thank you so much. Are you part of the crew?"

"Stunt crew." She laughed. "Running with all the tough guys."

"Speaking of tough guys," Brook said with a sly little grin. "Is the one with the black hair and the killer smile...you know, married or taken or anything?"

Zahara grinned. "He's not. And he's an absolutely fantastic guy. Okay, sort of a big goofball most of the time, but aren't they all?"

"Good point."

Zahara tilted her head toward the bar. "Go chat him up, but be prepared, he's a talker. Yap, yap, yap, let me tell you. And whatever you do, *do not* mention fantasy football or you'll be up with him all night."

"Really," she said with a sly smile.

"Really." Zahara matched her smile. "Just sayin'. You know, a woman-to-woman warning."

Brook's face split in a grin, and she held up a fist. "I owe you, girl."

Zahara tapped her fist to Brook's. "We gotta take care of each other."

Giselle and Zahara watched Brook make her way over to the bar.

"Does she like football?" Zahara asked.

"She hated it up until thirty seconds ago."

Zahara's laugh made Giselle smile. "Good. That boy needs to get laid."

It was Giselle's turn to laugh. "So does that girl."

They looked at each other and grinned.

Zahara said, "Our lifestyle sucks."

Giselle burst out laughing. "Seriously. Brook and I were just saying the same thing when you walked up."

Zahara rolled her eyes and shook her head. "I wanted to tell you we have a friend in common."

"Oh really? Who?"

"Nathan Ryker."

Giselle's smile turned to surprise. "Really?" Then excitement. "How do you know Nathan?"

"It's so weird to hear you call him Nathan. Everyone calls him Ryker except Rachel, which is how I know him."

"Oh…*Oh*…" All the dots were clicking in Giselle's mind. "Right. She works for the stunt company…"

"Same one I'm working for."

"Wow, small world." Her mind immediately veered from Nathan and Rachel to Troy. Surely this woman wouldn't also know Troy.

"Six degrees of separation and all that," Zahara said.

"Have you seen Nathan and Rachel lately?" Giselle asked, edging toward the questions she knew she shouldn't ask for the same reason she didn't ask Nathan.

What if she found out Troy was married? What if she found out Troy had kids? What if Troy had ended up with a perfect little family, like the perfect little family Giselle had always dreamed of? Like the perfect little family she and Troy had planned out together? What if Troy had used the names he and Giselle had picked out for their future children to name his children with another woman? What if he'd put Giselle completely behind him and never even thought about her anymore?

What if…What if…What if…There were a million of them.

And the answer was always the same. Troy had every right to have all those things. Giselle loved him. She wanted him to be happy.

"Yes, actually," Zahara said. "I saw Rachel just a few weeks ago when she came here to check on this filming site. Ryker was working, so he didn't come. But we see them pretty often, maybe every other month."

"That's great. I've only spoken with Rachel on the phone. I haven't gotten a chance to meet her yet with this darn schedule. But, God, I've never heard Nathan so happy. He's such a good man. He's been through so much. He desperately needed a good woman in his life."

Zahara's smile was warm and real as she nodded. "He definitely got one. They are fantastic together. Really complete each other."

Giselle chewed her lip as she nodded. She had to ask. She couldn't let it go. She just had to know. Not knowing was fine when the information was out of reach, but it would kill her not to know when the answer was potentially so close. "Do you happen to know a friend of-"

"Excuse me." A female voice drew Giselle out of the conversation. Gloria stood beside them with an apologetic smile. "I'm sorry to interrupt, but I'm going to be leaving soon, and I really just need five minutes with you."

"Not a problem." Zahara gave Giselle's arm a squeeze. "I'll be here awhile."

She smiled. "It was great to meet you." Giselle turned to Gloria. "I know you're frustrated with Chad-"

"I'm not going to waste my time talking about him, other than to ask if he told you about the offer from L'Oréal."

Giselle frowned, her mouth hanging open. "L- No. I haven't heard anything about L'Oréal."

Gloria exhaled and looked at the floor.

"Gloria?"

She lifted her gaze, her wide, dark brown eyes flashing with anger. "I'm digging deep for some professionalism here, Giselle, but, honestly, I'm coming up short. What direction you and Chad decide to take with your career is up to you. But you can't make the best decision unless you're getting all the information.

"L'Oréal would like your gorgeous face to represent their brand next year. They believe, based on how your career is growing, it will also be the year you break out big. I happen to agree with them and have been able to negotiate a substantial contract. And having your face all over their product line will certainly help your name-face-brand recognition.

"Since the copy of the contract I gave Chad seems to have evaporated, I'll send over another one directly to you by courier in the morning."

"Yes. Absolutely. Thank you." She reached for Gloria's arm. "I'm so sorry. I'll talk to Chad. And for the foreseeable future, let's agree that you'll let me know personally about any offer you extend to Chad. That way I'll know what's getting through and what's not."

"Agreed." She gave Giselle a quick hug. "Now get some rest, sweetheart. That man has you working your tail off. When you get tired of that, you let me know. There are all sorts of other ways to leverage the success you've already made. A hundred different directions to go with your career. Touring is lucrative, don't get me wrong, but it's not the only way."

Giselle nodded and forced a smile. But as Gloria breezed her way from the banquet room, Giselle's heart felt as heavy as a stone.

She glanced toward the bar and found Brook laughing with the stunt crew. The sight made longing stir.

She was about to turn that direction and join them, when someone touched her arm and a familiar voice said, "You finally have a free minute."

Chad.

With a ready smile, she faced him. But he wasn't alone. He stood beside Patrick Scott, one of the top acquisitions managers for Goldstone Productions. Which meant that instead of laughing with Brook and finding some lighthearted conversation, she was going to talk business yet again with a man who was eying her like she was on the dessert menu.

Six

Troy paused outside the concierge room and pulled his phone from his blazer jacket. At the balcony railing, he hit the speed dial for Ryker, gripped the metal with his free hand and closed his eyes. "Come on, come on, come on, Ry," he muttered. "Pick up."

The last thing he wanted to do tonight was walk in that room and shock the hell out of Giselle when she was surrounded by people. He wasn't particularly interested in getting his heart yanked out of his throat again either. But there was no good time to do this unless he could get her number and set up a private meeting.

"You've reached Ryker-" The voice mail spoke in Troy's ear.

"Fuck." He disconnected, then took a moment to settle into his conviction. He just couldn't hold on to this guilt anymore.

Face her. Be honest. Take the hit. Walk away.

Maybe then he could let go.

Really let go. And get on with his life.

Opening his eyes, resolved to the fate he'd created for himself, he squared his shoulders and stepped into the room. He'd been in a lot of rooms at a lot of the

Vegas hotels, but never here. The space was elegant and intimate. It was also filled with guests in fancy dresses and smart suits.

"Your name, sir?" the man at the door asked.

"Troy Jacobs. I'm part of the crew."

He slid his finger down the list and nodded. "Enjoy your night."

Before stepping into the mix, he moved into a shadowed corner and observed. Easing around the periphery, he found the room bigger than it looked. The lighting and the various levels-three steps up here, three steps down there-made the setting intimate despite the dark décor, lightened with touches of gold.

Four big screens scattered through the room played clips of Giselle-from her concerts, her music videos, backstage, rehearsing. A mix of her five current albums played over the speakers, really just background music to the lively conversation. Everyone looked happy and vibrant, drinks and hors d'oeuvres in their hands. A small dance floor off in the corner attracted a dozen or so guests.

He recognized many of the crew floating through the room, the producer, the director, the assistant director, the cast.

When he finally found Giselle, his heart stumbled. She was wearing light cream and the way that dress sculpted to her body made Troy groan out loud. When she shifted, he could see there was almost no back to the dress, leaving her beautiful body bare except for a strip of rhinestones down the center of her spine.

The sight felt like a lightning strike to his groin. Pain and yearning blended into the kind of feeling that made Troy want to drink.

A lot.

She was so fucking sophisticated now. So damn elegant. So...everything he wasn't.

Leaving him was the best thing she'd ever done. She'd had the ability to see the future, while Troy had been blinded by fear.

He shouldn't be here.

His body heat ramped up. His palms sweated. He couldn't do this. He should let her go on believing he was a stranger. He'd just have to find a way to deal with the guilt.

He turned for the doors.

And bumped directly into Zahara.

"Whoa." He grabbed her arms to keep himself from plowing her down. "Sorry, Z." She wore a simply elegant sleeveless black dress that showed off her great shape and olive skin. Her hair was up in a fancy, sparkly clip. "Wow, you look great."

"So do you. I didn't think you'd come."

"I didn't. Not really. Bad idea. I'm leaving."

"Really?" she said, challenging. "You went to all the trouble to get dressed up, do that...thing...with your hair to make you look rugged and sexy, and got all the way down here only to leave without even talking to her?" She crossed her arms. "Don't you think you deserve more than that?"

He huffed a laugh. "No. I absolutely don't."

"Huh. Even I talked to her."

His stomach turned icy. "What?"

"She's very sweet. Very down-to-earth. Not at all the prima donna-"

"Z, what did you say?"

"I told her we had a mutual friend-*Ryker*," she added just before Troy imploded. "We talked about how traveling sucks, hooked her assistant up with Keaton."

"*What?* Why would you do that?" The panic started to bubble low in his gut and rise.

"Because she's adorable, she thinks Keaton's hot, which he is, and wanted to know if he was taken, which he isn't."

Troy closed his eyes and searched for patience. "Please, Z, don't get in the middle. This isn't as simple as you might think."

"Obviously." She sighed and slipped a possessive arm through his, turning him toward the bar. "While you're here, you may as well get some free booze. Because if you're not going to talk to her, you'll need to be pretty smashed so you can pass out when you get back to the room, because, boy, she is smokin' hot."

"Thanks for pointing that out," he said with all the sarcasm of a pissed ten-year-old. "I hadn't noticed."

She just grinned as he took a seat at the opposite end of the bar as Keaton and a cute dark-haired woman who looked close to Giselle's age was completely absorbed in whatever Keaton was saying.

"I hope she took a few shots of caffeine," Troy muttered. "Did you tell her he can talk a freakin' blue streak?"

"She was warned."

Troy grunted and said hello to a few members of the crew nearby, but kept himself mostly hidden behind the cash register, watching Giselle when his line of sight wasn't obstructed by loiterers.

She had her elbow propped on one of the few tall tables, and the man mirrored her, his back toward Troy. He stood too close and touched her entirely too much—his hand covered hers, his fingers drifted up her arm, he'd reach out and wrap one of her curls around his finger.

Giselle didn't respond, but she didn't exactly discourage him either.

Which *didn't matter*, he reminded himself. What she did or didn't do with other men was *none* of his damned business.

Z elbowed him and Troy's gaze went to the bartender he hadn't noticed.

"Shots," he said. "Jamison. Half a dozen. Line 'em up."

The bartender's brows shot up, his eyes darted to Zahara, as if expecting her to veto that order, but she just smiled and said, "Thanks."

Casey strolled into a conversation nearby.

"I heard you bailed on Casey and Becca at the club for a blonde," Z said. When he didn't look at her, she added, "I thought you hated blondes."

"I do."

"Because of her?"

"Yep."

"How long are you going to let this eat at you?"

"Until I stop making stupid fucking mistakes, I guess."

"What the hell does that mean?"

He shook his head as the bartender lined up six shot glasses and filled them with whiskey.

Troy tipped back two in a row.

"I wish you'd talk to me," Z said, taking a sip of the cosmo the bartender left for her.

"Wouldn't do any good." He tossed back a third.

Keaton slipped onto the stool next to Troy, and he froze, aware Giselle's assistant was probably somewhere nearby. "Dude, you made it. Looks like you're making up for lost time." He reached over, picked up one of the shots, and drained it. "Thanks."

When Keaton didn't say his name, Troy relaxed again.

Duke came up beside Zahara. "Come dance with us, Z."

She slipped off the stool and tugged on Troy's arm. "Come with us, have some fun."

He nodded. "Let me finish these. Be right there."

Keaton tried to steal another one, but Troy smacked his chest hard.

"Dude," he said, laughing as he rubbed at the pain with one hand and grabbed the girl's hand with the other, turning toward the dance floor.

Troy sighed. "Finally alone with my booze."

Well, not exactly. Giselle was still smiling and laughing while she dodged the handsy guy. She was also on the screen above the bar, mostly in silhouette, wearing next to nothing, writhing on a wooden floor to the movie's title song, "Around the World."

Troy tipped back another shot and watched the screen where she arched her back and slid her fingers over her skin in a way that was clearly sexual, a way that matched the lyrics and style of the music. The sight pushed blood into his cock, and the ache that had lived in the pit of his stomach since the day Giselle walked out burned like a hot coal.

He pulled his attention off the video-the video that might very well have been what had driven her to the club-and tried to collect his thoughts as the alcohol seeped into his bloodstream. Across the room, Giselle had broken free of handsy man and now flitted from one group to the next, all smiles and glamour.

This was her life, one filled with the rich and elite, cocktail parties and special events, champagne and hors d'oeuvres, and men fawning over her.

That was fine. Good. *Great.* After her childhood, Giselle deserved to be showered with as much attention as she could stand.

"Don't you think you deserve more?"

But, yeah, maybe Z was right. Maybe he did deserve more too. Like closure. Maybet he deserved the right to move on too.

Giselle broke out of her conversation with an older couple Troy didn't recognize and strolled through the crowd, turning a balustrade and disappearing down a short flight of stairs.

Purpose burned a hole straight through Troy's chest. *This.*

This moment was the moment he'd been waiting for.

Giselle dried her hands, checked her makeup in the bathroom mirror, and added a little more concealer to her hickey, then feathered the edges. Going back to the club to see if she could catch him again was a really, really bad idea, wasn't it? Like the worst idea ever, she knew.

It was over. She wouldn't be going back. She wouldn't be seeing him again. She had to start looking forward, not backward.

With that new goal fixed in her mind, she straightened and turned for the door with her thoughts on the room upstairs. To the people who held her future in their hands. To the bathtub in her suite on the ninth floor-the lowest floor they'd had available-and the fragrant bubbles she'd fill it with when she returned.

She started up the short flight of stairs in front of her now with a grip on the iron handrail. The sight of men's black dress shoes and black slacks made her shift to the right.

She lifted her gaze and smiled politely at the man coming the opposite direction. "Excuse-"

The last word evaporated as she set eyes on Troy's face.

Denial blossomed even as her heart opened and swelled. Her feet stopped.

Not Troy. Can't be Troy.

Her eyes narrowed as the man stared back, still descending the staircase. Giselle had the strangest sensation of time slowing and warping and playing with her mind. She tried to see someone else in his face, someone she'd met upstairs, but all she saw was Troy-an older, wiser, sexier version of Troy with stubble heavy enough to be considered a beard.

Which only meant her mind was meshing memories of Troy with thoughts of the guy from...oh shit. The guy from the club.

"I'm in movies."

His words echoed in her head as her brain made split-second connections. Dread and panic swam in the pit of her stomach.

He lowered to the same stair and paused, his gaze still holding hers. Giselle's mind flooded with panic. She fought to focus, to collect her scattered thoughts, but a small smile hinted on his lush lips.

Lips that moved with "Hi, Ellie."

And her brain backpedaled, then stalled dead.

Ellie?

A spear of heat pierced the middle of her body. Her gaze jumped from his mouth to his eyes. And his identity hit her with absolute clarity: *Troy.*

Her heart did a funny twirl, jump, and flip, then took a high dive into the pit of her stomach. "What...? How did you...?" A flicker of doubt passed through her mind. She fell back a step, her hand grasping the railing. *"Troy?"*

She was so damn confused. Maybe she was going a little crazy. Because in that moment, every existing wrong collided and spit out an idea that absolutely did not register: *The man at the club had been Troy.*

"Oh my God." Panic tinged the words, and the stairs spun in her vision. She pressed a hand to her forehead, and her back hit the wall of the staircase. "Oh shit. *No.* No, no, no."

Her vision grayed around the edges. The strength in her legs gave out.

"Whoa, El..." He wrapped his arms around her, catching her before she hit the floor. "Holy shit."

His voice confirmed her dreaded realization.

Frustration, hurt, anger bubbled up inside her in something that felt a lot like hysteria. But everything was spinning and fading. Her limbs weren't working. And the fear kept rising like a tide, rolling in on wave after wave until it overwhelmed her.

Her chest squeezed so tight, she couldn't draw enough air. Her throat thickened until she thought it would close. She clutched at his jacket sleeves, as if having that fabric fisted in her hands would help her breathe.

From there, everything took on a dark haze. She had a vague notion of being moved, of being lowered to the floor, of someone speaking to her, but a buzz filled her ears, along with her every breath, her every heartbeat. Her brain remained soaked in panic and darkness. She didn't know how long. Didn't remember the what, where, why, or who of it all.

When the buzz finally quieted, a voice reached her. "You're okay. You're safe. Use your breathing, El. One, two, three..."

Her lungs responded as if they'd been trained to voice commands, and in the amount of time it took to snap fingers, air filled her lungs to his count of eight. Her head cleared. Her nerves smoothed.

"There you go," he said, his voice calm, warm, soothing. "Open those pretty eyes for me, Ellie."

Ellie. The name brought so much pleasure, her ribs ached.

She forced her lids up and blinked to focus into beautiful chocolaty brown eyes.

Troy's eyes.

Her heart flooded with emotion-love, longing, loss.

He smiled, showing a perfect row of bright white teeth and small lines fanning out from the corners of his eyes. Neither of which he'd had last time she'd seen him.

Seven years ago.

She sat up too fast, and her brain spiraled. She slammed her eyes shut and covered them with her hand, groaning a curse.

"You scared the shit out of me, El," he said before pulling her into the circle of his arms.

She wanted nothing more than to stay there, safe and warm and close to him. Oh, how long she'd craved the feeling of his arms around her again. Her mind seemed to stretch and expand, reaching for something. For time and place. For some sort of explanation.

And it all came back in a rush. The club. The devil. Troy.

"Oh shit," she rasped, scrambling away. The cold tile beneath her made her glance around, and a whole different reality hit her-she was in the bathroom of the banquet room, with a hundred people upstairs.

Her past, her present, and her future slammed together in the worst possible way.

"Good God." She rolled to her knees, and her head swayed. Squeezing her eyes closed against the spin, she steadied herself with a hand against the wall.

"Ellie, don't try to stand yet."

A sound bubbled from her throat, half attempt to speak, half denial. "Troy, what…? Why…? How…?"

Every syllable seemed to hammer another sliver of reality into her head, and it rattled her brain so hard, she felt it all the way to her teeth.

Holy mother of God. She'd *fucked* him.

A sob escaped her, and she covered her mouth with both hands. Tears swelled in her eyes, blurring her vision. Thoughts raced through her brain, but nothing escaped but sounds of dread and dismay. It was too much. All too much. She forced herself to her feet and used the counter to keep her there.

Someone tried to push into the bathroom, and the door hit Troy's back. Fear hit Giselle like ice water. She grabbed paper towels and pressed them over her mouth, stifling another sob.

"Sorry," he called through the door. "We just need a minute." Then to Giselle, "I'm really sorry, El. I never expected-"

She cut a look at him in the mirror that stopped his words. But she couldn't begin to come up with anything coherent to say from the mess inside. She spun and lifted her hands, fighting to keep her voice down, half-pleading, half-demanding, "*What the hell,* Troy?"

Someone knocked. "Is everything okay in there?"

She sucked a shaky breath, closed her eyes, and pressed a hand to her forehead. "Yes. I'm sorry. I just need one more min—minute."

She choked on the last word, and a flood of hysteria threatened. She clenched her teeth, willing it back. The fury wasn't as easy to contain.

Breathe.

Breathe.

She cut her gaze back to her own reflection, surprised to find she didn't look anywhere near as bad as she felt. Still, she touched up and turned to the door.

When he didn't move and opened his mouth to speak, she cut him off. "Let. Me. Out. *Now.*"

He raised his hands in surrender and took one deliberate step back with a "Yes, ma'am" filled with screw-you attitude.

Lies spiraled in Giselle's head as three women filed in. "I'm sorry. I received some bad news, and I just… needed a few minutes. Thank you for waiting."

She moved into the little alcove outside the bathroom and glanced up to make sure no one was standing near the railing, then faced Troy when he stepped out behind her. He was wearing clothes similar to those he'd worn at the club-tailored slacks and blazer that fit him to perfection, a smooth, light-colored button-down shirt beneath. He pulled off the carelessly sexy hairstyle well, especially with the beard. God, a beard. That still made her shake her head in dismay. The last time she'd seen him, he hadn't even been able to grow a full mustache. His face looked more rugged and seasoned, the same way his body was bigger and stronger.

Troy.

She was facing *Troy*.

The realization sliced something open inside her, and all her old emotions came spilling out. All the love, all the passion, all the hurt, all the loss, it filled her up until she was drowning. Until all she wanted to do was fall into him, take all the good, and let him make her forget all the bad, something he'd always been so good at.

"What the hell?" she repeated, unable to find anything else to say. She didn't even know where to start. Or if she even wanted to start. She was too shocked, too angry, too scared to even think straight. "Why are you here?"

"It's good to see you too, Ellie." He pushed his hands into the pockets of his slacks, rolled back on his heels, and all warmth disappeared. "I'm here because I was invited. You?"

"Don't even *start* with the attitude." A group of people laughed upstairs, making the nerves along the back of Giselle's neck ripple. "You decided to show your face to me here? Now? *Really?*"

His eyes narrowed. A black cloud darkened his expression in a way that signaled hurt feelings and a brewing temper. "I couldn't reach you at the hotel. I tried every alias I knew, but none worked. I've been calling Ryker to get your cell number for two days, but he's not calling back-"

"He's overseas on a teaching assignment."

She blurted the words, and the simple exchange of information slammed her back to a time that had defined the most important years of her life. The first time she'd ever been safe. The first time she'd ever been loved. Which all clashed with what had happened at the club, what was happening now, and confused the hell out of her.

The bathroom door opened, and the women filed into the hall, casting worried glances her way.

When they were gone, Troy said, "Look, I just wanted you to know it was me-"

"*Why?* So you could humiliate me?"

"*Humiliate you?*" His eyes burned with challenge. "How could I possibly humiliate you when you were at the club of your own free will? When you had every opportunity to leave of your own volition at any time with the use of two simple words? When you said yes to me after turning three other men away?"

Shame made the skin of her face flame. Her heart picked up speed, squeezed, and knotted. "Don't do that."

"Don't do what?"

"Twist everything. You recognized me at the club. You purposely hit on me, *knowing* I didn't recognize you. My God, look at you. Even your personality is different. You *knew…*" Hurt swelled in her throat and stung her eyes, and she couldn't go on. An irrational sense of betrayal stabbed at her. "*Why* did you do that?"

"Maybe, after seven long years," he said, his voice rough with emotion, "I just wanted to be close to you, El. Did you ever think of that?"

"Bullshit." The fact that he'd even try to sell her crap twisted the knife in her gut. "How long have you been in Vegas?"

He frowned. "What does that-"

"*How long?*" she demanded, unsuccessfully attempting to quiet her voice.

"Three weeks."

"My face has been everywhere for *six* weeks. I've been doing concerts almost every night for *two*. I've been in town for *four*. But I haven't heard a word from you until we happen to cross paths at a sex club? And even then you didn't tell me who you were? When you knew I was staying right across the street from the Venetian, where I know the cast and crew are staying?" She crossed her arms, but it didn't help calm the full-body tremor. Or the urge to throw herself into him and pray he caught her. "No, Troy, 'I just wanted to be close to you' is absolutely not something that ever crossed my mind. Just man up and admit it. When you recognized me and realized I was alone, you saw the perfect opportunity for a revenge fuck."

One big step forward, and he'd closed the distance between them. His hands curled around her arms and hauled her body up against his so hard, she gasped.

"You *know* that's not true," he said, teeth clenched, pain radiating from his eyes. A few deep, quick breaths later, his grip eased, and his gaze traveled hungrily over her face. "It had nothing to do with revenge. I've *never* wanted revenge."

She had her hands pressed to his chest, and his heart beat hard and fast beneath her palms. A heart that had once belonged to her, and only her. A heart that had more capacity for love and giving and sacrifice than almost any other heart she knew. A heart she'd crushed.

"After the way I left, maybe I deserved it." Her voice shook. "I just wish you had the guts to admit that's what it was about."

He shook his head and slipped one arm around her waist. All the skin along her spine tingled. "And I wish you had the guts to admit the chemistry between us is *real.* Seven fucking years and an anonymous meeting later, and it's still white-hot. It's still there, El."

His forcefulness, his confidence, his sheer dominating presence stunned Giselle. Made her insides quiver. This was a very different man from the one she'd left. The Troy she'd left was all heart and soul where Giselle was concerned. All about bending over backward to make her happy-until her career took off. Until her career came between them. Then he'd turned sullen and angry and unpleasable.

"Nothing about that club is real. Nothing about Las Vegas is real." Giselle didn't even know what "real" meant. She had very little of anything "real" in her life. "It was a one-time research trip for me that got out of hand, that's all."

"Oh, it got out of hand, I agree with you there." His free hand slid deep into her hair, his palm cupping the back of her head. "But it was real, Ellie. All that fire between you and me, it was one hundred percent real, and you know it."

His head lowered, and Giselle stiffened, expecting an aggressive attack. Instead, his mouth hovered a breath above hers, the tip of his nose tracing the line of hers in a way that brought back a rush of heartbreakingly sweet memories. "You still wear...*Forever*," he whispered, referencing her perfume as his lashes fluttered closed. "*God*, that makes me ache."

His lips touched hers. Just barely. Giselle was trembling, caught between pushing him away and grabbing on. Between anger and longing. She didn't know what to feel or how strongly to feel it. And all those old emotions from their five years together, all that deep, deep love they'd shared, all that time when he'd been her absolute everything, were mucking up her head and her heart and diluting her good sense.

"Troy..." She barely whispered his name, the single word shaky. "I...can't think...with you this close."

He kissed the corner of her mouth.

Her hands fisted in the back of his jacket. "I should knee you in the balls."

"But you won't." He dropped three kisses along her upper lip, then whispered, "Because you love the heat between us. You love the way we read each other, the way we give each other exactly what we need. You love the way I push you and test you. So, you're going to open to me. You're going to let me taste you the sweet way I should have tasted you for the first time again in seven years. Not the nasty way I did at the club."

He pressed his lips to hers, stroked his tongue across her bottom lip. And just as he'd predicted, she opened.

He groaned with passion and approval as he swept his tongue in and found hers. He was wet and warm, and his tongue glided over hers in the sexiest way. He tasted like a mix of whiskey and Troy, and Giselle moved her tongue against his even when everything inside her told her not to. His lips were soft, his beard rough, and he kissed her with his whole body. Hers instantly responded with a ball of heat in her pelvis, sliding deep between her legs, making her wet...

Stop, stop, stop. That voice of reason kept screaming in her head. She knew it was right, knew she'd regret this, knew she needed to push him away and turn her back, but...This was Troy. *Troy.* And, God, he felt so good, and when he was holding her, kissing her, she felt so...whole. So complete. So strong. Like she could do anything.

It won't last.

It will blow up in your face.

The fear finally broke through the pleasure, and Giselle pulled out of the kiss. She forced her fingers to unclench from his jacket and pushed him back a step. Her gut felt heavy and tight when she met his heavy-lidded gaze, his expression cautious.

"The chemistry may still be there," she said, "but the trust isn't. What you did at the club was wrong, and you know it."

All the heat in his expression drained, and the Troy she knew vanished with it. He straightened and pulled on his suit jacket to uncrumple the fabric from Giselle's hands. He gave her a lopsided smile, rigid with a mix of anger and hurt. "Trust is something we lost seven years ago, Ellie. That had nothing to do with the club."

He turned for the stairs, and that strange sense of panic licked her belly again. Confusion abraded her nerves. She was about to call after him, though she wasn't sure what she'd say. She wanted to tell him not to leave angry. Wanted to ask if they could set aside some time to talk. But she was glad she didn't get the chance, because the turmoil churning inside her like a tornado did not align itself well with rational ideas.

At the top of the stairs, Troy paused to speak to Jeff Michel, who stood at the banister, and from the surprised smile on Michel's face, she was sure he'd just witnessed their kiss. After a few quick words with the director, Troy darted a quick, none-too-happy look Giselle's way before striding out of sight.

She clenched her teeth and told herself all her sexy actions were good for her image.

But it sure as shit didn't feel good on her mind, body, or heart.

Seven

Giselle sat in the window seat of her suite, her gaze blurred over the Las Vegas strip below, picking chords and humming to herself, searching for a tune that struck her. She was worthless for anything more demanding, and many of her best songs started this way anyhow. Besides, she needed the feel of the strings beneath her fingers to keep her sane.

Few people would understand how many ways an instrument could act like a security blanket. Her guitar gave her a topic of conversation when she ran out of small talk. Gave her something to fidget with when she was anxious. Gave her somewhere to hide when she needed an escape.

Unfortunately, it was also a small-time problem fixer. It didn't rise to the level of your-ex-disguised-himself-and-screwed-you-in-a-sex-club-type problem.

Her backup singers, Helen and Simone, had asked her to go shopping with them earlier, and her band wanted an early dinner date after rehearsal, but Giselle knew the invitations were simply excuses to get time with Giselle so they could riddle her with questions. And she didn't have the patience or the strength to soothe their frustration with her lack of answers right now.

The stress had her so wrung out, all she wanted to do was sleep until the show, lose herself in the high of her music and the love of her audience, and fall back into bed. Not an all-around bad plan.

A knock sounded on her door before it opened, and Brook came in with a tray of food. Giselle winced. "Thanks, but I'm really not—"

"Don't even start." She set the food down on a four-person table and uncovered the plates. "Get your butt over here. You haven't eaten since dinner last night, and don't think I didn't notice how you pushed your food around to make it look like you ate something. I babysat a lot as a kid."

Giselle set her guitar aside and pushed from the window seat. "You're going to make a great mom, you know that?"

"Not anytime soon. Especially not after watching the hell you've gone through with love." As Giselle pulled her chair under her and picked up a strawberry, Brook said, "It's no wonder your songs are so...gut-wrenching."

That made Giselle chuckle, and her heartache loosened a little. "Hey, half of my songs are happy."

"But they still bring tears to your eyes." Brook took a seat next to her and finished uncovering dishes—eggs, bacon, toast, and fruit. Breakfast at noon, although it was her favorite meal any time of the day.

Giselle's stomach rolled with pleasure. "Oh my God. *That* brings tears to *my* eyes."

Brook gave a smug smile. "I know what my girl likes. Eggs and bacon first. You need some serious protein. No fainting on stage tonight."

"Mmm," she said around a strawberry, "that would seriously suck."

"Right?" Brook popped the top on a diet Pepsi with a roll of her eyes. "Imagine all the publicity I'd have to field."

They fell into a silence that would normally have been comfortable, each woman mired in her own thoughts, sharing when it suited her. Today, it wasn't like that. It hadn't been like that since Brook had found out about Troy at the mixer three days before. She'd known something major was wrong the moment Giselle had come back upstairs, despite her denials, even when no one else had noticed, not even Chad.

She'd told Brook about seeing Troy, but hadn't confessed any details about the club or their kiss at the mixer.

"Have you talked with your stunt hottie?" Giselle asked to ease the silence.

Instead of answering, she said, "I googled Troy. Do you want to know what I found?"

Her gaze cut to Brook. "You didn't."

"I did."

Giselle's air rushed from her lungs; her fork fell from her hand and clinked against the plate.

She already knew what Brook would find, which was why Giselle hadn't googled him herself. She was sure Brook had found out that Troy was an actor of some kind and the worst kind of playboy. She'd found images of Troy with woman after woman after woman on his arm. Which was fine. No, it was great. It was exactly the kind of life he should be leading. He was handsome and charismatic and intelligent. He'd obviously grown into a man who wielded the whole damn package, just like she'd known he would. And she was sincerely thrilled about that. Anything less would have been a true waste. He was a very special man.

Unfortunately, he was a very special man who hadn't been able to cope with the pressures of her demanding career. A career that was more than a job or even a way of life for Giselle. Her music was her calling. Her purpose. What she'd been born to do. And Troy knew that. He'd never once asked her to give it up.

"No," she said, "I don't want to know what you found."

"Yes, you do."

"No, actually, I really don't. I left him. I have no right to judge the way he's spent his life. I have no right to any pride in his success, no right to any disappointment in his failures. I have no rights at all where Troy's concerned."

Brook was silent for a long moment while Giselle felt like she was bleeding inside. Because she may have no rights, but she still cared. Would always care. And the fact that he was still hurting over their breakup enough to act so...fucked up, felt like a hot dagger in her gut.

"That's so..." Brook started, her voice dry, "mature."

Didn't feel mature. Just felt painful.

"You're going to have to talk to him," Brook said. "You know that, right? I hope you don't think you're going to get out of town without talking to him."

Her stomach coiled tighter. "There's really nothing more to say."

"Yes, there is. All this..." She gestured to Giselle with both hands in a chaotic burst of waving. "All this...turmoil. You can't live with that eating at you. You need to say what you need to say and get it out. You can't control what he says back, you can't control how he feels, but you can control what you do about how you feel. And keeping it all bottled up inside is not healthy, and you know it."

Giselle stabbed a forkful of scrambled eggs. "I'll think about it." She heaved a sigh and glanced at her watch. "I need to get out. Are you up for a Twitter drop?"

Brook's brows rose. "Really?"

Giselle nodded. The thought of randomly tweeting her location and having fans in the area show up for an impromptu, private, intimate mini-concert usually thrilled the hell out of her. It kept her grounded, kept her in touch, kept her real, kept her heart open, and reminded her of why she did this. Right now, she needed that reminder. Of why she'd walked away from Troy.

Right now, it kept her treading water.

"That is a great idea," Brook said. "Tell me when, and I'll put together the where and grab a couple of the hotel security guys."

"It's noon, and rehearsal starts at four. How about one thirty? I'll stay half an hour."

129

"Done. Who are the proceeds going to? Treehouse or Casa?"

"Didn't we donate to Casa last time?"

"Pretty sure we did."

"Then Treehouse."

"Are you singing, or are you letting your fans sing?"

"I can sing today. I just don't like singing after a concert."

"Oooo." Brook clapped and picked up her phone, tapping into some app. "Your fans are going to be sooooo excited!"

Giselle smiled, and a little spark lit up inside her. A spark she really needed right now.

Brook set her phone down, and that weird silence filtered between them again.

"Have you talked to Chad about this?" Brook asked. When Giselle frowned across the table at her, Brook added, "About Troy."

"*No. Why* would I do that?"

"Because you need to talk to *someone* about it and you're not talking to me—which is totally fine," she added quickly. "I don't expect you to talk to me about everything, I'm good with that. I respect that. I'm just really worried at the way you keep everything inside. Especially this. And to do what you do, to live up to the demands and expectations placed on you day in and day out, you need to be balanced. Your mind needs to be free and have room to move. Keeping this locked inside you isn't allowing for that and, honestly...you're scaring me."

"Brook, that's…I'm…" She exhaled. "Okay, look. I'm…different. We've known that from the beginning. I process things differently. I relate to people differently. You've seen me grow and change over the years. I've opened up, become more confident, which has allowed me to be more extroverted.

"Meeting up with Troy again has just, I don't know, sort of pushed me backward a little. I've started acting and reacting in some of the unhealthy ways I used to— like trying to handle everything myself, shutting people out, making rash decisions. It's—it's just my way of protecting myself."

Brook's hand reached across the table and covered Giselle's. "I hope you know you never have to protect yourself from me. I love you unconditionally. And I've always got your back."

This was the kind of closeness that rattled Giselle to the core. It felt awkward and uncomfortable. And it terrified her. This was the kind of closeness that could tear her heart out if—when—it was lost. Yet there was nothing she wanted more. It was the kind of closeness she craved. And the conflict created a constant inner battle.

But she didn't expect Brook to understand those twisted emotions—ones rooted in a traumatic childhood and a young life filled with repeated loss. So she smiled, turned her hand over, and squeezed Brook's. "I know. I love you too. I'm sorry I make you worry."

God, she was so messed up. So freaking broken. Even all these years and all her success later, she was still one crayon short of a full box. She still felt unworthy—of friends, of success, of love.

Brook eased back in her seat and picked at her fruit with a little grin tilting her mouth. "Did I already mention how totally, completely, raging *hawt* he is?" She fanned herself with her hand and rolled her eyes. "Like Vegas-in-August-during-a-record-heat-wave *hawt*."

Giselle cut her a glare. "About two dozen times in three days."

"Huh. So I have." She frowned at her fruit. "Have you talked to Nathan?"

"He's still in Syria," Giselle said. "And I wouldn't talk to him about this anyway. He never liked the idea of Troy and me together."

"The little-sister complex?"

"I guess. I never looked at either of them as brothers. We were friends. Equals. Three people with similar life experiences struggling to make it day to day together. My feelings for Nathan were always platonic. My feelings for Troy were *never* platonic. But Nathan's a leader and protector at heart."

They fell silent a moment, both of them playing with their food more than eating it. Giselle had never told Brook the story behind her relationship with Troy, though pieces had come out over the years when they'd talked about Nathan, about their pasts. Now, she felt the need to put it into perspective.

"The foster father where we lived was an alcoholic. A mean drunk, you know? But his wife, she was even meaner. So when he got sauced, he took out his anger with the world on the kids, because he was that big a coward. I was fourteen when I got there—it was my third home—and I was the only girl. Nathan and Troy were seventeen, and sort of took me under their wing.

"At first, I was wary, thought it was a ruse to get close to me and manipulate me. That wasn't my first time around that block. But I saw how they created a buffer between the father and me. There were times..." Her voice broke, and emotions rushed in. She paused and swallowed, forcing the memories back. Brook reached across the table and covered her hand again. "They took beatings that were meant for me. Beatings that I know in my heart would have ended in rape. Beatings that would eventually have killed me."

She took a slow, measured breath, fighting to hold the flood back. But she couldn't stand the contact any longer, and pulled her hand from Brook's. Sitting back, she crossed her arms.

"When they turned eighteen they got kicked out of the system. They had to leave. I had to stay. They'd done a pretty good job of teaching me how to take care of myself, but I couldn't bear the thought of being without them. They were my family and my best friends all rolled into one. We were each other's lifelines, you know?"

Brook's expression had darkened, but she nodded.

"I kept running away to their apartment, where I stayed until my foster parents sent the cops to haul me home. Finally, they just stopped coming. I dropped out of high school, and we all worked two jobs to make ends meet. But the guys made me study for my GED at night. Nathan bought this piece-of-shit car off a friend, and he and Troy would drive me to bars every weekend so

I could sing. They hung out to keep guys from hitting on me, make sure the equipment was set up right, and bring me water when my throat was raw.

"Then Nathan got into the army, and after he left, everything changed. When the three of us were together, we were the three musketeers. But once Nathan left, and it was just me and Troy..." She shook her head. "Looking back, I think I fell in love with him the first time he stepped between me and my foster father. I hid it because I didn't want anything to change. I never had those feelings for Nathan, but Troy...God, he was all I thought about. All I wanted. And when I discovered he felt the same about me, man..."

Her heart ached with the memories. Such sweet, powerful memories. "Back then, everything was a struggle—food, rent, gas. But he always found a way to get me to every gig. Always made the time to stay with me. He gave me inspiration for my songs, let me cry on his shoulder, supported my every attempt to live my dream." A smile tugged at her mouth and joy filled her heart. "He loved me. Loved me like I've never been loved.

"And it wasn't like he didn't have other girls interested. He'd had girlfriends before me. Had plenty of girls calling and coming to see him while we were together, but he told them straight up, 'We can be friends, but I love Ellie.' He was so confident with himself that way. Never needed to play games to feel secure the way so many of our friends did.

"I can't explain how intense our connection was. It's one of those things you can't understand unless you've been through the hell of abusive parents and violent foster care. But we were more than friends. More than lovers. We were...like...*part* of each other. Maybe we were so in love because we were young and reckless and stupid and broken. But I've never known love like that again—before or after."

She wiped her face on her sleeve, suddenly exhausted. She'd never given out so much information in such a short amount of time, and it drained her.

"And I guess I know the rest of the story from there," Brook said, voice sad.

Giselle laughed, but it was a painful sound. Theirs was a story of heartbreak shared by hundreds of others in this business where success tore people apart.

"So typical, right?" Giselle had spent many nights in those early months on the road crying on Brook's shoulder. "God, I *hate* clichés."

Brook sighed heavily and rested her chin on her hand. "Clichés exist for a reason, honey. It means you aren't the only couple that struggled with jealousy, the demands of the industry, and the influx of new and exciting people into your lives."

Maybe not, but that didn't make the memories any less awful. Or the breakup any less painful. She looked down at her plate and shook her head, still not sure what to do or how to handle this. "What a mess."

"I know more happened between you two than a chance meeting at the mixer," Brook said, "otherwise you wouldn't be this upset. And I don't need to know what that was. I just want you to remember that you're not the only one who acts a certain way to protect yourself. Troy's going to have the same kind of buffers in place. I'm not saying whatever he might have done or not done was warranted or okay. I'm just saying that if anyone would understand him, I mean really, honestly understand him, it would be you. But to do that, you're going to have to put your own hurt aside."

She dropped her head into her hand and massaged her forehead. "He's a grown adult. I'm taking responsibility for my flaws. He needs to take responsibility for his."

"True enough." Brook put up both hands in surrender. "I just thought it might help you wrap you mind around this and put it behind you."

Giselle's cell rang with Chad's ring tone. She and Brook groaned in unison.

"Has he left you alone for a minute in the last two weeks?" Brook asked, frustrated.

"He's just doing his job."

"No, doing his job would include telling you about that L'Oréal offer."

"I can only handle one difficult man at a time. And I think Troy counts as five," Giselle answered with as much ease as she could drag up. "Hey."

"Hey, sweetie. Can we talk a few minutes?"

"Sure. Be right there." She disconnected before Chat had time to ramble on about things he was going to tell her once she got to his room anyway, and pushed from the table. "The master has summoned."

"Whatever." Brook covered the food with the foil it had come in, her grumpy face on. "Don't forget about your Twitter drop at one thirty. I already posted it, so you can't back out. I'll lay out your clothes and be here at one to do your hair and makeup and make sure you've eaten more of this before we leave."

Giselle smiled, picked up room keys off a side table, then turned to hug Brook. "Thank you. For everything. I don't know what I'd do without you."

Brook pulled back and smiled. "Good thing you'll never have to find out."

Giselle was feeling a little lighter as she wandered to the next suite and used the extra key to enter.

"Hey," she called, stepping in and closing the door behind her. "What's—oh."

She stopped short at the sight of a second man in the room, sitting with Chad on the sofa—Jeff Michel.

Shit.

"I'm sorry." Her gaze jumped to Chad, and she wondered how much the director had told him. "I thought you wanted to talk now. I'll just come back—"

"No, no. I do want to talk to you now, but I would have told you to jump into something pretty if you hadn't hung up on me." He gestured to the director sitting beside him. He was in his fifties, wearing a tweed blazer over jeans and cowboy boots. "You remember Jeff Michel."

Suddenly self-conscious in her sweats, her hair up in a knot, no makeup on, she crossed her arms but approached him with a smile and held out her hand. "Of course. I'm so sorry about my appearance—"

"Not at all. My daughter lives in nothing but sweats."

He stood and shook her hand, his smile wide, his manner easy. That should have relaxed her, but it didn't.

She felt like a gazelle waiting for a lion to leap out of the tall grass.

"Sophie, right?" Giselle grinned and slipped on her professional veneer. One she used so often, it fit like a calfskin glove. "I think I signed a picture for her."

"Right, and she loved it, thank you. I think my ears are still popping from the squeal she let out when I gave it to her."

Giselle laughed. "How old is she?"

"Sixteen going on twenty-eight."

"Have a seat, Giselle," Chad said. "Jeff's brought us a very interesting offer."

"An offer. That's a surprise." She perked up as her mind started connecting dots. Offer plus movie director could equal the possibility of writing music for another film. Or, even better, writing and singing music for an animated production. As a girl, she'd fallen asleep every night for years fantasizing she was Ariel, Snow White, or Cinderella, and as she'd gotten older, dreamed of singing for a Disney or Pixar film.

She took a chair across from the sofa and curled her bare feet underneath her.

"Go ahead, Jeff," Chad said. "I think you'll explain the project better than I can."

He nodded, then focused on Giselle, growing intent and serious. "It seems we have a relationship—or two—in common."

Oh shit.

Her balloon of excitement popped, and she physically fought to keep her smile on.

"I've been good friends with Matt Sullivan for years. We worked on countless projects together before he bailed on movie production and started working on music videos. We had lunch yesterday, and I mentioned the mixer where I met you. He told me he was producing your music video and couldn't stop talking about how professional and talented you are in front of a camera."

The bubbles in her mind holding Arial, Snow White, and Cinderella popped, one by one.

"That's great to hear." Giselle kept a smile on her face, but her shoulders tightened with every new connection within this very small world of entertainment.

"And it got me thinking about the other relationship we have in common—Troy Jacobs."

Oh my God.

Alarm tingled through her belly.

Kill me now.

Giselle couldn't keep her smile from slipping a little.

Chad's head swung toward Giselle, his brows pulled together in a frown. "Who's Troy?"

That familiar metal band was back, cinching Giselle's chest tight. But she met Chad's eyes and said, "An old friend."

"He's also one of our top stuntmen," Jeff said. "Amazingly talented. Does the rigging for all the blockbuster action films in Hollywood. Works with a company called Renegades out of Los Angeles."

Stuntman. Troy was a *Renegade.*

That surprised Giselle more than if he'd been an actor. In his youth, Troy had been teased over his lack of coordination and skinny build. He'd never been particularly athletic, and sports had bored him.

"That's really beside the point," Jeff went on. "The point is that when I saw you with him the other night at the mixer, I realized what was missing in this film: passion. We've got the big stars, the big stunts, the big budget, but no *passion.*"

The band ratcheted tighter. Chad was frowning now. The vertical line between his brows indicated how hard he was trying to figure out how this all connected. And, man, she really didn't want to rehash her history with Troy again.

"I'm not sure how I can help," she managed, pushing the conversation along, wishing it would end. Wishing it hadn't ever started.

Jeff leaned forward, resting his elbows on his knees, and focused on Giselle with such intensity, she felt his magnetic pull. "I want to offer you a cameo in the film, Giselle. Just a small part, a few small scenes, really, as the love interest for our villain, Alec Guzman. I want the passion I saw between you and Troy in the movie on the screen. Matt and I actually came up with the idea together. He thinks a sexy part in a motion picture of this caliber would be right in line with your goals and give you a nice boost toward that jump you're trying to make in your career."

She darted a look toward Chad and found him already looking at her, still trying to unpuzzle this Troy situation, she was sure.

"You've really got the fresh country-star persona dialed in, and I would never have considered you for a sexy part like this unless I'd seen you on that music video at the mixer. But the camera loves you, Giselle, and you look absolutely at ease with your sexuality on film. It's beautiful and sensual. Add that passion between you and Troy, and bam"—he smacked his hands together, making Giselle jump—"we've not only got a blockbuster, we've got something really, really special. It's a win-win, in my eyes. What do you think?"

"I..." God, she didn't know what to think. "I'm not an actor. I don't know—"

"You don't have to be. If you need coaching, we can give you a little on the set. I talked to the producer about adding you in the background singing in one of the other major scenes. That would enable more of your work to appear on the movie soundtrack."

This was huge—her music on a major motion picture soundtrack? Personal exposure in a blockbuster film? There really was no better way to show her updated persona to the world. Of course, there was a love scene to think about. And working on the same film as Troy...

"Wow," she said, her heart squeezing. "What an amazing opportunity."

"For an amazing woman," Jeff finished with a charming grin. "I'll let you discuss it with Chad. If you're interested, we can finalize the nitty-gritty details later. And, just so you know, whatever's happening between you and Troy—"

She shook her head. "Nothing's—"

"As long as you can both handle it and do your jobs, it's fine with me. Troy's a really, really great guy. Maybe a little wild, but it's nothing a good woman couldn't cure."

He tapped a thick sheaf of papers lying on the coffee table. "This is the revised script. I've highlighted your part. I'd like you to take a look at it and get back to me— either way—within the next couple of days. I know it's short notice, but after talking with Chad, it sounds like it would fit into our production schedule and your tour dates. If you decide not to take it, we'll need to revisit the part to see if we want to keep it and cast someone else or just drop it."

"I understand. I'm honored, Jeff. Really. Thank you for considering me."

"My pleasure." Slapping his thighs, he pushed to his feet and offered his hand to Chad. "I'd better get back and see what my hellions are up to out there. Troy and his crew can kick up some serious dust when someone's not watching them. Their practical jokes are legendary."

Giselle stood and walked Jeff to the door with Chad. There, Jeff turned and shook Giselle's hand. "I hope you'll join us. And I can't lie when I tell you it would mean the world to my daughter. I'll be a hero in her eyes, and, well, at her age, anything I can do to connect is a blessing."

She smiled. "Thanks again."

They said their good-byes, and when Giselle closed the door, she held on to the handle for a long moment before finally facing Chad with a hand pressed against her pounding heart. "Wow."

"Yeah, wow." He pushed his hands into his pockets. "About this Troy…"

Giselle's eyes fell closed, and her shoulders sagged. "Such a long, painful story."

"Not too painful to take the part, I hope." His voice was deadly serious. "Not only is it exactly the exposure you need to get the sponsors to drop to their knees and drool at your feet, but it officially marks you as a triple threat in the industry."

She frowned at the title used for someone who could sing, act, and model. "I've never modeled, and I'm not sure you could consider messing around with a stranger while on camera acting."

"What do you think all those photo shoots for album covers and magazine spreads were? And if you're in the film, you're acting." His brows shot up. "They're also willing to pay you a nice hundred grand for the cameo. And since Gloria had no part in securing it," he said of Giselle's agent, "her fee won't come off the top."

A hundred grand. That was a lot of money, but not enough to sway her decision. That insight made her realize just how far she'd come from the dicey bars where she'd sung for hours and walked away with forty bucks.

The same dicey bars where Troy sat for the same long hours, listening to her sing, acting as agent, manager, bodyguard, and support system all wrapped into one. And what did he have to show for it?

"You should be bouncing off the walls, Giselle."

"I know. I'm excited. I am."

"But…?"

But her heart was in shreds.

She wandered back into the living room, sat on the edge of the sofa, and picked up the script, where the movie title, *Full Throttle*, stood out in big, bold print. "No buts. I'll do it."

Eight

Troy walked out the burn in his legs as he waited for the cameramen to move equipment. "You've shot this damn thing from every angle imaginable," he told John, the assistant director. "What more do you want?"

The cave felt like a pressure cooker today. The combination of Las Vegas sun and body heat from the crew made the space smolder, and after Troy's repeated sprints, jumps, and falls, he was about ready to pass out.

John answered without taking his gaze off the screen where he watched a replay of Troy's latest fall. "There's a cable shadow on that last drop. Just do it exactly the same. The new camera angles will take care of it."

Keaton was on his knees inspecting the decelerator while Duke scrutinized the grounding cables—the key safety measures that kept Troy from splattering all over the rock formations at the bottom of that damn cavern. But he couldn't say he cared all that much anymore. Given how he'd felt since he'd last seen Giselle at the mixer, dying in this cave doing what he loved most wouldn't be the worst way to go.

"Stop your pacing for a minute." Casey came at him with makeup in one hand, a brush in the other, and started patching up the foundation covering the tattoo on his chest and shoulder. "And while you're at it, stop sweating."

Troy would have laughed if his gut wasn't twisted into a knot. "I'll get right on that."

"Becca and I still want a redo on the club with you," she said, voice lowered.

No. God, no. "I won't be going back."

Her big brown eyes lifted to his. "Why not?"

He ignored her question and forced memories of the club out of his mind by focusing on catching his breath.

Keaton wandered toward him, offering a cold bottle of water. "My side's good." He frowned past Troy's shoulder. "But Duke doesn't look happy."

Troy finished the water and crushed the bottle, tossing it in a nearby trash can before glancing at Duke. His fellow Renegade wasn't inspecting the cables. He was scanning the cave floor. To retain the cave's structural integrity, Ed and his crew had drilled a metal post deep into the rock as the attachment site for all stunt cables. Duke scrutinized the insertion site.

"What's up?" Troy asked.

Duke shook his head. "Where's Ed?"

That was not what Troy wanted to hear.

Keaton keyed the radio. "Ed. Need you in the stunt cave ASAP."

After a moment, Ed came back, "On my way."

Troy wandered toward Duke, ignoring Casey's demand that he hold still. "What's wrong?"

"That's new." Duke straightened but kept his hard frown on the ground and pointed to a small crack originating at the metal's edge. The gap was hairline thin and only extended three or four inches toward the cave wall, something no one else would have noticed. "It's probably nothing, but I want Ed to look at it."

"Turn toward me," Casey said, pulling on his arm.

Ed's shadow darkened the entry to the cave. "What's up?"

As Duke, Keaton, and Ed discussed the crack, Casey used an airbrush to add shadow and depth to the foundation covering his ink, making his tattooed skin look like it had never seen a needle.

"No, that's normal," Ed was saying. "There will be some superficial cracks from the stress. I'm surprised we didn't see them earlier. They don't interfere with the cave's integrity or the stunt's safety."

At this point, Troy didn't give a fuck. He'd been dead inside from the moment he'd seen that holy-shit-what-have-I-done look on Giselle's face when she'd realized who he was and what she'd done with him—as if fucking him had been the worst possible thing that could have happened in her life.

He checked the straps on his harness, wondering if he should just unfasten them and end it all here and now. The only reason he didn't was because he knew Keaton and Duke would blame themselves.

"Come on, guys." Troy paced and stretched and jumped on his toes to keep his muscles warm. "Let's get going."

"We're all set," came from the lead cameraman.

"Hold on a sec, Hank." Jeff's voice dragged Troy's gaze toward the cave entrance again, where the director's silhouette cut out the Vegas sunlight at his back. And he wasn't alone.

As the posse stepped into the set lighting, Troy's gaze locked on Giselle, where she stood at the center of the group. His heart dropped to his stomach the same way Troy had been dropping to the bottom of that cavern all morning.

Her hair was in a ponytail, and she pulled mirrored aviator sunglasses from her eyes, tucking one arm of the glasses into the white tank beneath a breezy white blouse. Faded blue jean cutoffs showed off her shapely, tan legs. Her sweet little feet were slipped into cute sandals, her toes painted pink.

Goddamn she looked like the Ellie he used to know. The Ellie he'd fallen head over heels for the day she walked into their foster home, with a chip on her shoulder and a duffle filled with attitude, and even now, after everything that had happened, his gut twisted like warm taffy at the sight of her.

But he reminded himself she'd proven to him, both at the club and at the mixer, that she wasn't that girl anymore. She might still have the chip and the attitude, both now polished and carefully camouflaged, but the sweet, giving, nurturing soul that had been hidden beneath…He hadn't seen any sign of those.

He'd figured she would get a tour of the set at some point, but had hoped he wouldn't be here when that happened. He put on his dented armor and planted his hands at his hips, too aware of his sweaty, dirty, disgusting state.

He tensed his gut against the pain he sensed coming and asked Jeff, "What's up?"

"You already know Giselle, of course," Jeff said, then moved on to the man beside her, leaving him to wonder what she'd told Jeff. "This is Chad Moore, her manager. These two burly guys are her security detail courtesy of the Mirage. This pretty little thing"—he laid a hand on the shoulder of the woman Troy had seen with Keaton at the mixer—"is her personal assistant."

Giselle's gaze held on his chest, her expression just this side of sheepish.

"Brought the whole entourage, huh?" His question or his brusque tone got her to lift her eyes to his, and even in the dim lighting, he could see a storm brewing there. Just for the hell of it, he added a little lightning strike. "You're just in time to watch me throw myself down a cavern. I'm sure that will make your day."

He turned and set up at the takeoff point. "Let's do this."

"Everyone quiet," John called.

Troy shook out his arms, his hands, cracked his neck, shifted from foot to foot. He couldn't stand still. Needed to work out some of this anxiety. It helped him home in on the present. Helped him focus. Something he needed now more than ever.

The slate kid jogged into Troy's path, called out the scene and the take and snapped the slate. The sound ricocheted off the rock and echoed in Troy's head.

"Ready..." John called.

Troy lowered his gaze to the stone floor, secured his footing, and crouched like a runner at the starting line.

"And...*action*."

Troy pushed his body into a sprint. Strong. Solid. Measured. He felt good. In control. On target. He hit his launch point and lunged with all the strength in his legs. As soon as his feet left the ground, hyperfocus kicked in and time slowed. In split-second increments, he went through the necessary steps to execute the fall. His gaze surveyed the cavern's opening, he spread his arms wide to slow his flight, and gravity sucked him straight into the middle of the shaft.

Down, down, down...Air rushed past him, blowing his hair, cooling his skin, whizzing past his ears. His blood sang with the adrenaline. He loved free fall. No ties, no restriction, no past, no future, just now. Just that very moment. A moment when adrenaline and thrill and triumph mixed, producing a few blessed seconds of utter euphoria.

The same euphoria he felt when he was tangled up, body and soul, with Giselle.

Only Giselle.

The decelerator kicked in. The initial pull on his body always knocked the wind from him in a grunt. He came to a stop midair with only one thing filling his mind.

I want her the fuck out of my head.

"And, *cut.*" John's voice echoed through the cave.

Troy let his arms fall. Let his eyes close. The euphoria evaporated, and darkness settled in.

"Wrap it." Those words meant all the takes were good, the editors could piece together the stunt in various views, and he wouldn't have to run this again, which pleased him one way and disappointed him in another.

The machine holding him suspended now pulled him up, and he found himself hoping Giselle and her groupies were gone by the time he reached the cave floor. But when the lip of the cavern came into view, and the decelerator stopped, they were all still there.

Fuck.

Troy used his legs to swing himself toward the edge and caught Keaton's hand. His buddy pulled him in, and Troy climbed from the cavern to all the typical high-five fanfare that accompanied the wrap of every successful stunt—a reaffirmation of life for the stuntman, a celebration of good work for the crew. But the sense of satisfaction Troy always felt at this point in a stunt was absent. He felt more dead than alive with Giselle looking on.

Sweat slid down his face, neck, and chest. He needed space. Needed quiet. Needed air. Wanted to get out of this goddamned tomb and away from Giselle, who looked like a fucking goddess in those cut-offs, but Jeff approached, his hand out. "Kick-ass as always."

Troy caught a towel one of the crew members tossed to him and wiped down as he shook Jeff's hand. "Thanks."

Then Jeff wrapped his arm around Troy's shoulders and walked him toward the group. This kind of behavior generally meant Jeff had an idea he wanted to put past Troy. Some freaky new change to the script he'd whipped out of his ass overnight, and one that usually threw a wrench into the lives of the cast and crew, who were already escaping the cave as if they knew what was coming.

Giselle had her arms crossed, and she was leaning into one hip, but she didn't look comfortable. Considering how she'd suffered from claustrophobia most of her life after being stuffed away in closets, cellars, crawl spaces, or car trunks whenever her mother was high or sick of being a parent—which was just about every day—Troy was surprised she was still here at all.

"I wanted to tell you that Giselle's agreed to do a cameo for us." It took a second for Jeff's words to register. When they did, Troy's stomach dropped. Again.

He was destined to be tortured. Served him damn right. This was karma coming back to bite him in the ass. "Really."

"She's going to play Guzman's love interest. We'll be integrating her into several scenes over the next week."

Which meant Troy got to think about Guzman's hands and mouth all over her for the next week. *Perfect.*

He settled his gaze on Giselle and tried to act like the adult he should be by now instead of the two-year-old who was throwing a tantrum inside him. "I hope it will get you where you want to go."

Her brows pulled in a little frown.

"So…" Jeff's eyes narrowed on Troy's. "This won't be a problem?"

He shrugged, but he never let his gaze leave Giselle's. "There would only be a problem if she was doing stunts, because in stunt work, *trust* is required. But since she's not…"

He trailed off and held his hands out wide.

Jeff's face broke into a cautious smile. "I'm glad to see this is going to work out for everyone." He gestured toward the cave opening behind them and spoke to the group. "Let's stop to cool down and grab a drink in the dining hall."

They all turned, everyone but Giselle, who kept her gaze on Troy's.

"Giselle?" Chad said, waiting by the cave entrance.

She glanced over her shoulder. "I'll catch up."

When she turned back, Troy crossed his arms and set his feet wide, prepared for just about anything. But he was glad John had wrapped that stunt, because now Troy wouldn't have to spend any more time trying to focus on falling down a very tight rock hole without breaking his skull when the only thing filling his mind were flashes of images from their night together at the club.

She pushed her hands into the front pockets of her shorts. The move made her look ridiculously innocent and country-girl fresh. "You probably already know Jeff saw us at the mixer."

He shrugged.

"Based on our kiss, he's convinced I'm the perfect person to add *passion* to the film."

And what the hell did he say to that? He kept his mouth shut as the last of the crew took a break topside.

Troy found it *insanely* painful to just stand there with her. Pretend to be normal. Pretend to have a normal conversation when there was so much intense history between them. When she was the only person he ever had—or ever would—give himself over to, heart and soul. When she still owned both.

She heaved an uneasy sigh as her gaze darted around the cave before landing on him again. "I realize I might have overreacted at the mixer, and I'm sorry about that. I'm still really confused about how I feel and what I think about all this. And I don't have the time or the..." she gestured to her head, struggling for a description, "brain power, I guess, to work through it all right now. But I don't want any more conflict between us. It's too complicated to explain now, but this part is really important to me, and it's going to be hard enough as it stands. Stress with you would push me over a very brittle edge."

Anger and pain collided, eclipsing rationale. "A word of advice, El. Think before you talk, because when you don't, things like what you just said come out, and eventually you'll piss off someone who really *does* matter to you."

He turned his back on her and ripped the harness open. The harsh sound of Velcro echoed through the cave.

"What did I say?" she demanded, sincerely upset.

"It's all about *how* you said what you said, and what you *didn't* say." He dropped the harness into a pile and turned on her. He felt raw and gutted and wanted to be anywhere but here, talking to anyone but Giselle. "You just apologized for bitching me out only because you want something, yet I'm not important enough to waste your valuable time trying to figure out how you feel about seeing me again, trying to decide how you feel about me now or even to explain why this thing you want is so important to you. Of course, you fully expect me to comply with your not-so-cleverly-disguised attempt at manipulation. I'm your key source of stress, and I could ruin everything for you. That's what you said."

"But that's not what I meant." She scraped both hands into her hair, pulling it off her face as her eyes fell closed. She looked as tormented as he felt. "God, you've changed so much."

"You mean the part where I don't contort myself to fulfill your every wish? Yeah, I guess that's changed a little. People change over the course of seven years in the prime of their lives, El. But I guess there's something comforting about the fact that you're still willing to compromise anything to reach the top."

He turned away, exhausted from the relentless ache eating him alive, and fished out a water bottle from the cooler. She'd get sick of him and walk out soon. The sooner the better, because the ugly band of two-year-olds who made up this ridiculously immature side of him were running rampant in his psyche.

"Hold on," she said, anger making her voice rise. "What the hell is that supposed to mean?"

"It means you're not thinking twice about getting naked with some guy you've never met and getting busy on camera in a cave so you can take that next step up the ladder, just like you didn't think twice about fucking a stranger in a club so you could get sexy for a music video to push your song to the top of the charts, just like you didn't think twice about walking away from me to get your break."

She sipped air and held it. Pain and anger flashed across her face, and a very familiar self-hatred welled inside him.

She closed her eyes and lifted her hands to her head. In a low voice, likely more for herself than for Troy, she murmured, "I'm not going to get mad. I'm not going to get mad." Then louder. "I'm not going to get mad, because one: you don't know what you're talking about, two: you're speaking out of anger and you know what you're saying isn't true, and three: you probably have half a dozen little brats running around in your head right now turning you into a lunatic."

He scowled hard, but a bittersweet balm swelled somewhere deep inside him. "Don't pretend you know me."

She crossed her arms again, and tilted her head with that knowing look. "I bet they're playing cops and robbers, chasing and shooting each other, creating chaos."

God*dammit.* "It's cowboys and Indians. They haven't been into cops and robbers in years. See, you don't know."

Her lips quirked. "Anyone burning at the stake yet?"

He laughed, totally against his will. He didn't want this. He didn't want to know how well she still understood him. Didn't want to be reminded of what he was missing. He didn't want amiable. He didn't want forgiveness. He didn't want letting go and forgetting and putting it behind them. It might be wrong, it might be backward and fucked up, but he'd rather have the hurt to hold on to than nothing.

Only now he realized that maybe Giselle needed something else. Maybe she did need to let go. And maybe he needed to let her.

"The cowboys keep breaking the ropes. But my Indians are resourceful. There will be burning flesh," he warned with a wag of his finger. "Soon."

She smiled, a sweet, authentic smile Troy recognized as pure Giselle. A smile that brought a wave of loss so deep, it had the power to drop him to his knees if he let it. He purposely lowered his gaze to the cave floor, holding on to the anger. Because without the anger, without the fighting, all the pain and the loss bubbled to the surface. And Troy had experienced enough of that for ten lifetimes.

His energy for keeping the battle alive waned. His drive to hold on to the hurt flagged. And a heavy beat of silence filled the cave. Voices drifted in from a distance. They were alone, with nothing but a few feet of air separating them, yet he felt like they were separated by miles. And he had no idea how to close that distance—or even if he should.

"Are you over your claustrophobia?" he asked.

"Not exactly, but I'm better at dealing with it."

"Does your manager know?"

"Yes."

He lifted his gaze without moving his head. "Does he *really* know?"

She shifted on her feet. "No." With her lips pressed tight, she scanned the cave again. "You think this is a really stupid idea, don't you? Me working in these caves."

He huffed a laugh with absolutely no humor in it. "When's the last time you gave a fuck what I thought?"

Her gaze sharpened and drilled into his like fiery blue ice. "I hung on your every word right up until the day you told my manager to go screw himself with a pogo stick after he'd gotten me a goddamned tour with Lady Antebellum."

The past spun back at warp speed and hit him square in the forehead. Damn, that would leave a mark. But he still cracked a smile. "Yeah. I did that, didn't I?" He shook his head. "Man, Ellie, you should have dumped me a lot sooner than you did."

A mixture of volatile emotions twisted her face before she pulled in a breath to speak.

"Giselle." Chad's voice rang out from the mouth of the cave. "They're ready for you."

She clenched her teeth and growled in frustration, which was about as threatening and adorable as a kitten's hiss.

"Go get your sexy on, girl." He wandered away, busying himself with some unnecessary equipment gathering and a distracted "Don't keep the star waiting."

As Troy listened to her footsteps fade from the cave, he let the harnesses drop from his hands and covered his face, rubbing his eyes with his palms. The best thing he could do for both of them was keep his distance—physically and emotionally—until they parted ways again. And they would, because they spent their lives crisscrossing the world.

Letting her go, letting her move on, might be the hardest, most painful thing he'd ever done, but it was the best thing he could do for her. And he might not have done a lot right in his life, but all the best things he'd ever done had been the things he'd done for her.

Giselle's mind couldn't stop pinging. Thoughts ricocheted against her skull like little sparks, bursting, then fading only for another to burst somewhere else, then fade. Over and over and over. Troy. Her career. Alex, the man on top of her. Troy. Tonight's show. The club. Troy. All the eyes on her mostly naked body. Alex. Troy. Jeff, the director. Troy. Troy. Troy…

"Nice, Giselle," Jeff said, his voice smooth and encouraging. "You love this. You need this. Arms overhead, arch your back. Good, nice. You're so hot. So turned on. Alex, tilt your face a little more this way. Cathy, shift the lighting…"

Jeff's direction continued to cast and crew as Alex's lips traveled down the middle of Giselle's chest, between her breasts, over her stomach. She'd lost track of how long the guy had been kissing and groping her, but every time they started over and filmed it again, she had the same numb sensation, like she was only half there. And she wondered if that was why they'd had to refilm so many times. But no matter how hard she tried, she simply couldn't engage herself in these acts with this man.

He was handsome, friendly, warm, and patient. Alex also had a body as equally built as Troy's, a smile that lit up a room—or in this case, a cave—a sexy laugh that turned heads, and had all the women on the crew swooning over his every breath.

"And hands to breasts…" Jeff said.

Alex's hands slid up Giselle's sides and covered her breasts. Her fingers curled into fists. Her belly quivered. But not in excitement.

"Writhe a little, Giselle. Perfect. Push into his hands. Yes, just like that."

Why didn't she feel anything? His mouth was warm. His hands practiced. His body supple and strong.

"All that fire between you and me, it was one hundred percent real and you know it."

Troy's voice filled her head bringing a rush of anxiety. Her thoughts rushed back to the pleasure he'd brought her, to the euphoric sense of hope she'd experienced when she'd believed she might be able to find another man who could make her feel even a sliver of the fulfillment Troy always had.

Only that man had been Troy.

So where did that leave her?

"And…Cut," Jeff said.

Giselle eased back to the thin foam mat on the rock behind her and waited to hear what he said next, praying he didn't want another take. They'd run this scene six times already, with cameras at every possible angle.

But instead of wrapping, Jeff said, "Great job, guys. Let's take twenty."

Her shoulders dropped. "This is way harder than it looks," she told Alex. He straightened his arms and grinned down at her. "And you've been incredibly patient with me."

His smile was warm, and the interest sparkling in his hazel eyes was real. If she were smart, she'd grab on to that and run with it. If she were smart, she'd find a man who wasn't as screwed up as she was and love him as hard as she could.

"You're an easy woman to be patient with," he said, "and you're doing great."

"Alex," Jeff called. "A word?"

His smile vanished, and he made an impatient sound in his throat. "Evidently, I'm not doing quite as well."

Giselle didn't know what that meant. Didn't really want to know. This world of movies was not only foreign but counterintuitive.

Alex pushed to his knees as one of the crew handed Giselle a silk robe. She slid her arms in and pulled it across her body, then climbed off the cave's ledge with the help of another crew member. Someone else handed her a cold bottle of water, while another laid flip-flops at her feet. They treated her like royalty.

"Do you think I could get some air?" she asked the young man whose name she couldn't remember.

"Sure. But I wouldn't go outside. You'll melt."

She wandered toward one of the cave's many entrances, and the closer she came to the mouth of the cave, the hotter it got. So she found a shadowed alcove where she eased to a seat on a small ledge, closed her eyes and took deep, slow breaths of the fresh but hot air, soaking in the natural light. She was glad she'd asked Chad and Brook not to stay for the shoot. They would only have fussed and worried, which would have raised her anxiety level.

"Penny." Jeff's voice touched Giselle's ear. "Go find Troy for me. I need to talk to him."

Her heart skipped. Her eyes popped open. She didn't want Troy here, of all people. She swallowed back her anxiety, but her stomach had tied itself into triple knots by the time Troy entered the cave through the door where she sat in a dark corner.

"What?" he asked, clearly not pleased over the summons.

His deep voice shivered over her, and her body lit up the way it should have during her scene with Alex.

"Hey, Troy, yeah." Jeff met him at the entrance, and Giselle held her breath, hoping she sank into the shadows. "Listen," he said, voice low. "Giselle is doing great, but she and Alex just don't have the chemistry I'm looking for. We've done the take six times, and it's good, don't get me wrong. She's absolutely gorgeous on camera. Stunning. But I'm not getting that raw passion I saw between you two. You've played great parts for me in the past, I really need you to—"

"*No.*" Troy cut Jeff off with the quiet but final word. He'd cleaned up at some point in the last couple of hours. He was no longer covered in grime and sweat. His hair was combed off his face, and he'd thrown on a T-shirt. "What you saw was…a moment. Nothing more."

A stab pinched her heart, one that surprised her. He was right. What they'd had was nothing but a moment.

"Tell yourself whatever you want to get through the day, kid, but I've done this long enough to know real emotion between two people when I see it. And I need you to bring that to life for the camera."

Giselle's stomach churned in a waterfall of acid. She'd failed at depicting the passion Jeff had wanted. And if she couldn't pull off this part, if Jeff canceled the cameo, she'd fall right back to where she'd been before the part had been offered—with her future riding on a wing and a prayer.

"Alex is an amazing actor and a great guy," Troy said. "If you aren't getting the spark you want with him, you won't get it with me."

"Okay, okay..." Jeff's voice soothed and placated. "What about giving it one try. Just one take. If it's not there, it's not there."

"She'll never go for it."

On impulse, she stood and stepped forward. "Yes, I will." They both startled, their heads snapping toward her. Her stomach jumped and her heart raced. She was doing exactly what he'd accused her of doing earlier—whatever it took to benefit her career. She'd have to face the truth of that later. "I'll do whatever you want."

Jeff grinned. "That'a girl." He turned toward the main space in the cave. "Holly, grab me a script."

Troy's gaze drilled into her, challenging, questioning. "You are fucking *relentless*."

She held it even as Jeff assured them both this was going to work out great. Even as a young woman rushed over with a script. Even as Jeff spoke to Troy about the part.

"Take thirty," Jeff said. "Do a dry run if you need to. We'll meet back here at—"

"I don't need thirty minutes." He snapped the script from Jeff's hand. "I'm ready now."

Still holding her gaze, he reached behind him, fisted his shirt, and dragged it over his head. Fire licked through Giselle's body. The move was so let's-get-it-on carnal, wetness spread through her sex. She fisted her hands, hating the way she responded to him and no one else.

"Casey," Jeff yelled across the space. "Get Troy into makeup. Thin out his beard to look more like Alex's scruff, cover that tat again, and slick his hair back."

"Already there," Casey said, taking Troy's bicep and dragging him toward her chair.

"Jill," Jeff called to another girl, "touch up Giselle."

A little blonde waved Giselle toward her.

"Get all the cameras you want set up now, Jeff," Troy said without looking up from the script. "'Cause you're getting one goddamned take. I'm not doing this twice."

Jeff snapped his fingers at some of the cameramen, and the room whirled into action like Troy wielded the power of movement. The entire atmosphere of the set changed, everyone focused and serious. Jill powdered Giselle's face, touched up a few spots, opened her robe, and powdered her breasts and belly.

With his head bowed, his brow furrowed, Troy gave his rapt attention to the script, as if Casey wasn't fussing all over him with makeup and gel. Then Jeff was back, facing Troy with an open look of expectation.

"Okay, look." He closed the script and met Jeff's gaze. "We'll get close, but it won't be exact. We'll flow with it. You film until we stop, then cut and paste the way you want it in editing. She's done it several times, and I've read the script, so don't be yelling directions at us. Keep your mouth shut. Don't screw the mood. We've got this. As long as Ellie's on board, you'll be happy with what you get."

The way he spoke for her, took control of the situation, wielded the confidence and the balls to order the freaking director around made her nerves rise to the top of her skin and vibrate. Yeah, he'd been dominant at the club, but that was sex, and he'd known Giselle was Giselle. This...this was true power born out of respect, out of trust, out of talent.

And Giselle was ridiculously impressed. And strangely...humbled.

"Giselle?" Jeff's voice pulled her gaze from Troy's handsome profile, his features stronger with his hair slicked back.

"Yes?"

"Are you on board?"

Troy's chair spun, and he stood, facing her. Those dark eyes met hers with expectation. The expectation that she would obey. That she would follow. That she would not question.

She swallowed hard and broke the powerful eye contact. His chest was wide and strong, his abs tight, his skin tan.

"Y-yes," she said.

Jeff turned and yelled at the cameramen, making her jump. Troy picked up a bottle of water on his way to her, took her hand and pulled her off to the side near the ledge.

He uncapped the water, took a long drink and offered it to her. After she did the same, he set it aside. Then he gave her two hundred percent of his undivided attention, and Giselle felt it all the way to her soul. He stroked her hair off her face and tilted her chin back. His touch made her body shiver to life. "Look at me."

When her eyes were on his, he scanned every inch of her face slowly, intimately, as if the atmosphere in the room wasn't ratcheted up to high gear. His gaze flowed over her, dark and liquid. His fingers stroked her face and neck with a feather-like touch, making her ache for more.

"We're in no rush," he murmured. "We have all the time in the world. It's just you and me. In the moment. No past. No future. Just Ellie and Troy. Right now."

Pain bit at her heart, and her eyes slipped from his.

"Only good thoughts. No pain. No regret. Just now. Just us. Just the perfection of you and me, angel. It's still in here." He touched the spot over her heart with the backs of his fingers, rubbing gently. "Close your eyes. Slow, deep breaths. That's it. Let go."

In those two minutes, she swore she relaxed one hundred percent.

"That's my girl." He pressed a soft kiss to her lips. "Remember how good it was," he whispered against her mouth, then kissed her again. "Remember how close we were. Remember the way you used to finish my sentences. The way I could read your mind."

He quickly became her only reality. He'd always been able to draw her in so completely, she lost track of everything but him. She relished the escape, the comfort, the pleasure. Her entire body released three levels of stress she hadn't realized she'd been holding on to until they vanished. Until she felt fifty pounds lighter.

He pulled her lower lip between his and suckled gently. He smelled like soap and heat and sweat and Troy. Raw, real Troy. Excitement blossomed low in her belly. She swayed into him, and he was just like she remembered, solid, steadfast, supportive.

"Very nice." He pressed his hips into hers gently, just enough to brush his erection against her. Just enough to make her moan for the feel of it. "Mmm, baby, you are delicious."

"Ready on set." Jeff's voice was either quieter or Giselle's hearing had faded in the pump of blood in her ears. But as Troy eased away, the entire cave seemed quieter, more still, like Troy had put everyone into a trance.

"I want your mind filled with me, Ellie." His fingers pulled on the tie of her robe. "Just me. Just me, and the way I make you feel." He brushed the robe off her shoulders, and she was naked except for flesh-colored panties. "Christ, you are gorgeous."

He bent at the knees, wrapped his arms low on her waist, and lifted her effortlessly. Giselle's legs parted and wrapped around his hips. His cock rode her heat, and he murmured, "Perfect."

He took the few stairs to the ledge smoothly, lowered to one knee, and laid her back as if he'd done it a million times.

Distantly, a soft "And action" registered.

But Troy instantly drew her attention again. "Do you ever fantasize about us, El?" He was on his knees and elbows, his gaze so soft and intent on hers, he really did make her feel like they were alone. Like there were no lights shining on them, no eyes beyond the lights watching. "Ever dream about us?"

He tilted his head and licked her lips. Heat streaked across her ribs, and she opened to him, the way she always opened to him. Then met his tongue, and they swirled together. He tasted strong and male, forbidden and dangerous, and heartbreakingly familiar.

He eased his hips between her thighs, resting against her. His weight created a decadent pressure, the rigid swell of his cock in line with her heat, and she bent her knees, sliding her thighs along his hips, his sides, then back down. His bare belly pressed hers and she pulled in a breath at the contact. The warm, sizzling contact. His fingers combed through her hair, tightened in the strands, and dragged her head back. Then his body covered hers, and his mouth came down on her throat, his teeth nipping at her skin, making her body move the way it should for the scene, but with absolutely no thought. Skin against skin. Warmth. Pleasure. Sensation. Lust. Need. They filled her heart, tightened her breasts, quivered in her belly, melted between her legs.

Her mouth dropped open, arms stretched overhead as Troy palmed one breast before swirling his tongue around the opposite nipple. A sound escaped her throat, part sigh, part moan, and offered herself for more. He opened wide, covering as much of her breast as he could, sucking hard, scraping her skin with his teeth.

She lifted her hips, her sex aching for pressure, but Troy was sliding south, his hands covering her breasts while his mouth traveled across her ribs, down her breastbone, over her belly button. Giselle closed her eyes, focused on the feel of his mouth and hands on her skin. Troy's mouth. Troy's hands. Emotions blended— love, excitement, loss, pain, confusion—each heightening the others, all intensifying her reaction to his touch.

And when his mouth traveled lower than the script called for, Giselle's fingers curled into fists, her head rolled side to side, and her hips lifted into the heat and pressure of those amazing lips. He closed his mouth over her and hummed. The vibrations shivered through her skin, tantalizing her clit. Giselle writhed. So close. She was so close.

"And... *cut.*"

Jeff's voice shattered Giselle's fantasy world. Worse, Troy lifted his mouth off her, pulled his hands from her breasts, and pushed up to all fours, hovering over her. He licked his lips, his dark eyes drilling into hers with fiery passion.

Then Jeff's voice cut between them again with, "It's a wrap. Great job."

And everyone started clapping.

Chatter broke out around the cave, voices echoing. One of the crew offered Giselle's robe. Troy sat back on his heels, took the robe, and passed it to her. She was still shivering with pent-up need, while Troy was rolling to his feet.

"Great shoot." His tone was as cold as his gaze was hot. All the concern and sweetness and charm he'd shown at the beginning of the scene were gone. Now he was just flat and distant. "Hope this role gives you that leg up you want so badly."

He climbed from the ledge, grabbed a water bottle from a crewmember standing nearby, his shirt from another, and exited the cave.

Giselle held the robe to her naked body, dazed, her heart throbbing against her ribs, staring at the passageway he'd just disappeared through, and realized not only didn't she know him anymore, she didn't even recognize any part of the man he used to be in the man he'd become.

Nine

Giselle had been on the road for so long, different places and different faces had become her normal. She'd learned to make small talk with everyone from the hostess at the local breakfast spot to the CEO of a prospective record label. She'd learned to work a party the way she worked an audience. And while she didn't always want to be at every event she needed to attend, she rarely felt out of place anywhere.

But this was one of those rare places.

She stood at the window of yet another concierge room, this one at the Venetian, surrounded by the cast and crew of *Full Throttle*, where everyone had gathered for some food and a viewing of something called the dailies.

She'd done her due diligence as far as socializing was concerned, making the requisite pass around the room, chatting with the various producers, production assistants, directors, assistant directors, other crew members.... Movies employed one hell of a lot of people. While everyone had been polite and gracious, it hadn't taken more than fifteen minutes to realize that these people were more of a working family than coworkers, just as she and Brook had noticed at the mixer. And for the first time in a long time, Giselle was an outsider.

Beyond the window, the Mirage lit up the Vegas skyline, her face splashed across the hotel's top ten floors. That couldn't have been easy for Troy to look at every night. Not that it gave him the right to hurt her in retaliation...

"It had nothing to do with revenge. I've never wanted revenge."

She lowered her gaze to her club soda and lime. She was exhausted after a day of filming and performing, and all the emotional drama surrounding Troy sucked her dry. She hadn't even stopped back at her room to change after her concert, still wearing a black halter dress far too sexy and too revealing for this setting. After days and days and days of relentless stress, she felt snappish. And as if her body was trying to tell her she'd reached her limit, tonight after her concert, she'd come down with a sore throat.

So she was using it as an excuse to take some downtime from socializing, because she really wasn't in the mood to put on a happy face and pretend everything in her world was perfect.

Troy, on the other hand, had no problem doing just that.

Across the room, raucous laughter filled the space, turning every head. Troy was sitting on the arm of a chair, long, jean-clad legs stretched out and crossed at the ankles. With his long-sleeved black Henley pushed up on his forearms, a drink in one hand, and a joyous smile splitting his face over something his fellow Renegades were talking about, Troy had never looked happier.

The star of the movie, Channing Tatum, who was also one of Giselle's favorite male actors and just as charming and sexy in person as he was on screen, wandered over to the group and said something that made them all break out in laughter again. Channing fistbumped Troy.

Giselle had learned over the course of the day that Troy was stunt-doubling Channing in the movie, which demonstrated just how far Troy had come. He was as big a performer as Giselle, just without all the fanfare. He moved through the various groups at the party with ease, with the ability to talk to everyone on all levels with comfort. He was secure with who he'd become, and it showed in every relationship. Which was a one-hundred-and-eighty-degree shift from seven years ago and the immature, insecure guy forever out of place at industry parties with no one to talk to and nothing in common with the guests.

His frustrated, jealous behavior had only made the existing animosity between him and other members of her team worse. In the end, the festering animosity had led to the end of their relationship.

And now, here he was, seven years later, the life of the party, fitting in with everyone.

She shook her head at the irony of it all and glanced around the room. Brook and Keaton were over in the corner talking and laughing where they'd been most of the hour. Chad was busy schmoozing with the movie moneymen since they'd walked in. And standing there alone, while everyone else had a connection to someone in the room, Giselle got a glimpse of that awkward feeling Troy must have felt all those years ago at the parties surrounding her gigs. If she multiplied that by at least a hundred, she might have a good idea of what he'd suffered on a regular basis. Because the big difference between those parties and this one was that everyone here treated Giselle with respect. Troy hadn't been afforded the same courtesy.

From the corner of her eye, she saw Troy push to his feet and saunter to the bar. He leaned on the counter, waiting for the bartender to make him another drink, and Giselle saw her opening to break this burning ice between them.

She took a deep breath and moved through the room to his side. "Hey."

His dark eyes slid toward her, then away.

Anger prickled up her spine like hackles. She bit the inside of her lip to remind herself to be patient. When the surge had mellowed, she said, "I wanted to tell you—"

"Hey, handsome." Casey, the makeup girl, slid into place on Troy's other side, her hand roaming intimately up his bicep. To the bartender, she said, "White wine, please." Then to Troy. "Can't wait to see those clips of you in the cavern today."

Troy turned toward her, leaning one elbow on the bar and giving Giselle his back. Hurt and fury blended into a fiery cocktail all its own.

He laughed, the sound cocky and flirty. "You just want to see your cover-up job on my tat."

"I'll take any excuse I can get to look at that hot body of yours."

Zahara stepped up beside Giselle. She ordered a rum and Coke from the bartender, then said, "You look drop-dead gorgeous. How'd your concert go?"

"Thanks, but I can't wait to get out of this." Giselle took the opportunity to turn away from Troy and Casey, grateful for the distraction. "As for the show, my guest violinist tripped on stage and fell on his ass, and I ended the night with a sore throat. Other than that, it was great."

Zahara made a pained face and sucked air through her teeth. "Ooo, ouch."

Giselle laughed, smiling at the memory of Craig hitting the stage floor, the band, the backup singers, and herself breaking out into laughter, which allowed the fans to bust up and almost brought down the house.

"It happens." She shrugged. "And he's got an amazing, self-deprecating sense of humor the crowd loved. I made a crack about a live concert being nothing like a movie set where you can just do another take, and everyone left happy. The audiences here are truly fabulous."

The lights dimmed, then brightened. Giselle darted a look toward the door and found Jeff playing with the lights. "Time for the show, folks."

"Crap," Giselle said, turning toward a screen lowering on one wall. "I haven't been looking forward to this."

"I remember those days." She gave Giselle's arm a reassuring squeeze. "You're going to be great."

Giselle smiled, but when Zahara found a seat on a nearby sofa, Giselle wandered away from Troy and Casey. She didn't need to listen to the woman gush all over him. Didn't need any help imagining the two of them in bed together.

Images flashed on the screen, creating tension all along Giselle's back and shoulders. Nausea burned beneath her ribs. Her head ached. And she suddenly longed for complete isolation and three days of sleep.

"For those of you who are new to dailies, these are either rough cut or uncut. You'll have to use your imagination until the finished product is available."

Giselle couldn't keep her gaze from drifting toward Troy. And while Casey still stood nearby, when Giselle scanned her way up his body to his face, she found him already looking at her, his eyes intense but his expression...unreadable.

She was grateful when the lights dimmed again, and she had the clips to distract her from the inner turbulence.

The clips ran quicker than Giselle expected. A few action shots of a fight between Keaton and the villain, Alex, were followed by several different views of Troy falling down the cavern, which made Giselle's muscles tense so hard, she ached. After the third clip, she had to close her eyes.

Finally, her love scene with Troy filled the screen. It had to be her imagination, but compared to the others, this clip seemed smoother. And infinitely longer. She swore the images dragged on and on. Swore her naked body filled the screen on the wall for hours, not minutes. And seeing herself from this vantage point, watching what Troy did to her while remembering how it had felt...

Shit.

She was wet again.

And so damn embarrassed.

She was so turned on and so pissed off—all at the same time.

She wasn't ready for the lights when they came back on, and rubbed at her hot cheeks as everyone turned their applause on her and Troy. She received applause every night, but this wasn't welcome or comfortable, yet still appreciated. And the emotions spiraling from her chest to her toes were both terrifying and gratifying. And so confusing.

But what made the biggest impact on her was how she couldn't share any of those thoughts with Troy. In fact, as soon as the lights came up, he started saying his good nights and making his way toward the door, never meeting Giselle's gaze.

She felt like some creature was inside her, gnawing at her ribs. She couldn't take this anymore. Couldn't just accept this angry silence. It was tearing at her, twisting at her, slowly eating at her. There may only be a few days left on set, but she had to at least try to clear the air, because if she didn't and they parted with this... this...*ick* still between them, it would fester, the way it had been festering for the last seven years. And if Giselle had learned anything from seeing him again, it was that she needed to find a way to deal with this so she could move on.

"Are you ready to head back?" Chad came up beside her.

"Go ahead. I'll be over soon."

Brook stopped in front of her, blue eyes sparkling. "Keaton and I are headed down to the bar for a drink."

Giselle made sure the stuntman of interest wasn't watching, then lifted her brows. "Oh, *really.*"

"Really. Why don't you come? Keep me from totally embarrassing myself."

"Hardly." She laughed the word. "You two have been talking for an hour, and by the way he can't look away from you, I'd say you're doing just fine. Have fun. I won't wait up, but I want details tomorrow."

On her way out, Giselle stopped to thank Jeff again and said good-bye to a few members of the crew. She started down the long hallway of hotel rooms with anxious energy tightening every muscle. Logistics crowded her mind—she didn't know what room Troy was in. Didn't know if he was sharing a room, or—shit—what if he'd brought Casey back to his room?

Okay, she'd go down to the desk and ask them to call him. She'd ask him to come down to the lobby. That might work. But what then? What should she say? How should she say it?

As she approached the stairwell, voices pulled her gaze up. At the end of the hallway, Troy and Duke paused in front of the hotel room doors, talking across the hall.

Something at the center of her body pulled hard. A complex, edgy sensation that made her restless. Maybe even a little reckless. And her mind started pinging with all the unanswerable questions she needed answered but that were as meaningless as the square root of infinity. Why was he acting like such a prick? If he hated her so much, why didn't he just walk away from her at the club when he'd had the chance? Why hadn't he humiliated her then? And what about the club? Why did he go there? Was that part of his lifestyle now? Who had he become over the last seven years? And why?

She didn't really want or expect answers. Even if she got them, they wouldn't change anything. But she did need to settle things between them for the here and now. Her future depended on it. She also had to get something from the past off her chest. He didn't have to care one way or the other, but she had to tell him. It needed to be said.

"Troy." She called to him while pushing her feet forward. Both men looked back.

Then Duke said, "Catch you tomorrow" and disappeared into his room.

Instead of turning to face her, Troy disappeared into his room as well.

"Troy—" She hurried forward, but the hard click of the door snapped in her face. A millisecond of shock stilled her. Then her heart raced. Her temper spiked. And she lifted both hands to pound on the door. "Troy Jacobs, grow the fuck up and open this door."

The door opened a foot with Troy's body filling the space. "Ellie," he said, his voice infuriatingly condescending, like he was talking to a child. "Don't yell in the hall."

"Let me in. We need to talk. This tension between us is stupid, and it has to end."

"I've had a really long day, with another really long day ahead in about six hours. And unlike you, princess, I don't have a manager, bodyguards, and personal assistants. I have to take care of all my shit myself. So, no, I'm not letting you in, because talking is the *very last* thing I feel like doing with you."

He started to close the door, and Giselle felt as if she were on the verge of insanity. As if she'd been pushed past her breaking point. Her brain felt like it was vibrating inside her skull. Like it was going to short-circuit and explode.

She pushed against the door again. "You're driving me batshit crazy."

"No, honey," he laughed. "You managed that all by yourself."

Snap. That was it. She'd had it.

She shouldered her way into the foyer of his suite, then spun on him. "I'm done with the eggshells. I have shit to say. If you don't want to talk, fine. You can listen."

He slammed the door so hard, the walls rattled. The pictures on the wall shook. Giselle jumped but stood her ground as he turned on her, hands at his hips, gaze furious. And, yes, in the suite's small hallway, with only one light filtering in from the living room, he was menacing.

"Maybe I don't want to hear it," he said. "Did you ever think of that?"

"Why wouldn't you want to hear me tell you that *I'm sorry?*"

He pulled in a breath as if he were going to yell, but held it instead, his expression shifting from anger to surprise back to anger. He finally said, "Because it *doesn't matter.* You can be as sorry as you want, and it won't change a goddamned thing. I'm sick of rehashing all this pain."

Pain. That coupled with the look on his face when she'd first seen him on those stairs at the mixer gave her a little glimpse behind his constant wall of snide disinterest. Something inside urged her to push forward, to dig deeper, validate the fact that he was, in fact, the same man who had once loved her so completely. But to what end? He was right. Bringing back the painful memories wouldn't change anything in their current lives.

"I don't want to dredge up bad feelings, I just need you to know—"

"*Don't*, Ellie." He took one big step toward her, his eyes hot.

"I know you felt out of place with the people in our lives all those years ago. And I knew they didn't treat you right even after I asked them to."

He closed the distance and gripped both her arms hard, a flicker of panic in his eyes. "Stop it."

She flinched at the pain but lifted her gaze to his. She talked fast to get all the words out before he threw her out the door. "But tonight, our situations were sort of reversed. And being the outsider gave me a tiny taste of what you went through then. I knew it was bad, but feeling it made me realize how bad it must have felt for you. So much worse than I realized."

"God*dammit*, El. *Shut. Up.*" He pressed her against the wall. Her heartbeat spiked. "It doesn't matter now."

"Maybe not. But I just wanted you to know that I always knew they were the problem, not you, and—"

"I know that, El—"

"But I've never told you how sorry I was for all the unhappiness it—"

He pinned her arms to her sides and lifted her, hitting her back against the wall again, knocking the words out of her mouth. A little cry of surprise popped out of her throat. "You *never fucking listen.* I knew it then, and I know it now. That was only one piece of our broken puzzle."

"I *do* listen." The weight of her body dragged at her arms, and she squirmed against the wall until he pushed his body against hers, all hard and hot. She forced herself to finish what she'd come to say. "You may not care anymore, but I'm sorry I couldn't find a way to make things right for you."

She was breaking his fucking heart.

Again.

Goddammit. He wasn't going to let her do this.

"What do you want from me?"

"N-nothing." The tears brimming in her eyes finally spilled over, and, Christ, the sight tore him straight down the middle. "I just wanted to make sure you knew…"

"Why? So you could ease your conscience? So you could walk away feeling all better? Fuck that, El. *Fuck you.*"

He fought to lower his voice, but the lust and the need he'd been fighting from the moment he'd seen her in the cave in those goddamned cut-offs was roiling through his veins, mixing with anger born of hurt that had been simmering for years, creating a dangerous combustible on the verge of explosion.

"No," she said, eyes wide, "that's not what—"

"Then *what?*"

When she didn't answer, Troy's patience snapped, lighting the fuse on his volatile emotions. He was done with her goddamned games.

He bent his head and covered her mouth with his, pushing her into the wall, and kissed her the way he wanted to fuck her, long and hard. She gasped and stiffened. Troy plunged his tongue into her sweet, sweet mouth. He took and tasted and licked and took some more. She mewled, then moaned. Her fingers fisted, her body softened, and her mouth loosened, opening to him, taking him, and finally, *finally*, giving back.

The sensation eased all his muscles, and lust swept over him in a hot wave. His mind hazed. His body took over. God, he needed her. Needed her so badly, he ached with it. Needed her to want him as Troy, not as some stranger who could give her a thrill. Needed her to want him for him, not to fulfill some part that would edge her up the ladder toward success. Yet, he didn't want her to want him at all.

He broke the kiss violently, fisted his hands in her hair, and pulled her head back. "Let me make this crystal-fucking-clear, Ellie. If you don't leave this room—and I mean *right now*—I'm going to fuck you as long as you let me fuck you. I'll call in sick tomorrow. I'll get fired. I'll die of starvation before I stop fucking you."

She slid her tongue over her lower lip. "Why do you keep testing me?"

"Because I want you to *get* the hell *out*."

"Then push me out the door." She was breathing fast. Her throat rolled as she swallowed. "You weigh a hundred pounds more than me. You're five times as strong. If you really want me out, push me out."

She'd called his bluff, and now he was stuck with their bodies molded together, her big beautiful eyes staring at him with heat and need. And he couldn't move. Physically couldn't push her out the door.

A soft huff of dry laughter exited her mouth and ruffled her hair. "We're both still *so* screwed up," she murmured. "And I still want you *so bad*."

Bittersweet pain ripped through his gut. He clenched his teeth and growled, "*Goddamn* you."

He should throw her out, rail at her in the hallway, embarrass the hell out of her, get a restraining order, anything to keep them from self-destruction.

Instead, he took her face in both hands and kissed her, gaining instant relief from the feel of her lips against his, reveling in the euphoria of being wanted by the one woman who knew every dirty little corner of his soul and still wanted him. It was wrong. He didn't know how, didn't know why, didn't know anything but the feel of her legs wrapped tight at his hips, her arms clutching his neck, her mouth begging for more.

He tasted her mouth one way, then tilted her head and slanted the kiss the other. He couldn't get enough. Would never get enough. Had to take everything he could while he could. Because he'd lied. He was kicking her the hell out as soon as he regained control. She might be able to compartmentalize her life to deal with the loss, but he couldn't. And he refused to live in that kind of constant pain. It had to end.

She moaned into his mouth. Her hands pulled at the tail of his shirt until it cleared his jeans. Then her hands were on his skin, and she could have had electrical current in her fingers. He unfastened the strap of her dress at the base of her neck. She fought with his belt. Fumbling and frantic, they couldn't get at each other fast enough. Troy wanted it over and done with. Wanted to put her behind him.

Then her breasts filled his hands, and he forgot all about shoulds or shouldn'ts, goods or bads, rights or wrongs. Her supple mounds melted in his palms, and he squeezed and teased and groaned with pleasure. But it wasn't enough. He bent his head and dropped his mouth to one breast, sucked and licked, then bit and scraped. There was nothing gentle or sweet about this need. This was a fierce, dark need. The need to take. To claim. To own.

Then release. And do his best to forget.

She had his jeans open by the time he turned his attention to the other breast. And when her hand slid along his length, he winced at the excruciating thrill of it. Of having Giselle's hand on him.

He pulled his mouth away from her with a raspy "Fuck, yes." Then lifted her and pinned her against the wall with his body. She scraped the fingers of both hands into his hair, tilted her head and scanned his face with those gorgeous eyes, denim with lust, before kissing him deeply, pleasuring him with her tongue, her lips, teasing him with her teeth.

Troy fumbled with his wallet, dragged out a condom, and let the leather fall to the floor. Ripped open the foil, let it drop, and rolled the condom on, then immediately slipped his hand between Giselle's legs and yanked her panties aside.

She sucked a shocked breath, breaking the kiss. Hadn't regained her composure when he roughly stroked her, positioned his hand among her wet, warm folds, and thrust as deep as he could.

She cried out and dropped her head back. Her pussy clenched his fingers. God, he loved this. Loved the wild, frenzied lust of sex. Missed the thrill of giving that pleasure to someone who mattered to him.

He parted his fingers and drew them out, slowly. Waited for her head to loll sideways, for her tongue to slide along her lower lip, then thrust again. Deep. Hard. She arched. Cried out. A mixture of euphoria and pain etched her face. Her wetness coated his fingers, making him slide easily. He gave three shallow pumps, tapping that little ridge deep in her body, making Giselle mewl.

This was delirium. He repeated the pattern until Giselle was rising into his hand for more. Then he pulled out completely. Because now, even that wasn't enough. He needed so much more. Needed to taste her, to feel her pussy clench around his tongue and ride his mouth.

He crouched, pulled her thighs from his hips to his shoulders, gripped her ass in both hands and stood again, balancing her against the wall.

"Oh my God..." Her hands dug into his hair. "Troy."

Hearing her say his name while his face was between her legs sent a shock of warm triumph through his belly.

He pressed his mouth to her pussy and licked. Musk and tangy sweetness. So hot. So erotic.

She tensed and gasped in surprise.

"Spread for me, Ellie. Let me eat that pretty pussy."

He encouraged the spread of her thighs with the position of his hands, and when he had Giselle trapped between the wall and his mouth, he smiled. He smiled and memorized the beautiful sight of her perfect pink pussy, the tight folds glistening with her excitement, the plump little clit half-hidden beneath her swollen lips.

"Mmm, good girl."

Her barely there crop of blonde curls was trimmed into a perfect landing strip, leading directly to the center of her pleasure. He circled the juicy little nub lightly with his tongue while he fingered her opening, slid her juices all through her folds and worked one, then two fingers deep inside her. Never enough stimulation to bring release, only enough to make her insane with pleasure.

He pulled the swollen folds back to expose the plump bud and flick, flick, flicked it with his tongue. Giselle's head fell back on a growl, eyes closed. She pressed one hand to the ceiling and wound one in his hair, lifting her hips toward his mouth.

"Open your eyes, Ellie," he said, giving her clit one luxuriously slow lick while sliding a finger deep inside her. Pleasure vibrated in her throat, then her head fell forward and her heavy lids parted to midnight-blue eyes. "Now watch me eat you."

"Too much," she said between pants. "Need to come."

Her sex clenched, squeezing out juice Troy lapped up, making her shiver. He was sweating like he was in a sauna. His cock throbbed with every beat of his heart. "Have I told you how demanding you've become?"

She whimpered.

"If you want to get off, watch me eat you. As long as you watch, I eat. The minute you stop, I stop. Simple, right? And when we're done there, I'm going to fill your hot, wet, tight little pussy with the divining rod you've created. Now shut the hell up, because I'm fuckin' hungry."

He opened wide and covered her pussy. Her face crunched in pleasure-pain, and her head fell to the side. Her hair fell in a pale waterfall, whispering across his face. And those big blue eyes of hers watched every lick, every kiss, every tug, every nip, and every suck, until her teeth were digging into her bottom lip, and her hips rocked toward his mouth, begging for the touch of his tongue. And watching her watch him eat her.

Man, that was crazy hot.

"Troy..." she murmured, her body trembling, her hand fisted so tightly in his hair, his scalp burned. "Please..."

Christ, he'd give her anything, absolutely anything when she begged like that. He groaned, long and deep as he positioned his mouth over her pussy and, with a frenzied combination of licking and sucking and tongue-fucking, pushed her right to the edge. And her eyes stayed on him right up to the end.

"Oh...*God*..." Her hips bucked, her body bowed. "Troy... *Troy*..."

When she finally broke, calling his name—*his name*—Troy closed his eyes and rode out her pleasure, licking and sucking her essence into his own body.

Giselle quivered uncontrollably. Aftershocks trembled through her muscles. Her entire body felt light and relaxed and tingly. Thinking straight was out of the question, but she still tried, and thoughts tumbled sluggishly through her brain, disconnected and random.

He rocked his shoulders, and her thighs fell to his sides, supported by his arms. And with his hands still on her ass, he lowered her along the wall, straight down and onto his cock. She moaned as his wide head pushed inside. Her nails bit into his shoulders, but she ended up just getting fistfuls of shirt.

With one hand at her hip, he used the other to brush her hair off her face, and drilled into her with those liquid chocolate eyes, so intense, so serious. So familiar. With his hand tangled in her hair, he searched her eyes, her face, then her eyes again, as he slowly invaded her body. Spreading her, stretching her, pulling out, pushing back in, going deeper, stealing her air, making her tense. She had no words.

"You are so fucking tight," he murmured, almost to himself, but he was looking deep into her eyes. "Damn that's…so good. *So good.* Mmm." The hum of pleasure coincided with a shake of his head and the jump of a muscle in his jaw. "So fucking good."

The sight of his satisfaction was a crazy aphrodisiac. She loved seeing fierce desire twist his face. Loved watching his lids go heavy, watching his eyes roll back. Loved the growling, teeth-grinding, lip-licking, nostril-flaring, sweat-dripping signs of rising lust and need.

And the act of forcing her body to fit his while he searched her eyes was intensely intimate. This was so raw, so animalistic, so blatant, so deliberate, so…erotic. And all the sensations created by his slow penetration— the stretch and push and tug and burn and pressure— had her wriggling for more. She released his shoulders to try for more leverage on his forearms and managed to push off the wall, lift her hips, and take him deeper.

Excitement rippled through Giselle's pelvis. "Ah, God…"

His eyes fell closed, and a growl rolled from his throat.

She pulled back and thrust again, taking him a little deeper. He joined her rhythm, and within seconds, he was so deep, Giselle's throat ached with the fullness. When he opened his eyes again, his gaze was fierce and hot and determined, a look she recognized from the club. A look that shot the unique thrill only he produced through her blood. But there was something else there too, something softer, something deeper, something more human, more Troy. Something that pulled hard at Giselle's heart.

How had she lived so long without him? How in the hell was she going to go back to that way of life when this was over? The thoughts made tears cluster in her eyes again, blurring his handsome face.

He dug his fingers into her hips and drew his length almost completely out on a long low groan, then pulled her in as he thrust home, their meeting so hard and so fast, Giselle cried out, her eyes closed, and the tears spilled down her cheeks. If Troy noticed, he didn't care. He immediately repeated the motion in a way that told Giselle this was the ride to the finish line. And she was on board, locked in, because it was just that damn good.

Each and every thrust was the same complete, powerful stroke. Steady, steady, steady perfection. The kind of perfection that took her completely out of place and time. The kind she never wanted to end.

Sweat gathered along her neck, her chest, between her breasts, beneath his hands on her thighs. His face glistened. Dark areas stained his shirt. The muscles in his arms and legs quivered. But he never paused, never slowed. Just drove her higher and higher, then quickened his pace when she showed signs of climax.

And with her body still thrumming from the first orgasm, she rose quick and broke hard, gripping fistfuls of his shirt to ride out the spasms.

Troy paused only long enough to lean in and kiss her deeply, his mouth loose and warm, whispering, "Ready for another?" before pulling back and gripping her hips again.

"No, no..." She dropped her head against the wall, still trying to catch her breath. She was exhausted from the day, from the stress, from two full-body orgasms in a row. "No more."

"Thank God," he rasped, wiping his forehead on the shoulder of his shirt before pressing it to hers. "I forget I can't promise you the moon."

He cupped her face in one hand and kissed her deeply, slowly, while he rocked his hips. His cock slid easily inside her. He growled a groan and picked up that same sweet rhythm, quickly rising to his own orgasm, one that raged through his body, twisting his muscles and pulling guttural sounds from his throat.

He slumped against her, pressing her to the wall for long, sated moments while he caught his breath. But he eased out of her too soon, lowered her feet to the floor, and replaced the clip of her dress at the base of her neck. Then he stepped back and hiked up his own jeans a little.

Still dizzy, she pressed a hand to her temple and lifted a smile to him with a quip about him stealing her brain's blood supply on her lips, but the look on his face froze the words on her tongue. He wore the same cool, closed-off expression he had that morning in the cave. As if the last twelve hours had never happened.

"Troy?" she said, suddenly off-balance again. "What's…?"

"Now, I *am* kicking you out." His voice was casual, but cool enough to prickle a chill over her skin. He ran both hands through his hair, pushing it off his face and met her gaze with a deliberate, "And don't expect a repeat performance. This won't happen again. It's over, El. Time to put the past behind us."

The harsh rejection stung. "Troy—"

He turned away and started toward the suite, slapping her ass in the process. A squeak of surprise pushed aside the argument brewing in her heart just before he dismissed her with, "Make sure the door closes when you leave."

Without looking back, he sauntered down the short hallway and turned into a room, closing the door behind him.

All Giselle's air leaked from her lungs and left a sharp ache throbbing beneath her ribs.

What the…?

Water ran behind the closed door, snapping Giselle out of her shock. Hurt flushed her system, quickly transforming into anger. Anger exploded in fury.

That piece of shit.

Rage, hurt, and shame took turns slicing at her heart and self-worth.

The burning need to barge into that bathroom and tell him just what she thought of being treated like nothing more than another one of his slutty one-night stands made Giselle fist her hands and clench her teeth.

Then the water turned off, and reality cut into her thoughts. Where would that get her? Deeper into heartache. Deeper into resentment. Deeper into self-hatred.

No.

She purposely exhaled, pivoted, and swung the hotel room door open.

He was damn right—this was *definitely* over.

She walked out of the room, slamming the door at her back, a punctuation to officially leaving Troy Jacobs behind her.

Ten

Sweat ran down Troy's left temple and into his eye, but there wasn't anything he could do about it unless he wanted to lose his grip on the rock, fall into the cavern, get jerked around by his harness, and start the damn climb all over again.

All ten of his fingertips were raw, the muscles of his forearms were chanting an ear-piercing curse, and his biceps were tuning up to join the choir.

"Fuckin' heat," he grumbled, squeezing his eyes tight and giving his head a shake. But when he opened his eyes again, the sweat burned like a chemical. He found his toeholds and tested his bounce. "Let's go."

"Slate," Jeff called without hesitation. The slate kid called out the scene and take. Troy lowered his head and listened. "Ready...And...*Action*."

Already coiled for release, Troy pushed off the wall and opened his body wide as he fell at full speed down the cavern. But today, like yesterday and the day before and the day before that, no euphoria filled Troy. The air swept past him, his heart rate picked up, his reactions kicked in, but there was no joy. No thrill. He was just... numb. Worse than numb. He was *nothing*.

The decelerator jolted Troy in a drastic speed reduction, and an involuntary grunt rolled from his chest.

"And *cut*," Jeff called from the top of the cavern. "Looked great. You've just got one more shot, the one-armed hang, and you can take a break while we let Channing play."

"Dude," Channing called down to him. "Are you leaving blood on those ledges? I might need a full medical disclosure before I follow in your fingerprints."

Troy rolled to a seated position as the machine slowly wrapped the cable on a giant spool and drew him toward the top. "Why do you think I went first? I'm the smart one."

Channing made some quip Troy didn't hear over the crew's laughter, but at the moment, he wasn't up for their usual sparring. His fingertips throbbed, and he lifted his hands to blow on them, but his mind was on Giselle. Nothing new there, only that today was her last day on set, and he hadn't seen or spoken to her since he'd fucked her dizzy in the hallway of his room, then kicked her out—four days ago.

If he defined success by goals achieved, then he'd been successful at silencing her unstoppable declarations of regret. There was no need, no place, no purpose for those now. And he couldn't stand to have that knife plunged into his heart over and over and over. It had to stop.

He couldn't see it now, but he had to believe it would benefit them both in the long run. They needed to let go of something that had been destined to fail from the start, something that still had no future, and focus on the success they'd found.

The fact that she hadn't fought him harder, the fact that she hadn't contacted him since, told him he'd finally done it. Finally chased her off permanently. Which was the only way. She had bigger, better things and people in her future than the likes of him, and she'd eventually move on. He couldn't take that kind of heartbreak again.

The cable stopped Troy before he reached the top of the cavern, and he stared dully at the rock wall.

"Hey." Keaton's voice sounded above, and Troy looked up. His friend stood at the edge, hands on knees. "Finish up so we can all head over to the air-conditioned cave, listen to Giselle sing, and eat cake."

A tiny spark burned a path through his heart. Hearing her sing in person one more time was the last thing he needed before he could permanently close the door on that part of his life.

"Then let's get this done." He swung himself to the wall, caught himself by the fingertips on a narrow ridge of rock, and clenched his teeth against the pain as he maneuvered himself into position for the shot. "Go, Jeff."

He set his feet, fit and refit his bloody fingertips on the rough stone edge, and focused. But a new pain resided deep at the center of his body, one with sharp edges that cut on every breath. Heartache—he knew it well. The feeling of someone you love more than life slipping through your fingers. The knowledge that no matter how badly you wanted to hold on, forces in the universe took control. The idea that there was a bigger meaning to life that you couldn't see but that needed to be fulfilled, which could only happen if you weren't together.

"Ready," Jeff called. Troy refocused. "And...*action.*"

Troy let his feet slip off the foothold and pretended to scramble for traction while he clung to the side of the cavern by five raw, bloody fingertips.

"And...*cut.*"

Troy grimaced and swore as he released the ledge and let his body fall into the harness, then blew on his fingertips as the cables drew him up. That was his last major scene in the movie, and while on one hand he was relieved, on another it unnerved him to have time on his hands. Time to think about Giselle. Time to think about all his mistakes—then, now...

"Wrap Troy's role," Jeff said. "Take thirty, everyone. Channing's up when we get back."

By the time Troy reached the cave floor and wrestled out of his harness, everyone was headed to the other cave, and, Don, a guy from Ed's crew was crouched near the metal spike, a toolbox at his side.

"Hey." Troy wandered that direction, grabbed a hand towel, and wiped down as he checked out the crack that had begun as a hairline fracture but which had grown over the course of the week. "What's up?"

Don glanced over, then returned his gaze to the floor, fitting a long, thin metal stake into the thickest section of the crack. "Just checking the depth on this. Ed doesn't think it's anything, but I've seen a couple of others pop up at other stress points in other caves, and I want to make sure they don't go deep enough to damage the structural integrity or connect or do anything weird."

"Anything weird," Troy repeated. "That's the really scary stuff, right?"

Don laughed. "How much longer are you going to be using this stake? I might just put in a new one somewhere else."

"Only a couple more scenes," Troy said. "And we'll just be using the harnesses for support in those. No more throwing ourselves into the cavern."

"Hallelujah. You guys are hell on engineers." Don pulled a drill out of the toolbox. "I'm going to do a few tests while you're all next door."

"Knock yourself out." Troy wrapped the towel around his neck. "I'll bring you back some cake."

He wandered from the cave, wincing at the ruthless Vegas afternoon sun. Passing equipment trailers and tents, he tossed the towel over his head to give himself a shield as he trekked across the desert set, then paused after stepping inside to let his eyes adjust to the new darkness.

An excited buzz filled the cave with lots of chatter and light laughter, but Troy's ears homed in on the strum of a guitar. The simple sound evoked a rush of sweet memories—wildflowers stolen from a random garden, washing, brushing, and braiding her hair as she played with new lyrics or new chords, staying up late to catch *Saturday Night Live* even when they both had to work in the morning, but unable to take his eyes off her face when she fell asleep on his lap...They went on and on, overwhelming him in a sudden wash of emotion—so much love, so much loss. Sometimes it still mystified him how something so good could have gone so bad.

"Quiet, everyone, quiet."

Jeff's voice dragged Troy's thoughts back to the present, and he wandered deeper into the cave and stepped off to the side, into the shadows. He gripped the ends of the towel tight, anticipating both pleasure and pain when Giselle opened that beautiful mouth.

Jeff went through the motions of instructing everyone watching to stay quiet, gave the actors in the foreground a couple of notes, and checked the camera angles.

Giselle leaned against a simple wooden stool on stage, one heel of one cowboy-booted foot hooked in the rungs. She wore ripped jeans that hugged her beautiful legs and a translucent blouse with a floral pattern. Her hair was braided down one side and hanging over one shoulder, almost touching the body of the guitar where it rested in her lap.

She could still steal his breath.

"Ready..." Jeff said.

Giselle started strumming, and the crisp, smooth notes filled the space. Troy instantly recognized the song "All These Regrets," from her latest album. A song that emphasized both the range and power of her voice, a song that could rip Troy's heart out and bring him to fucking tears when he listened to it alone, the volume cranked up, his headphones on. He'd always thought that was as close to touching Giselle as he'd ever get again.

"And...*action*."

The camera's lights flashed red, the actors read their lines, the extras played their parts, but all Troy saw or heard was Giselle. Her voice had grown even richer, deeper, and stronger than he'd been able to appreciate on her album recordings. And just as it always had, her voice moved him. His chest filled. His heart squeezed. His eyes burned. Tingles spread through his body, raising gooseflesh along his skin. The emotions she could elicit with the simple combination of voice, words, and guitar chords remained unfathomable.

She closed her eyes and tilted her face up to the ceiling, opening her throat to belt out a line in the song with such passion, such talent, no one could doubt that voice was a gift straight from heaven. A gift she was now using to bring joy to millions, not just Troy, reminding him that everything happened for a reason.

But in that moment, he would have sold his soul to the devil for one chance to make different choices in his life. One chance to go back in time and handle everything with Giselle in their last months together, in this last week together, differently.

A murmur rumbled in the back right corner of the cave. The unacceptable noise during filming drew everyone's gaze. Giselle continued singing, oblivious to the fact that the shot had been ruined and would have to be redone.

"Cut, *cut*..." Jeff turned to Giselle as she sat back on her stool, stilling her guitar strings. "Sorry, honey." He turned toward the back of the room again. "Whoever's making noise, get the hell—"

A louder clatter came from the far corner, followed by a female scream, a cloud of dust, then Jeff's rough "What the hell's going on back—"

Rocks tumbled from the ceiling. Screams and yells echoed through the cave. The hair on Troy's neck prickled. He pushed through the crowd toward the commotion. Until more rock fell. And dust erupted through the cave in a murky cloud.

Alarm stopped Troy's feet and turned him toward the stage. Giselle had pushed from the stool and pulled her guitar strap off, but held the guitar close like a shield, her eyes wide, darting and scared. Before he could take one step toward the stage, more rocks tumbled from the ceiling.

Like falling dominos, rock cascaded, the devastation running toward the stage. Stalactites dropped and toppled. Screams ricocheted through the space. Panic erupted. And Troy became a salmon swimming upstream, trying to reach Giselle while everyone else rushed for the exit.

Troy fought his way between and around people pushing to get through. He kept his eyes pinned to Giselle, which was easy because she was frozen in terror, standing in the middle of the stage—beneath a cluster of stalactites.

"Ellie!" His yell drowned in the chaos. His gaze darted to the ceiling, to Giselle, to the nearest exit. And panic burned up his spine. "*Giselle!*"

She didn't hear him. Just curled around that damn guitar like it was a magic shield.

Urgency drove him forward. Someone elbowed him in the ribs. Someone else kicked his shins, knocked his head, nailed his jaw. Still, he drove through the surging, panicked crowd toward Giselle.

He gained five feet and reassessed—ceiling, Giselle, exit.

Fuck.

His strategy shifted from getting her out to getting her to safety. And he was almost there. Turning sideways, he pushed between two production assistants, diving onto the stage. "Ellie—"

But he didn't have time to say more. The ceiling came flying at them. Troy grabbed her arm, dragged her into him, and yanked her into a dive off the stage and beneath the nearest table. He landed on his back and immediately flipped her over, covering her body with his.

The room thundered around them. The table cracked and caved in, slamming Troy's back. He forced himself to his knees, dragging his body off Giselle's so he didn't crush her.

Long moments of terror loomed as the thunder continued and absolute darkness closed in. Dust filled the small space, making them both cough. Then a sudden and unexpected quiet cut through. An eerie, consuming, end-of-the-world-type silence that made ice streak through Troy's veins.

"Ellie?" his voice came out harsh and low. He leaned into one hand so he could run his other hand over her, searching for injuries. "Ellie, baby, say something."

"O-out." Her hand clasped onto his wrist with the desperation of a drowning victim. Her raspy, quick breaths filled the space. "Need...to get...*out.*"

He twisted his wrist from her grasp and stroked her face. "Shh, Ellie, it's Troy. I'm right here, baby. I'm"—he paused for a coughing fit—"right here."

Her breaths quickened, labored. Her hands darted out and around, feeling, searching. "Out. *Out!*" Terror turned her voice shrill. She struggled, squirming under him, and the rock around them shifted. She coughed. "Get me *out.*"

Troy grabbed both her hands and pinned them to the cave floor. "Stop moving."

"Let me go. I can't breathe. *I can't breathe.* I have to get *out.* Please, let me out!"

"Ellie!" He screamed, purposely startling her brain out of the panic pattern, then had to stop to cough again. "Listen to me. The only thing keeping tons of rock off us is this broken table. If you don't hold still, it will all come down."

"But, but—" The uncontrollable terror filling her voice tore at him. "*No.*"

"I need your help to get us out of here." He kept his voice measured and soothing. "Are you listening to me?"

"I can't help. I can't *breathe.* Please. *Please*, let me out." A sob escaped.

Troy squeezed his eyes shut, praying this wasn't the start of a complete mental breakdown. "Baby, we'll get out, but you *have* to stay calm. And all this screaming and sobbing is damaging those perfect vocal cords. Please don't do that."

A terrified, heartrending mewl started deep in her throat and grew, rolling out of her body as she fought his hold like a goddamned demon.

Troy held her down while reining in his own fear and fighting new and rising pain in his head, back, and shoulder. This snap of PTSD would pass, she would calm, and Troy would start the reasoning process all over again. She'd had several severe panic attacks during their years together. Countless night terrors. They'd get through this trauma just like they'd gotten through all the others.

Only, after long minutes of unrelenting terror, Troy was losing strength against her fight. And if he let go, if she tried to dig and claw her way out of this avalanche…

No. He couldn't let that happen.

He tightened his grip on her arms, drew her up with the last of his strength, and slammed her back against the floor, screaming, *"Ellie! Stop!"*

She froze, but tremors shivered through her body. While she was lucid, he said, "If you don't hold still, we will both be *crushed.* Do you understand what I'm telling you? We will both *die here,* if you don't get ahold of your panic."

"H-h-holy hell." She breathed heavy and fast. Her hands flexed and fisted. "I can't…I can't…"

"Use your breathing, El. Focus on my voice. Long, slow, deep breath in, two, three, four…" He counted to eight, cautiously releasing her wrists. "Good. And out, two, three…"

The dust had died down, making it easier to breathe. And as he continued to count in a steady, reassuring voice, he pushed himself into a sitting position. "And again," he said, repeating the count as he grasped her arms gently and eased her slowly toward him, pulling her into his lap and the circle of his arms. "Good. And out, two, three..."

He shimmied his butt backward until he felt something solid behind him and tested his weight against the rock. When nothing shifted or crumbled, he relaxed, tucking her head beneath his chin. But she remained stiff.

"Everything's going to be okay."

"*Nothing's* going to be okay," she bit back, shaky but adamant and angry. "*Nothing.* This is a perfect metaphor for my life right now—I was finally making headway. Getting serious name recognition, great sales, sold-out concerts. I have a good manager, an ambitious agent. Here I am, telling myself, 'Push yourself just a little more Giselle. Do the sexy video, do the sexy part, it's no big deal.' I'm this close to reaching that breakthrough level, where I choose my concert dates, and I choose my venues, where I get courted instead of being the one to court others. I can see that glimmer of finally having some control over my life—and then *you* show up, and everything threatens to cave in around me. Just. Like. This."

She was rambling. She did this when her anxiety wound out of control with no outlet, and he didn't want her winding up so tight, she blew in this dangerous setting. "Ellie, you need to—"

"And not only are you *you,* as if that wasn't bad enough, but you're *not* you. You're some wickedly bastardized version of you who screws up my head and makes everything worse. In case I haven't mentioned it, I hate you, just so you know." She paused only to draw air, then yelled at the ceiling, "Either get me the hell out of here, or put me out of my misery!"

And then she burst into tears.

Troy exhaled and pressed fingers to his closed lids.

She hated him.

Beautiful.

His miserable life was now complete.

God, she hated this. Hated the shaking. Hated the nausea. Hated the gnawing fear. Hated the chills. Hated the aches. Prolonged anxiety attacks affected her like a rabid case of the flu, and her body was being ravaged while she struggled to keep a grip on her mind. And that crying jag she'd just gotten a hold on had wiped her out.

Her automatic instinct was to lean on Troy. But she didn't trust him. Not now. Not after all the Jekyll and Hyde shit he'd pulled. Which she still didn't understand. But after that degrading dismissal he'd given her from his hotel room, she'd written him off as a major douche bag she no longer even wanted to know.

"How long does this amount of air last?" she asked.

"We're not in an airtight container, El. We'll be fine if we just hold tight. Rescue crews are probably already mapping out a plan."

She fought to hold the questions back, but the silence crept in and pried them out like a crowbar. "How long have we been in here?"

"Maybe twenty minutes."

"Why does it feel like hours?"

"Because you're scared. And because you're stuck with me."

She wrapped her arms around her bent legs and rested her chin on her knees. "We're going to be down here forever, aren't we?"

"I imagine rescue efforts of this size take time, but they probably already know we're missing. Depending on what happened up there, they may not be able to access the cave to start digging right away."

"How did this happen?"

He didn't answer right away. "I don't know, but we'll figure it out."

His voice held an and-heads-will-roll edge that only intensified Giselle's anxiety. "I don't hear anyone else. Did they get out? Or are they…" Her stomach cramped. Her throat swelled. Her mind started to fray again. "Oh God…"

"Ellie, don't. I think most people got out." His hand stroked down her back. "We're going to—"

She shrugged his touch away. "Stop. What is this? One of your nice moments?"

When he just hissed through his teeth, something inside Giselle snapped. Because even though her mind knew she should write him off, her heart still struggled with all his contradictions.

"*Who* the hell *are you?* Every time I see you, it's like seeing a different person. You're nice, then you're mean, then you pretend you care, then you're an ass, then you're nice again. You're like a psychotic yo-yo. Sometimes I think I see the man I fell in love with, then I'm sure there isn't even a flicker of that man left in who you've become."

"I'm not that kid anymore," he bit out, sullen. "I've grown up."

"Really." She didn't care how much attitude dripped from her voice. She was so done with the façades. "Because *that kid* was ten times as mature as you are. *That kid* had compassion and honor and loyalty and decency and fucking *impulse control.* Those are the things you're supposed to *gain* when you grow up, not *lose.*"

"If *that kid* was so awesome," he yelled back, "why'd you dump him?"

"That's a stupid question, because you already know the answer. If you need to hear me say it, fine, you made it impossible for me to stay. After a lifetime of having nothing, you made me choose between you and my music." She sucked a lungful of dusty air. "Now it's my turn. If you hate me so much, why'd you fuck me at the club? Why didn't you just walk away?"

Troy heaved a muttered, "Jesus Christ."

"Or even better yet, why didn't you let *me* walk away? I was headed toward the door twice. But no, you taunted me back. I want to know *why*, dammit, and I'd rather focus on this than on our potentially insanity-inducing situation."

He winced. "Can you stop yelling? It's really, *really* bad for your voice, my head is killing me, and I'd rather not have you dislodge more rocks."

"Don't pretend you care now."

"I didn't want you fucking some other random guy, okay?" he yelled, right after asking her to stop yelling. "You don't know what kind of shit goes on in clubs like that, El. I could have been anyone. I could have gagged you in addition to cuffing you and done any goddamn thing I wanted, as long as I wanted, and there wouldn't have been a damn thing you could have done about it. Didn't you see the whips and chains hanging on the wall? Don't you think half a dozen other people would have come running if I'd opened that curtain and snapped my fingers? If you don't know what you're doing in places like that, you could get physically and mentally scarred."

That wasn't what she'd expected him to say. And the pictures he painted made her shiver with disgust and unease. "Is that why you go? So you can do whatever you want with whoever you want?"

"No, El," he snapped. "I go because it helps me forget, okay?"

"Forget *what?*"

"*You,* goddammit," he yelled. "What do you think?"

Her mouth dropped open. Damn this darkness. She wanted to see his face, read his expression. She couldn't believe what she was hearing. "Bullshit. I haven't heard from you in seven years, and you've treated me like shit from day one."

"You chose your career over me, and then the first time I see you again after all that time, you jumped down my throat when I tried to do the right thing and tell you it was me at the club. I don't like the way you've disrupted the life I've pieced together after you left. I don't like having you on the set. I don't like having to think about or watch you get it on with Alex. I don't like being reminded of all the dreams I've missed watching come true for you. Your presence is a constant reminder of how badly I fucked up the only good thing in my life, and it hurts, goddammit. It hurts like hell. Yet I can't seem to keep my goddamned hands off you when you're within five feet. So yeah, I'm treating you like shit for a reason. I want you to stay the hell away from me and get the fuck out of my life."

He stopped yelling as suddenly as he'd started, and the silence was so complete, it rang in her ears.

"I"—she took a few shallow breaths and blew them out to take the edge off the tears tightening her chest. This pain felt deep enough to break her open, and she couldn't do that—not here, not now—"didn't see that coming."

She lowered her face to her knees and tried to hold herself together, but as his words sank in and touched on memories, pain swelled in her heart. He was right. Her mind scrambled with the ramifications of everything he'd said and how it all related to the past, the present, how it would alter the future. Her mind spun and spun, tying her heart in a knot so tight, she was sure it had lost blood supply.

Part of her wanted to confront Troy on what he'd just said, delve deeper into what that might mean, but she knew she couldn't take it. Not under these conditions. Her brain felt frayed, her nerves fried, like she was one trigger shy of losing her mind. Her skin was crawling. Her muscles ached from trembling. Every part of her felt raw and exposed and vulnerable.

"Troy?" A male voice pierced the quiet from a distance. Giselle thought it was her imagination until she heard, "Troy, can you hear me?"

"I'm here," he yelled back, his voice so loud, Giselle's heart bounced against her ribs. "I have Ellie. Get us the fuck out of here."

"Working on it. Hang tight."

Troy grabbed her arm. "Hear that, El? We're gonna be fine." His hand slid down and covered hers, threading their fingers. Then he pulled her in until she was leaning against him, wrapped his other arm around her, and kissed her temple. "We're gonna be fine, baby."

For a guy who wanted her out of his life, he sure had a twisted way of showing it. But then their relationship had always been different from most—deeper, more intense, more passionate, a hell of a lot more confusing.

And she was definitely not fine. Nothing about her was fine, not her head, her heart, or her body. Her emotions were slipping little by little from her control. She could feel them sliding out from under her like sand through her fingers. And even though she knew the cave was stifling hot, she was growing cold.

"I'll be good. I'll be good," she whispered to herself, a soothing mantra from her childhood. She knew it didn't make any sense, knew this situation was very different, but she couldn't stem the compulsion to repeat the phrase over and over, words that gave her hope when no hope existed. Words that helped stem the slide of her mind and body. "I promise. I'll be good. Promise, promise, pinkie promise."

"Shh, honey." Troy held her close and rocked her. "You're okay. We're okay."

He was so warm, but she couldn't absorb his body heat. Her head grew fuzzy, and her mind drifted where it always had during her childhood while she'd been trapped alone in spaces like this—to death.

"I thought about calling," she said, letting her eyes close. "I need you to know that I thought about calling. I picked up the phone a hundred times, wanted so badly to hear your voice, to make things right, but it was so complicated."

"Ellie, don't. You're not dying. It's just anxiety. You're going to be fine."

"I couldn't find the words." She had to get it out. The guilt had weighed on her so heavily for so long. "Nothing seemed right. The more time that passed, the harder it got. And as long as Nathan assured me you were fine, I told myself I should just leave you alone…"

"Troy." Zahara's voice, closer to their location, cut off Giselle's words. "We're setting up a rescue op. Tell me where you're at."

"I grabbed Ellie from the stage and dove under the first table I could find."

"You've got cover?" Duke's voice penetrated the stone.

"Don't get too excited. The table's already broken."

"We've talked to the engineers, and we're going to get the top layer of excavation started. There may be some sift and backfill as we go. Let me know if it gets bad. The engineers will be here soon."

"Those propeller heads are the reason we're down here," Troy said, angry.

"Wait till Josh hears about this," one of the Renegades said on the other side of the darkness. "He's gonna shit a cow. A full-grown fucking cow."

The thud of rock made Giselle's nerves fray a little more. The group's banter was foreign to her, just like their dedication and total trust in each other. And the process of disturbing the precarious cocoon terrified her.

"Shouldn't we wait?" she asked. "For, I don't know, the fire department or someone? Don't they get people out of disasters?"

"All kinds of people rescue others from disaster, honey. It's a hundred and ten degrees outside. Without the air conditioning, plastered together like this, without air circulation, we're going to be smoldering soon." We can't wait."

The scrape and thump of rock invaded their tiny space. The trickle of sand slid into their only fresh air. A sliver of light penetrated the darkness and seemed cuttingly bright to Giselle's eyes, and it gave her a view of the small, rubble-filled space surrounding them. The sight flipped one of those terror triggers inside her brain. It didn't matter that there were people outside trying to help her. It didn't matter that Troy was in this with her. She felt the life getting squeezed from her body. Saw gray edges lining her vision.

"I'll be good," she whispered. "I'll be good."

"Hold on," Troy said, his voice soothing now. "Just hold on."

"Duke," Zahara said, "help me with this big one."

The sound of scraping rock seemed to rip at Giselle's skin. She pressed her face to Troy's shoulder, dug her fingers into his arm. "Pinkie promise."

"Just a little longer," he said.

But when they lifted that rock out of place, the opening destabilized and sent the far wall falling against Giselle's back. She screamed as the mass forced her against Troy, and she found herself layered with dirt, sand, and rock from the back of her head to the backs of her heels. Her face smashed against Troy's chest, and dust darkened the cave again.

"No, no, no. Can't do this...Can't do this." She coughed hard as the dust filled her lungs. "Gotta get out. *Out, out, out.*"

"I'm sorry, baby," Troy said, "I know this scares you, but we'll come out okay."

He would. She wouldn't. She could feel her sanity taking that last thin slide out from under her.

She curled her fingers into his biceps hard, digging her nails into his skin. This was that moment to say what needed to be said before she never got the chance.

"Nothing's been the same since I walked away from you, like half my soul was missing. But it was better for both of us. I must have known it would be somehow..."

The darkness swept across her vision, and she clutched Troy tighter.

"Giselle, don't talk. You're going to be fine."

"I never stopped loving you." Fingers of darkness invaded her brain. "Never stopped thinking about you. I'm sorry it ended so badly..."

And unconsciousness dragged her under.

Eleven

Troy sat on a chair beside the gurney next to Ellie in her room in the emergency department and stroked her hair. He'd unbraided the honeyed strands once all her urgent care had been finished, planning to brush out the dirt, but he'd found it surprisingly clean from the braid. The nurses had focused on sterilizing her wounds, but Troy had cleaned the grime from any exposed area with paper towels and hospital soap after the nurses had gone.

Now, he heaved a sigh and pulled the chair closer so he could sit beside her. Then he pulled one of her hands from beneath the blanket and curled her hand into his. Emotion welled inside him as he stared down at her long, slim fingers and felt her chord-calloused fingertips against his.

"I never stopped loving you."
"I never stopped loving you."
"I never stopped loving you."

It just played over and over in his head and heart like a skip in a record. The words brought hope and fear, joy and pain. So much confusion. She'd said them under duress, when her mind was twisted, when she'd believed she was going to be crushed to death. Not exactly a profession of free will.

And what if it was? That didn't mean she planned on acting on those feelings. She'd loved him when she'd walked away before. The fact that she'd never stopped loving him—yet never contacted him over the years—didn't give him any sort of hope anything would change now. That she'd want to try again.

The room's curtain moved, drawing Troy's gaze. Zahara motioned to him. When he stepped outside the room, he found his makeshift family of Renegades and their women clogging the ER's corridors, including Jax Chamberlin, Renegades' owner, and worse, Ryker.

Ryker's presence at this fragile time between Troy and Giselle could ruin everything.

"Jesus Christ," Troy said to Jax, exasperated. "I told you we could handle this." To Ryker, he said, "You're supposed to be in Syria." To Rachel, he said, "Why didn't you tell me you were coming?"

"Good to see you too, bro." Ryker stepped forward and pulled Troy into a quick hug. And just like always, Troy's frustration melted.

Maggie, the nurse who'd been taking care of Giselle gave Jax a stern look. "Take this into room six, Jax. You've got twenty minutes. Not a second longer. We need that room."

Jax grabbed the hand she used to wag a finger at him and dragged her close for a hug. "Thanks, Mags. You're the best."

She hugged him back, then pushed him away. "Go on, get out of here."

Troy looked back at Giselle. "I don't want to leave—"

Maggie gave his arm a squeeze. "I've got her. I won't let anyone in until you get back."

He exhaled. "Come get me if she wakes?"

"You bet."

Troy gave her a smile of thanks and followed the others into a room nearby, where Wes, the Renegades best stunt driver, closed the glass door behind them. Troy scanned the stoic faces in the room—Jax, Wes, Ryker, and their girls, Lexi, Rubi, and Rachel. Zahara also stepped in. She'd been acting as liaison between the crew and the hospital all night.

Ryker spoke first. "How's Giselle?"

He hooked his thumbs through his belt loops and leaned against the glass wall to the room. His hands were too torn up to shove into his pockets, his arms too bruised and cut to cross. And he couldn't find a comfortable spot on his back to press against the glass. "Physically, not as bad as she looks. She has a concussion, a few cuts that needed stitches. Mentally, she's a mess. They had to knock her on her ass with some heavy-duty drugs just to get X-rays."

"I can only imagine." Ryker said, then explained to the rest of the group. "She's claustrophobic and nosocomephobic. One freaks her out bad enough to be problematic, but together they're obviously—"

"Noso—what?" Zahara asked.

"Fear of hospitals," Troy explained. "She spent a lot of time in them as a kid. Abuse involved cops. Cops involved custody battles, custody battles involved more beatings. It was an endless cycle that created a horrible fear of hospitals."

"Sounds like you've been through it before," Rubi said.

He rubbed his eyes. "A few times."

"It's amazing she's done so well in her career with those emotional issues," Lexi said.

"The woman has a goddamned will of steel."

"Speaking of her career," Zahara added, "her manager and her assistant are wearing holes in the waiting room carpet."

"I know. I've been focused on keeping her calm and didn't want to leave in case she woke and freaked. I'll have to deal with them soon enough. And he's just..." Troy shook his head. They didn't need the details of how hard Chad pushed her, how much stress he caused for Giselle instead of alleviating it for her the way he should. "Never mind."

"What's the word on Don?" Jax asked of the engineer who'd been trapped under the rubble. Both caves had collapsed when Don's exploratory drilling had tapped into a weakened area of the caves' core structure.

"He's out of surgery. Stable. They say he'll be okay."

Jax exhaled, his shoulders releasing some tension. "Great news."

"And everyone else has been released," Zahara added. "Troy and Giselle are the last of the crew here."

"Good," Jax said, his expression tense. "Wes and I will pick up the job from here with Z, Duke, and Keaton. We're going to figure out how this happened so it won't ever happen again. And I'm going to try to pull Josh on board full-time."

"Oh, thank God." Troy exhaled the words. "The guy's OCD can make me crazy, but I'll take his crazy to this any day. I know this would never have happened if we'd had Josh running risk assessment." He ran his hand through his hair. He'd cleaned up in one of the bathrooms and changed into clothes Duke and Keaton had brought him from the hotel. "And we were lucky. It could have been so much worse."

A knock sounded on the door, then Maggie slid it open, her gaze on Troy. He pushed off the exam table he was leaning against. "Her manager is getting unmanageable. I really don't want to call security on him."

Ryker turned, shoulders back, chest out. "I'll set him straight."

Troy huffed a tired laugh. "She's got enough trouble with him as it is." To the nurse, he said, "I'll deal with him. Thanks, Maggie."

Jax, Wes, and Ryker filed out of the room. Lexi hung back and faced Troy. She gripped his forearms and lifted those big blue eyes to his. "Anything you need, and I mean anything, you know that, right? If she's important to you, she's important to us. She's instant family. We take care of each other, and there's nothing we won't do for either of you. Ryker and Rachel are staying with us at the beach house. I hope you'll bring Giselle home to stay there too."

Troy lived on the bottom floor of Jax and Lexi's mammoth home on Malibu beach, one of two homes they owned and the one they stayed in on weekends when they weren't working in downtown LA.

Gratitude and joy swelled inside him, making him ache with the kind of acceptance and belonging he'd never believed possible. The kind he wanted to share with Giselle. He pulled Lexi into a hug and whispered, "Thank you. So much."

"Don't be stubborn or proud," she said, scolding like the sister she'd become. "Because if I find out you needed something and didn't ask, you'll be sorry."

He laughed and released her. "I do *not* want to suffer your wrath. Thanks for coming."

"Always."

She left the room with Rachel, but Zahara and Rubi lingered, and Troy knew he was in for another talking-to.

Zahara didn't waste any time digging in. "I heard what Giselle said when we were digging you out."

People say all kinds of things when they're panicked."

Z got that determined look in her eyes. "They say things that are automatic, things like 'I'm scared,' 'I'm sorry,' 'Don't leave me.' They don't say things like, 'Nothing's been the same since I walked away from you, like half my soul was missing.' *That* was real."

"And in the very next breath, she said, 'It was better for both of us.'"

"Give me a break. She meant it was better for both of you *then*, not *now*. Times like these make people reevaluate their lives. Facing death makes people realize where their priorities lie. They see holes in their lives they never noticed before."

No fucking kidding. Troy had maintained his distance from Giselle over the last four days by clinging to the belief that she deserved better. But after watching that ceiling fly toward her, holding her while the cave wall crushed her to his body, witnessing her mind fray, cell by cell…It all brought back a reality that he lived with on a daily basis in stunts—life was short, and you never knew when it would be stolen from you.

So, yeah, he was second-guessing all his previous convictions pretty damn hard.

"Neither you nor Giselle can work right now," Zahara said, "and sitting around will drive you both crazy. I suggest you two go away together for a few days and take some time to really talk. Really think about what you want the rest of your lives to look like. It may be the last chance you get to do it together."

Rubi stepped forward, picked up his hand, and pressed a ring of keys into his palm. "The keys to my father's house in Malibu. He hasn't set foot in the place for six years, and he's in Thailand for another month. There's a car in the garage. I'll have clothes and food delivered to the house. Z has clued me in on Giselle's sizes from her costume fittings. And no one will know you're there but me and Z."

That overwhelming sense of gratitude tightened his throat again. He swallowed past the lump and closed his fingers around Rubi's. "I don't know—"

"You don't have to know," she said, giving his hand a squeeze. "Just know it's there for you. Just know I hope you use it."

Troy exhaled heavily, swallowed his fierce independent streak, and wrapped an arm around each of the women's shoulders, holding them tight. "I love you guys."

"Love you too," they said at the same time, then released him.

"You're an amazing man," Z said, "a man any woman would be lucky to have in her life. You *do* deserve more. Now go put that prick in his place."

Troy laughed, nodded, and followed them from the room. With more doubts than he'd had in years, he watched Zahara and Rubi leave the ER. But as soon as he turned back into Giselle's room, as soon as his gaze slid over her profile, soft cream against the crisp white pillow, the churning in his chest eased.

He scanned the busy ER and found Maggie. Once she met his gaze, he nodded. She returned the nod and started toward the waiting room. In Giselle's room, he flipped off the overhead lights, returned to her bedside, and stroked her soft cheek with the backs of his fingers. The act lowered his blood pressure and eased his stress, but the sight of her so broken tore at him. This was the result of too much stress built up over a long period of time. It was Giselle trying to be everything to everyone—the star, the businesswoman, the mediator, the employer, the employee, the friend. And when she found herself in need of those reserves to hold herself together, she'd come up empty, with no one there to give her the kind of support he was getting from his Renegades family. Except for Brook, Giselle was essentially alone, and it broke his heart.

"What are we gonna do about this, angel?" he whispered.

Deep blue bruises were developing in various places on her cheekbone and chin. Troy wished he had a magic wand to erase them. Wished he had a magic wand to erase every mistake he'd ever made.

Movement at the door drew Troy's gaze. Chad wore khakis and a polo shirt and carried a duffle bag. Worry creased his pale face. Beside him, Giselle's assistant, Brook, tore a Kleenex to shreds, her eyes and nose red and swollen. Troy forcefully curbed his frustration.

"What took so damn long?" Chad demanded. "Why haven't we been able to see her?"

"She had to be sedated. She needed tests and stitches. Her medical care comes first."

Brook nodded fervently. "Of course."

Chad pushed past Troy. At the sight of Giselle, he dropped the duffle. "Giselle? Honey?" When she didn't answer, didn't move, Chad swung back toward Troy. "If you had anything to do with this—"

"Don't you worry about a thing." Brook's sweet whisper contrasted sharply with Chad's anger. She'd rounded the bed and gently curved her hand over Giselle's, stroking back Giselle's hair with the other hand. "We both know what a miracle worker I am. I've got you completely covered. You don't even look that bad. Nothing a little concealer and bronzer won't fix."

As Brook bent to kiss Giselle's forehead, Chad barked at Troy, "How did this happen? How bad is it? What did the doctor say?"

"We're still looking into the exact cause, but at this point, it looks like the engineers Paramount used for risk assessment fucked up." Troy crossed his arms, fighting against a grimace when his own injuries shot pain through his body. "Physically, her cuts, bruises, and concussion should be healed in a week or two. Her voice"—he shrugged—"there's really no telling how long it will take for that to heal until she wakes up, but judging by the amount of screaming and sobbing she was doing, I'm guessing at least three weeks, but probably more. Mentally"—he heaved a sigh—"she's shattered."

Chad pried his gaze off Giselle to glare at Troy. "You underestimate her."

"You don't know her like I do."

"Like you *did*. She's not a scared girl anymore—"

"She hasn't been a girl for decades. Abuse has a wicked way of making you grow up real fast. And you didn't see her in that cave or coming into the hospital. She was absolutely terrorized. Her issues aren't things you outgrow. They're things you learn to manage, which she may control under normal circumstances, but days like today create setbacks. There's no way to tell how quickly she'll bounce back until she's had a few days to recover. And even then, PTSD has a weird way of striking at the oddest times, from the slightest trigger."

"You know she still won't take the elevator," Brook said, staring at the floor and tearing her Kleenex. "And if we stay somewhere with a big, like, you know, a really big walk-in closet, I have to put her clothes away and get them out, and, oh, she just hates that. And when we're at a dark restaurant, I always get her the brightest table. Sometimes, sometimes, sometimes...."

Brook gasped for air as she fought tears. Troy's frustration toward Chad faded in the face of Brook's pain, and he slid his arm around her shoulders, as his own fears over Giselle's health resurfaced. Brook turned into him and started crying. "Sometimes I bring over a-a-a lamp from a-another t-table."

"You're a good friend," Troy murmured, hugging the girl.

Chad's jaw twitched. "I want to take her home."

"Home as in a hotel room? After she was nearly crushed to death in a cave when she's intensely claustrophobic?" Troy's temper slipped. Brook turned her head to look at Chad but didn't leave the circle of Troy's arm. "Who are you thinking about right now? You or Ellie? Because that might be convenient for you, but sticking her back in a hotel room alone where all she can do is relive the hell she's been through or worry about how this could affect her career is not in her best interest.

"The best thing you can do for her now is focus on canceling her appearances for the next two weeks in a way that won't hurt her chances at the next step she's worked so hard to get. That peace of mind will go a long way toward letting her relax and heal."

"Oh yes," Brook said, relief filling her voice. "Yes, yes, good idea. I can take care of—"

"*Two weeks?*" Chad balked. "That will wipe out the rest of her concerts here."

Brook curved her lips inward and cast an uncertain look up at Troy.

"I'm not canceling anything until I talk to Giselle," Chad continued. "This could be nothing more than a temporary setback. She might just need a couple of days to—"

"Dude, she has a *concussion*," Troy said, releasing Brook. "Have you ever had a concussion? I have, and I can tell you, your head hurts like a mother. That alone would keep her from singing. But like I said, her vocal cords are ragged. I can guarantee you don't want her singing *anything* in public right now."

Chad's fingers closed tight around the gurney's metal side. "You don't know shit about—"

"Yeah, as a matter of fact, I do." Troy stepped up to the gurney and leaned in to get as in-your-face as he could in the small room with this damn bed separating them. "I know that any change in her head, neck, or chest affects her ability to sing. I know that if she tries to sing before her concussion has healed, the pressure it would create in her head would cause blinding pain, and she could pass out. I've *seen* it happen. I've also seen her try to sing with a sinus infection, strep throat, and a tooth abscess. And I'm telling you she can't do it. Once, she screamed her lungs out over a damn Super Bowl game, and she couldn't perform for a month. A god-damned *month*. Don't fucking tell me I don't know her. We were together five years. How long have you been her manager?"

Chad's mouth tightened, his hand twisted on the gurney, his gaze turned to Giselle.

The doctor who'd been taking care of her approached, pausing just outside the door to speak with a nurse.

"There's the doctor," Troy told Chad. "Ask him. As for Giselle, I'm staying with her until she's well enough to leave the hospital. I'll have her call you as soon as she's awake."

Chad walked out without a word.

Troy turned to Brook. "I'm really sorry about—"

"She really loves you."

He froze, stunned. "Wha...?"

"Giselle. I've been her assistant since she went on the road with Lady Antebellum, right after you two broke up." She snuck a look at Giselle. "I love her like a sister, and we look out for each other, you know? And we've talked so much about you that I feel like I already know you. I know how much you loved her, and I don't believe that kind of love ever ends, even if you aren't together. Not that I'd really know, because I've never been in love like that. Just call it women's intuition or whatever."

She paused only long enough to draw a quick breath and started rambling again, never giving him time to process anything she was saying, and making Troy's head spin.

"And she's really open about how messed up her childhood was, and gets really frustrated sometimes because she wants so badly to be normal, but she's just not, you know? So I'm stepping in as her normal, I don't know, spirit friend or something, because at this point, normal people in love would tell each other how much they mean to each other and find a way to talk things out and work around the obstacles. But, I know Giselle, and the first thing she'll ask for when she opens her eyes is her phone, even if what she really wants and really needs is you. Just you.

"I know I'm talking really fast, but I'm sort of sandwiched between two people here who don't want me saying what needs to be said, but I've seen you with her a few times over the last week, and she and I have talked some, and after living with her day in and day out for seven years—I beat you by the way, my seven to your five—I can read so much more into her feelings than what she's telling me. Her facial expressions, the inflections of her voice—"

The door slid open. "Brook," Chad barked. "We're leaving."

She perked up with a bright "Be right there." But as soon as the door closed, she dropped back into her serious, confidential quick-talk. "When she freaks out, you tell her I've got her back. Tell her I'm taking care of everything I can take care of from this end. You tell her that she'd better not come back to work until her voice is one hundred percent, because I won't let her sing any sooner than you will. You tell her," she said with more emphasis and a wicked little gleam in her dark blue eyes, "that she won't be singing again until she gets a written release from *Jacque.*"

Troy rubbed a hand down one side of his face as the fatigue settled in deep. "And who's Jacque?"

Brook's mouth tipped up in a tired little smirk. "Only the very best laryngologist in the country. He treats all the big stars, and he's someone who will knock Chad on his ass when necessary."

Troy laughed and nodded. "Perfect. Shoot me his contact information when you get a chance, will you?"

"You bet. Take care of our girl, will you?"

"You bet." Troy pulled Brook into a hug and whispered, "Thank you. For loving her. For being with her when I couldn't."

Brook sighed and patted his back. "It takes a village to raise a country music star."

Troy laughed and let Brook slip from the room.

At Giselle's bedside, he dropped into a chair, moved it to the side of the gurney, and lowered one metal arm. Resting one hand on her thigh beneath the blanket, he curled the other hand around hers and laid his head on the foam mattress and watched her sleep.

"Ellie, Ellie, Ellie," he murmured as fatigue settled in. "Why did we cross paths now? And how do I keep you from slipping through my fingers again?"

Giselle floated out of a deep, deep sleep. The kind of sleep that made her feel like a rock in the bed. The kind of sleep that made her eyelids feel like cement and her mouth feel like a cotton ball. She tried several times before she finally forced her eyes open a sliver, then searched for orientation—day, time, place. But her brain was as groggy as her body.

She was warm but uncomfortable. Vague pain in her head made her wince. When she tried to shift her body, more pain erupted all over, and she groaned. Something flinched around her hand, and she forced her eyes that direction. A large male hand cradled hers. A hand with callouses and dirt-encrusted nails.

Her slow, heavy gaze followed the hand up a muscular arm marred with scrapes and bruises, then skipped to a full head of deep brown waves. Then jumped to Troy's face, where his cheek lay on the gurney near her hip. His eyes were closed, his face loose in sleep.

Troy.

Her heart leapt with pleasure and spiraled with affection while a smile curved her mouth—until the condition of his face registered in her sluggish mind. More scrapes and cuts had been covered in strips of tape, bruises marred his smooth tan, a black eye made Giselle wince. Alarm sang along her nerves. She lifted her free hand to run her fingers through his hair, but her wrist jerked to a stop. Confused, she darted a look at her arm. Something was wrapped around her wrist. Fabric? Rope?

She didn't understand. She just pulled at the fabric again and again. Fabric tied to a metal railing. A metal railing on a gurney. A gurney in a hospital room.

"Troy?" With each thought, panic jumped another rung. "Troy. *Troy!*"

She wasn't thinking, just reacting, jerking and yelling.

"Shh, honey, I'm right here." He was on his feet, pressing her shoulders to the mattress. "Everything's fine. You're okay."

"W-what is this? Why…" She jerked both hands at once. "Get these *off.*"

"Okay, okay," he said. "Just show me you can calm down first."

Anger immediately replaced panic, but she clenched her teeth and forced herself to lie back and stay still. Which made it easier to fill her lungs. Helped her brain clear.

With two tugs, Troy freed her hands, and relief engulfed her, followed by a mess of other intense emotions she couldn't define and didn't understand. All she knew was she needed security, and she went directly to her purest form—Troy.

She threw her arms around his neck. Holding him tight, she closed her eyes as deep relief swept in with such force, she shivered. "Oh my God. Oh my God."

Memories rushed in—the cave, Troy, nearly getting crushed and buried, losing it when they reached the hospital. Mortification made her bury her face in his neck.

"The others?" she asked. "Were there others?"

"One of the engineers was caught in the stunt cave, but he's out and he's recovering. A few others had minor injuries, but they've all been treated, and they're on their way home. Everyone is going to be okay."

Thank God. She closed her eyes in relief. "How long have I been here?"

"About eight hours. They had to sedate you."

"When can I leave? I need to get out."

"I know. We were just waiting for you to wake up."

He held her tight. Spoke softly, but firmly, never treating her like she was crazy or weak. And remembering how insane she'd acted after that cave wall had collapsed, the way she'd fought when she realized they'd brought her to the hospital...She'd definitely earned a looney-tunes label.

He pulled back and met her eyes. "The doctor wants to check you over one more time. If you're all good, you can go."

She nodded and let one arm fall from his shoulders to wipe at wet cheeks. "Okay. I'm ready."

Troy grinned and shook his head, then pressed a button on a remote nearby. "You still fuckin' amaze me."

A nurse slid the glass door to her room open and offered a tentative smile for Giselle. "Look who's awake. How do you feel?"

She nodded. "Better."

"The doctor's seeing another patient, but I'll send him your way when he's finished."

When she slid the door shut again, Giselle dropped her head and covered her face with both hands. "Oh my God. Please, tell me I'm here under an alias."

"Yes, ma'am, Miss Susie Cue."

A puff of laughter escaped her, and she dropped her hands. "You named me Susie Cue?"

"I wish I'd thought of it, but no, actually, the hospital named you. Turns out they're quite familiar with the rich-and-famous protocol. But the press is already swarming. There were some big stars at the site today, so this is going to stay on the radar awhile."

"Does Chad know?" Dread flooded her belly. He would be so bent out of shape. So worried about every show she missed, every conceivable contract glitch, every potential endorsement blip. "Is he here?"

"He brought you some of your things and went back to the hotel to reschedule your concerts. Everything's fine."

"Reschedule—No. No, he can't. I can't...Oh God. No, no, no. Where's my phone?"

"Ellie." Troy lifted her chin until her eyes met his. "Can you hear yourself? You sound like an addict who needs a hit. And if you even try to sing one line of 'You Are My Sunshine,' your head's going to hurt so bad, you'll be begging someone to shoot you."

As if the mention of her head made the injury a reality, pain stabbed her skull, and she winced.

He took her face gently in both hands and smiled so sweetly, she wanted to melt. "It's *okay*. Performers get sick all the time. They have accidents. Family emergencies. They're *human*. Venues schedule backup acts for situations just like this."

She closed her eyes and her shoulders slumped. This didn't happen to her. She never missed a concert. She never let a venue's manager or her fans down. None of this had to be her fault for her to still feel bad. And even though she had enough money saved to live the rest of her life comfortably if she used it wisely, she doubted she'd ever get over the ingrained fear of going hungry or homeless if she failed.

"This is one of the reasons you pay Chad to manage your career. Let him manage. He wants you to take the time you need to get better so you can come back full steam."

Tension ebbed from her shoulders, but she frowned. "He...does?"

"Do you doubt that?"

"No, no." She shook her head and looked away, but she was having a hard time envisioning Chad saying such a thing. Then again, she'd never been gravely ill or seriously injured, so she couldn't say she really knew how he'd act in this situation. "It's just, I'm at a sort of pivotal point in my career…"

She trailed off, her mind filling with all the promotional networking they had planned. All the concerts she still had scheduled…

Troy's dry laugh drew her gaze to his smirk. "When was the last time your career *wasn't* at a pivotal point?"

Her brow pulled harder. "What does that mean?"

"It means that when you're in entertainment, every step you take seems pivotal, especially as you gain notoriety." He took a deep breath and blew it out, his shoulders relaxing. "When I'm under a lot of pressure to get a stunt right, say, one I can't repeat because it will cost a ton of money or because it would be too dangerous or simply because it's a one-time-only situation, I always, *always*, take a moment to step back and assess the big picture before I go for broke.

"I can't tell you how many times that's saved money, time, injuries, and even lives. It also makes for better filming, because that moment of perspective gives me one more layer of security, allowing me to give the stunt my all.

"Sometimes," he said, his voice softening as his focus eased off his work, "it makes the most sense to step back during the hardest push, to make sure you're on target, that you have everything you need in place to make the project successful…and sometimes, even to make sure it's still what you want."

God, that was so…true. His advice so sage. How did he do that? And why did that suggestion sound so rational, so reasonable coming from Troy? But so unthinkable in her own mind? Unimaginable coming out of Chad's mouth?

"Wow," she said softly, half in awe, half teasing. "That's…deep."

A grin flashed across his face. "And I'm good-looking too."

Laughter popped from her throat. Only Troy could make her laugh at a time and in a place like this.

He ran the backs of his fingers down her cheek. "Feels good to hear you laugh."

But she was too exhausted to laugh for long. And even that pressure made her head ache, which meant Troy was right about singing. If she tried to get up on stage now, she might just snap her vocal cords and blow her brains out her ears.

"I should call Brook," she said. "I'm sure she's talked to Chad, but she's a worrier." She glanced around for anything that looked personal. "Where's my phone?"

"Brook's already been here."

Giselle's gaze jumped to Troy's. "Oh no. If she saw me like this…Oh God, she's going to be freaked."

"She's stronger than you think, that one." A sly smile tilted his mouth. "A little devious too. I like her. She's an amazing friend to you."

A soft spot opened in Giselle's chest. "What did she say?"

"A lot. Like, *really* fast."

Laughter rolled from her throat, but pain stabbed her brain. She grabbed her head with both hands, rocking back and forth. "Oh, ow. Ow, ow, ow."

Troy massaged her scalp, and the pain faded into a dull throb. "She wanted me to tell you that she has you completely covered on the home front. Your mail, e-mail, social media—everything. She wants you resting and healing, and she doesn't want to see your pretty face until you're one hundred percent again."

"Is that right?" she asked with a smirk.

"That's right. She also said, don't plan on singing until you're cleared by Jacque, whoever the hell that is."

Giselle gasped, and her mouth hung open in an expression of irritation. "That little…"

"Uh-uh." He put a finger underneath her chin and forced her mouth closed. "*That little* has your best interest at heart."

She heaved an exasperated sigh. "I know." A moment of sweet silence filled the room, but memories quickly invaded her peace. She scanned his face, grimacing at the injuries. "Did I…do any of that?"

"The black eye with your elbow." He pulled down the collar of his T-shirt, showing four raw, linear welts. "These. A few miscellaneous bruises. You're stronger than you used to be, but, still, it's nothing I haven't dealt with before."

She drew air through her teeth. A fresh wave of tears burned her eyes. How and why he'd put up with her and all her problems for as long as he had all those years ago, she'd never know.

"I'm so sor—" Her throat choked off her apology, and she lay back on the gurney, hands covering her face.

"Baby," he said quietly, "you can't afford any more crying. You're already looking at a long haul to get your throat back to singing status, but more urgently, after the way you came in here, you need to get ahold of yourself before the doctor checks on you, or he's going to hold you on a seventy-two-hour psych eval. That's not going to do anyone any good."

Ice chilled her skin, and Giselle gasped. Her hands slid down to clear her eyes, and she focused on him. Their past came spiraling back at her again in vivid, terrifying color. No, she couldn't go through three days of lockdown and zombie-inducing drugs. That had never crossed her mind, and if word leaked to the press…"Oh my God. I totally forgot…"

"I've got your back." He covered her hand with his, using the other to tuck a strand of hair behind her ear. "I know getting you out of here as fast as humanly possible is what you need most right now."

Her heart flooded with a level of gratitude she couldn't begin to describe. No one in the world knew her better than Troy. Brook ran a close second, but Troy knew her every flaw, inside and out. He knew her every vice. Her every fear. And after all that had happened between them, he was the last person with any obligation to help her, because everything he'd said in the cave was true. Yet, he was here, comforting her without judgment.

But the only words she could find among the torrent of emotions were "Thank you."

A smile fluttered across his lips before it fell again. He picked up a piece of her hair and twirled it around his finger, his gaze distant, the way he used to whenever his mind drifted.

"Do you remember?" he asked, voice quiet and hesitant. "What happened in the cave, I mean?"

She swallowed the surge of anxiety pushing up her throat. "Yeah. I mean, I think I do."

"Do you remember…" His eyes flicked to hers, guarded, a little shy. "You said some things…I mean, I know we all say things we shouldn't or things we don't mean when we're angry or stressed. I've made a million mistakes since I set eyes on you again…" He dropped the hair coiled around his finger. "Never mind."

The sliver of intimacy they'd developed in that moment vanished, and Giselle felt it like a cut to her heart. She grabbed his hand back but couldn't meet his gaze when she said, "I remember. And I meant what I said." She pulled his hand to her heart, eyes squeezed shut. "Things I should have said a long time ago. I've made just as many mistakes as you have."

He wrapped his other hand around the back of her neck and pulled her into the circle of his arms. He dropped a kiss to her head and buried his face in her hair, holding her tight. "God, I've missed you."

His pained rasp sounded almost violent in the quiet, drawing her gaze to his face. His dark eyes were warm and swimming with tears. All the pain from their breakup, all the loss she'd felt over their years apart flooded back, filling her chest until she ached. "I'm so sor—"

He covered her mouth with a hard shut-up kiss. When he broke away, a tear slipped over his lashes and down his cheek. Giselle wiped it away.

"No more apologies, okay?" He cupped her face, his gaze open and vulnerable. "It's all in the past. We're different people now. When I heard you sing today"—he shook his head, his expression filled with awe—"I was blown away by how your voice had matured. How sophisticated and professional you'd become. And I thought, everything happens for a reason, because if we'd stayed together, you wouldn't be where you are now."

Pain twisted her heart, and her mind scrambled to make sense of this. "Troy, that's...Nobody knows what—"

"But now you're here," he said, gripping her arms to punctuate his words. "You and me, here, together. That happened for a reason too. This is a gift, Ellie." His hands lifted to cup her face, thumbs stroking her wet cheeks. "I want to get to know you again."

"Oh," she breathed, her heart fluttering with both fear and excitement. "I...I...want that too."

"Neither of us can work right now," he said. "Just spend a week with me."

"I..." She shook her head, the idea impossible at first thought, but she couldn't come up with one valid excuse to reject it.

"Ryker's back from Syria. He and Rachel are here."

"Here?"

He nodded. "They're probably not in the waiting room anymore, but they'd love to see you. And everyone on my team wants to meet you. We can all stay with my boss, Jax, and his girl, Lexi. They've got a house in Hollywood and another on the beach in Malibu, where I live on the bottom floor. We'll take long walks, sleep late, eat out, talk, laugh, relax. They're good people, El. They're my family. They're Ryker's family. They should be your family too."

Family. Her heart floated, and a longing pulled deep inside her. But something else inside, something deeper and smaller, felt suddenly overwhelmed. And scared. She didn't know how to do family. "I really need to talk it over with Chad…"

But even as the words exited her mouth, she knew he would hate the idea. And the thought of arguing with him over her going away where he couldn't hover with constant access instantly drained her.

"I'll talk to him." Troy pulled her gaze back to his, those dark eyes imploring her. "Just say yes, Ellie. Just say yes to seeing who we are together now, say yes to meeting these great people who treat me and Ryker like brothers, and I'll take care of everything else. I'll call Chad, I'll get you sprung from this place, and we'll grab a cab to the airport. We'll be in LA in a couple of hours. Anything you need that's not in this bag, we'll get in the city."

She laughed, trying like hell to force all the irrational unease away. "Troy, look at me." She held out her arms, marred with bruises and scrapes where they extended beyond the hospital gown. "I can't go anywhere like this. If anyone saw me, I'd be headlining the tabloids tomorrow as a battered woman."

"With a ball cap and sunglasses, you'll just be any random hot chick returning from a Vegas bender. Believe me, I've worked with enough stars to know exactly how to get them from one place to another incognito. You can relax and take all the time you need to recover once you get there." He gave her a slanted grin, the charming, quirky, secretive, little smile that made her insides jump. "Come on, you know you want to escape as bad as I do."

A knock on the glass cut in, and as the door opened, a dark-haired man in a white lab coat walked in. The sight swamped Giselle with anxiety.

"Say yes to a week of healing," Troy said softly, one hand sliding down her back, "and I'll take care of the rest."

"Are we talking about a vacation?" The doctor was in his mid-forties with a buoyant, easy manner, and Giselle forced back the irrational unease. "I'm Dr. Davenport." He shook her hand. "And I would be highly in favor of that idea. I told your manager, Mr. Moore, the same earlier. I strongly suggest two weeks but insist on at least one. After that, I'll leave it up to your discretion." He set her chart on the gurney and scanned her face. "You look much better with color in your cheeks."

Giselle smiled, but Troy wouldn't be ignored.

"Ellie," he said, easing toward the door with his phone out. "Should I make that call?"

Half-giddy, half-terrified, Giselle exhaled and nodded. Troy's mouth kicked up into a lopsided smile.

When he turned for the door, Giselle said, "But, Troy?" He paused and she took a breath, then dove in head first. "Can we spend that week together—just us?" Her belly fluttered with the thrill of having time alone with him. "I'd love to meet everyone eventually. But right now, I really want just you."

His face split into a brilliant smile, one that lit her heart and almost washed away all her concerns over Chad and her immediate future.

Almost.

Twelve

Giselle stood outside the door to the master bath-room, leaning against the wall, her head and hands resting on the doorframe as Troy ran the water in the tub. He was on his knees, in a gray tank top and tan car-go shorts, his bare feet still a little sandy from their walk on the beach. She loved watching the way his muscles rolled beneath his tan skin when he moved. Loved the way his hair flowed over the nape of his neck, all unruly and wavy from the wind.

But she found herself wishing it looked that way from having her hands fisting and combing and twist-ing the strands while they made love—something he'd deliberately avoided during their last two full days and nights together.

She scraped her lower lip between her teeth and scanned his body again. The dull ache that lived low in her pelvis sank between her legs and throbbed. God, she hoped he planned on getting in that tub with her and rocking her hard enough to spill water over the sides. Hope he came so hard the sound of his excitement echoed off all the marble and stone.

"El?"

"Huh?" her gaze snapped up to his, and she found him wearing an adorable little smirk.

"You didn't answer, so I added bubbles." He shrugged. "You used to love bubbles."

A languid, sweet pleasure spread through her, one that had become familiar again over the last forty-eight hours. The best forty-eight hours she could remember in years. He'd made her feel so utterly treasured during their time together. So totally wanted, absolutely adored, completely cherished. She'd forgotten the comfort and joy of being so well loved and cared for. Of spending time with someone who understood her better than she understood herself.

But she still didn't remember what it felt like to have him make love to her because he'd avoided any sexual contact with her since they'd arrived, and the encounters they'd had before had been about lust, not love. And Lord, how she longed to be reminded of how he could make love to her.

"I still love bubbles." She strolled through the door and paused behind him to run her hands through his hair. It was thick and soft, and she loved the way it curved around her fingers.

He moved the water around with his hand. "It's hot, but the steam will do your throat good."

She'd forgotten until these last two days with Troy how much she used to depend on him as her sounding board, her barometer for everything from help with the lyrics in a song to the best business decision. Now, with all her experience in the business and the consultants surrounding her—her agent, her manager, her accountant, her sponsors—she didn't feel like she needed that gauge anymore, but knowing he cared still felt good.

She reached for the oil on the bathroom counter, the one infused with lavender that she'd been using on his hands to help with healing, and poured some into her palm, then spread it over the skin of his neck and upper back exposed in the scoop of his tank. "And this will do your sore muscles good."

While he played with the water temperature, Giselle sank her thumbs into the supple muscle of his neck and upper back, slowly kneading the tension away.

He groaned, and she smiled, happy he was letting her do something for him for a change. He'd been determinedly focused on her every need since they'd arrived at the house—her every need barring any sexual need.

She massaged the tension from his neck, starting at the base of his skull and continuing down until he lowered his forehead to his arm where it lay on the edge of the tub.

"God, you are good with your hands."

She liked the want dripping from his words, and took a break from the massage to pull his tank toward his head.

"No." He glanced over his shoulder. "This is your time. Get in the bath."

"It's not even half-filled yet, and if this is *my time*, I want to spend it with my hands on you."

He relented with a groan, lifting his arms enough to let her pull the shirt off. She settled in behind him on her knees, poured more oil on his skin, and relished the warm, smooth, supple feel of him beneath her hands.

"It's still hard for me to believe I'm touching you." It was more of a thought than a comment.

He exhaled heavily, and his voice was thick and languid when he said, "Believe me, baby, I'm still waiting for someone to slap me awake from this dream."

Her heart filled like a balloon and blossomed like a flower at the same time—a sensation she'd had a lot since seeing Troy again. And as she worked her way down his spine, avoiding the bruises he'd gotten during the cave collapse, his groans of pleasure gave her as much gratification as a cheering crowd.

"Your bruises look better," she said. "All your cuts are healed over."

He hummed in acknowledgment of the news.

"What do you want to do tonight?" she asked, hoping his answer held the words *naked* and *under the covers* and *together.*

Their first forty-eight hours alone together again after seven years apart had been spent very quietly. They hadn't left the house other than to walk on the beach. Troy had regulated her talking time to make sure she rested her voice. And in between talks, they'd spent a lot of time kissing, cuddling, feeding each other, listening to music, or watching the waves. But one of Giselle's favorite pastimes had become watching films Troy had worked on and hearing all his behind-the-scenes tales from his stunt work.

He exhaled a groan. "I can't think when you're doing that."

"I can decide for us, if you want."

"Why am I sure that will get me into trouble?"

She leaned close and kissed his temple. "Because you know me so well?"

He chuckled. But when he didn't take the bait, she rolled her eyes and turned back to other topics to keep him talking. "Tell me something else I don't know about the new Troy Jacobs."

He groaned as she rubbed out a knot at the base of his neck. "I found my dad a few years ago."

Surprise snapped in her gut, spreading tingles. Neither of them had known their fathers growing up or ever thought they'd meet them.

She leaned around to look at him. "Seriously?"

He grinned. "Seriously."

She sat back on her heels and continued rubbing his muscles. "Wow. What's that like? Is it as cool as we always dreamed it would be?"

The bubbles almost reached his nose, and Troy reached up to turn off the tap. "If you mean the way we always hoped they'd swoop in and fix everything, no, it's not like that. But, it's still pretty cool. He's a good guy. Says he didn't know about me, that my mom didn't tell him."

"Do you believe him?"

"He's divorced with three other kids, and he goes out of his way to see them, pays child support, remembers their birthdays and all that, even remembers mine now. So, yeah, I think he would have made an effort with me if he'd known."

Her heart filled with all sorts of giddy feelings. "Oh my God." She slid her arms around his torso and pressed her chin to his shoulder. "You've got *siblings?*"

He turned his head toward her and covered her hands with one of his. "A brother and two sisters."

"Holy shit." She swung around and sat on the floor, her back against the tub, grinning at him. "Troy," she said, her hands gripping his arm. "You've got a *family.* You've got a *real* family."

He laughed and cupped her cheek. "Christ, you're so fucking adorable."

"I'm *so happy* for you. It's what we always dreamed of having."

"No, honey," he said softly. "I mean, they're great people, and yes, they add a lot to my life. But *you* were what I always dreamed of having. *You* were always my family."

Her heart overflowed. She pressed her forehead to his and closed her eyes on the intense pleasure. He tilted his head and kissed her, firmly and sweetly. But instead of taking it further, he pulled her to her feet, took the hem of her tank top in his fingers, and drew it up and off over her head, then reached for the bra clasp between her breasts.

She lifted her gaze to his and held it purposely. Surely this would lead to sex. How long could they stay together alone without it? He wanted it. She felt his erection against her lower body every time he pulled her close, every time she leaned into him, as he'd held her until they'd fallen asleep. But he hadn't made any move to get it, which left Giselle feeling... awkward and oddly unsure about making the first move.

Her bra fell open, and his gaze lowered to scan her breasts. The sigh that passed through his lips transitioned into a growl of hunger. Her nipples tightened at the sound, at the way his eyes stroked her skin. But instead of touching her, instead of taking handfuls of her breasts or pulling the sensitive flesh into his mouth, he just tugged on the tie to her shorts and bent to lower them over her hips. Then dropped to his knees to pull her panties down. And as the silk slid down her thighs, desire flooded her sex until she bit her lip to keep from moaning.

"*Fuuuuuck.*" He drew out the word filled with awe and desire. "You are so ridiculously gorgeous."

His hands slid up the sides of her thighs, slowly over her hips, pausing at her waist, where his fingers dug into her flesh firmly and drew her forward until his face was buried low in her belly.

Yes, yes, yes. Her eyes fell closed, and a moan ebbed from her throat. He pulled back and pressed kisses from her belly button toward her sex. Her breath caught, fingers tightened in his hair.

But he eased away and pushed to his feet far too soon, leaving Giselle dizzy and confused. Before, he hadn't been able to do her hard enough, fast enough, or long enough. Now...

This sense of rejection was stupid. Logically, she knew that. Emotionally…

He turned her to face the mountain of bubbles and she huffed a laugh. "I might get lost in there."

"I'll find you." He pushed a mound of fluffy white suds away from the head of the tub and took her hand as she stepped into the giant bath, then sighed as warm water and fragrant bubbles enveloped her.

"Oh my God." She settled back against the sloped end and stretched out, closing her eyes on a long, pleasure-filled groan. "I didn't realize how much I needed this."

The clink of metal brought her eyes open to Troy pulling the handheld showerhead from its holder and flipping a lever on the handle to turn on the water. He used one hand to cover the stitches on her forehead and the other to wield the spray. Giselle closed her eyes and relaxed as he gently massaged shampoo into her hair. Her mind drifted over the things they'd talked about over the last two days, the things they'd avoided talking about—like what would happen when real life hit again—and the tattoo on his shoulder came to mind. The one that flowed across the right side of his chest and onto his shoulder, depicting a ship at sea, and the one he hadn't wanted to talk about when she'd first seen it last night when he'd taken his shirt off in bed.

"Will you tell me about the tattoo on your chest now?" she asked.

He hesitated, but his voice was soft and open when he said, "What would you like to know?"

"Why a ship?" He'd never shown any interest in boating or the ocean when they'd been together.

"I worked on a fishing vessel for several years," he said. "It's sort of commemorative of that time."

Giselle's eyes jerked open, and she cut a look at him over her shoulder. Out of everything she'd learned about him over the last forty-eight hours, this was by far the most shocking. "Fishing vessel?" She searched her mind for some sort of reference. "Like that show, what's it called? Deadliest...something?"

"*Deadliest Catch.* Sort of." He pushed on her shoulder. "Relax." When she sank back into the water, he said, "Most days it felt more like a mix of *Deadliest Catch* and *The Perfect Storm*, but that's a good reference."

She was having a really hard time picturing him in slickers, working like a slave in torrential rain. "When did you do that?"

"After you left, it took me a while, but I realized there was no reason to stay put."

With sudden clarity, Giselle realized why he'd been putting off this talk. This was the painful stuff. This was what his life had been like after she and Ryker had gone off to live their dreams, leaving Troy alone to fend for himself.

"One of the guys at work had a brother on a boat in Alaska," he said, "and he hooked me up."

When he didn't go on, she asked, "What's that like? I mean, is it a day-trip thing? Or a few days at a time?"

"It depends—what you're fishing for, what season you're in, who you're working for, how big the operation is. I needed to stay busy, so I took everything anyone threw my way, no matter how little it paid. Swore there was one year I didn't touch dry land for more than an hour in nine months."

Her heart felt heavy. Her eyes burned. He'd needed to stay busy to forget about her. To drown the pain. She knew, because she'd done the same. "Sounds...lonely."

"It was good for me. Changed my body. Changed my mind. Gave me a work ethic, drive, stamina, business sense, a brotherhood. Honestly," he sighed, his voice growing soft, "I think it saved my life."

Giselle's breath whooshed out like she'd been hit, and an ache developed at the center of her belly.

He picked up the shower nozzle and rinsed the shampoo from her hair. "Those were some dark years. There are periods I don't even remember. I must have blocked them out. It's strange to think back on them. I don't recognize the person I was then—someone different from who I'd been before, different than I am now, almost...I don't really know how to explain it."

"Empty," she said. "Like a shell. Going through the motions of life, meeting your obligations, but numb, because if you felt, the pain might take you under."

He shut off the spray and fell silent for a moment. She knew he understood she was talking about her own experience, one that mirrored his. He must also have heard the guilt in her voice, because he said, "It's not your fault, El. You may have walked away, but I pushed you to the door. And I'm a better man for the years between then and now. It wasn't fun, I'd rather not do it again, but they were pivotal years I wouldn't give back.

That's why I had the tattoo done, to remember the lessons I learned on those ships. Those were important for you too. Years that you devoted completely to your craft, to your career. And look how far you've come."

But at what cost? What level of success was worth your happiness? Your health? Your sanity? Those were questions that she asked herself with increasing frequency over the last year. Questions she hadn't been able to answer.

As he massaged conditioner into her hair, she asked about his other tattoo. "And the one on your hip, extending down your thigh?"

"The Terminator tat? That's just for my love of machinery, gears, how things work."

"Is that why you got into stunts?" she asked. He'd talked a lot about his work over the last two days, but never about how he'd gotten started.

"No. Stunts came as a fluke. I was deep into my fourth year of fishing, trolling the Pacific for Chinook salmon, when we had engine trouble and had to dock in Los Angeles for repairs. Jax was shooting a stunt at the harbor and needed help rigging a fall. Word spread, and they came to me. Asked if I wanted to give it a shot. I said, sure, what the hell else did I have to do?"

He rinsed the conditioner from her hair. "I spent a couple of days rigging various stages of different stunts for him, and he offered me a job with Renegades. I took it. That's another one of those meant-to-be stories. Right place at the right time. If I had said no to rigging the stunt because I'd never done it before, I would have missed that opportunity. If I had gone back to what I knew, what was familiar and safe and gotten back on the boat instead of taking a chance on the job with Renegades, I'd still be gutting fish and breaking my back on the open ocean."

He dropped a kiss to her shoulder and stood. "I'm going to start dinner."

By the time her mouth dropped open to protest, he was at the door, then gone. And Giselle sat there, staring at the door with frustration mounting as she wondered just what the hell was—or was not—happening between them.

Troy chopped off the tops of three baby carrots, then flipped them around, but had to wipe sweat from his forehead with the back of his hand before he could cut the tips. He set the knife down and tossed the carrots into the bowl along with the snow peas, peppers, watercress, and ginger.

Troy wiped his hands on a kitchen towel, then reached down and repositioned his erection.

"God damn," he growled, turning toward the fridge for the steak. He didn't know how in the hell he was going to sleep holding Giselle again tonight. "Stupid. You're not going to sleep." He unrolled the meat from pink butcher paper and dropped it on the cutting block, then grabbed a different knife. He was going to owe Rubi forever. She'd delivered on every promise—the house, the car, the food, the clothes, and the complete privacy. That woman was a magician, a spy, and a confidante all rolled into one fabulous human being.

The buzz of a phone drew his attention to the kitchen island. He moved some grocery bags around and found Giselle's cell vibrating against the granite with the name Chad lighting up the screen.

Troy clenched his teeth and picked up the phone. Giselle had misplaced it early on, but they'd been so caught up in each other since, she hadn't been looking for it. And the fact that Chad just couldn't stop hounding Giselle even after the doctor had told him she needed this time off to heal pissed Troy off.

The phone quieted, but Troy's temper still burned.

Just as he set the phone down, it chirped with a new text message.

"Fucking A." He tapped the face and pulled up Chad's message.

GET. BACK. HERE. NOW.

"What the…?" Troy set the knife down and scrolled through Chad's previous messages, all unanswered by Giselle. He also found a handful from Brook. His gaze darted to the lower bar showing missed calls and waiting messages, and he swore, then returned his attention to the texts, which started about the time Giselle was in the emergency room.

He skimmed through Chad's rants over Troy keeping him out of her room and skipped to the ones that had come in later, all of them designed to lure Giselle back to work.

Met with Pepsi today. They're offering a three-month military tour in Asia. Call me.

Anheuser-Busch has approached me about a headliner tour in North America. This is BIG.

Word's spreading. I've gotten sponsorship offers from four big hitters. Where the fuck are you?

I'm on the edge of panic. AEG Live and Live Nation are on board with sponsors. CALL ME!

Giselle, get your priorities in line! This is your career. Stop fucking around.

And the one she'd just received: *GET. BACK. HERE. NOW.*

"Just fucking beautiful."

Troy had made enemies of the people closest to Giselle in the past, a mistake he didn't want to repeat. But this was different. Troy wasn't alienating Chad because he was jealous or felt challenged. Chad had the Type A personality that fed into Giselle's ingrained drive to achieve. A drive stemming from a childhood of poverty and strife. Chad wanted her back at work and away from Troy, who Chad saw as interference and competition. But work wouldn't help Giselle heal.

Only Brook asked how Giselle was feeling, how things were going with Troy, and if she needed anything.

Troy's head throbbed. He closed his eyes, propped his elbow on the granite, and rested his forehead on his hand. He was sweating. His heart was racing. He was thrilled for this rise in her career and terrified for her at the same time.

These messages told Troy she'd finally done it, finally risen to the level of her idols. He saw her hitting the big time in the very immediate future, and he couldn't have been more thrilled for her. But it also couldn't have come at a worse time, because in her current physical and emotional state, that kind of pressure put her on a direct fas track to burnout. The kind of burnout that didn't just go away with a few days of rest but that killed careers. Killed relationships. Killed *people.*

He also knew Giselle would work herself sick before she'd take the break she needed. He'd watched her do it over and over again while Ryker had been off playing army and before Chad had ever met her. He could tell that hadn't changed by the number of concerts she put on, the number of albums she produced, and the number of charity events she participated in. She was one of the most driven people he'd ever met. He respected that, admired it, but he also knew that compulsion had to be tempered or it would run her aground. Run *them* aground. Again.

To grab hold of these tour offers, she'd jump back on the first available plane, even with a concussion. She'd promise the sponsors the moon, even if her voice wasn't ready to deliver, even if her body wasn't ready to handle the stress. Troy was certainly no stranger to workaholism or vices, but his brotherhood of fishermen and then the Renegades had given him the support he'd needed to stay balanced. He could easily see Giselle didn't have that network. And traveling around the world certainly wouldn't create one.

He exited to the main message screen where Chad's *GET. BACK. HERE. NOW.* stared back at Troy. He wouldn't put it past this guy to trace Giselle's phone to get ahold of her.

He pressed the power button, turning the phone off, then pulled the battery out, threw it and the phone into the nearest drawer, and slammed his hands on the granite.

Giselle might think this guy was a great manager, but in Troy's opinion, Chad looked a lot more like a greedy narcissist, looking to wring every drop of blood he could get from her. How he didn't see the effect this would have on Giselle in the long run, Troy didn't understand. Or maybe the guy just didn't give a shit. Maybe, when Giselle burned out, he simply planned to dump her and move on to the next hot ticket.

But Troy knew attacking Giselle's agent wasn't the way to get her to see what he was doing. His best hope was to show her that she could have a life outside her work and still be successful. Maybe that couldn't have happened in the beginning, but they had a lot more flexibility now, so many more options now. He just needed more time with her. Time to bond. Time to fit. Then, when they'd found more comfort together, he could breach those topics with her.

It was a good plan. The only plan. But he still felt a powerful undercurrent pulling Giselle away even while she was still here, and he couldn't help but wonder: Was losing her inevitable? Was this draw so ingrained that she would ultimately choose her career over him the same way she had seven years ago? Or would she be able to swim against that current and make the sacrifice required to find balance in her life?

"We need to talk."

Giselle's voice startled him, and he jerked his head up to find her standing five feet away wearing nothing but a towel. A very small towel. One that barely covered her breasts and stopped way too high on those delicious thighs.

"I didn't hear you." Dragging his mind back to her demand was a struggle. *Talk.* "Uh, sure." He moved to the cutting block and picked up a knife. "Dinner's almost ready. Go ahead and get dressed. This will only take fifteen minutes."

Giselle stepped up beside him and covered his hand holding the knife. "No. Now."

Her tone shot the sizzle of oh-shit across his skin. He took a closer look at her face and found those blue eyes serious and intense and determined. There was no sidestepping that expression.

He set the knife down and wiped his hands, trying like hell to keep his eyes on her face. God, he was such a damn animal. He couldn't think about anything but touching her and kissing her. About doing things to her that made her moan and gasp and scream. About pushing inside her, again and again and...

"Okay," he said, and pressed one hand to the counter, stabilizing himself for...whatever.

She licked her lips. "I need to know"—her eyes flickered away for a split second—"if you only like sex when you want to fuck."

His mouth dropped open. His brain hit a wall. He narrowed his eyes. "*What?*"

"I know that's direct, but I can't spend days here with you expecting one thing only to find out another. I'd rather just know up front so I can...just...deal with it."

Her voice was matter-of-fact, soft, understanding, not the curt, cold tone the words implied.

She crossed her arms and met his gaze again. "So, is that what you want now? Fucking? No emotional connection when you're having sex? I mean, I get it. It's safer. You're not putting yourself out there. I...put you through a lot when I left. And it's probably the only way you could operate in those clubs—"

"I don't go to *those clubs*." He cut her off, confusion over this strange ramble drawing frustration. "I go to that one club—*occasionally*." He gripped the granite with one hand, pressed the other to his hip. "I'm sorry. What is this about? I thought we were on the same page about the club—"

"I don't have a problem with the club or why you went or what you did there." The thin veneer of control she'd been using slipped, and hurt frustration seeped through. "What I have a problem with is your disinterest in sex as we get closer. Because as good as sex is between us, that's not what I want—just sex. Because... because..."

Tears filled her eyes, flooded over, and spilled down her cheeks, and Troy had a sensation of time speeding out of control without any idea of what was happening. He put his hands on Giselle's arms.

"Baby, slow down..."

She shook her head and met his gaze head-on. "Because I love you. *I love you*," she said again with more intensity, more purpose, as if confirming she'd said it the first time, "and I can't just have sex with you. Even if I could, I wouldn't want to, because the more I get to know who you've become over the years we've been apart, the more I realize all I've missed, and the more

I'm sure that I don't want to miss another minute. I want *all of you.*

"But I know this is all happening fast, and I know there are unsettled hurt feelings between us, and if you aren't sure or if too much has happened or if we're just too different, and you can't love me back…" She closed her eyes and exhaled heavily. "Shit, I shouldn't have gone there. I want to tell you it's okay, but…Shit…" She pressed her hand to the middle of her forehead. "I shouldn't have—"

"Ellie." He gave her a shake to stop the ramble. Holy shit, he was only half-sure she'd just told him she loved him. *Twice.* His heart was on a freaking trampoline. "Just…*stop* for a second."

She did that adorable thing with her lips, where she curved them over her teeth, her eyes on the floor. The exact same expression she'd had coming into their foster home that first day. The day he'd fallen in love with her.

Now, his heart was beating just as hard as it had then. A dozen damn years later, and the girl owned more real estate in his head and his heart than anyone else in the universe.

"Baby…" Emotions overwhelmed him, and he didn't think letting them spill all over her now was such a great idea. So he picked something tangible. "I'm trying really hard to show you my better side, the side that has been blown completely out of view by every damn shitty thing I've done since I saw you again. Our time here isn't about sex, El. We already know we are absolutely, utterly, perfectly compatible there. So if you think I'm not interested in you because we're getting closer emotionally..." He stepped in, took her hand, and pressed it to the rigid line of his cock through the canvas of his shorts and rubbed the length. Lust rushed his groin, and he clenched his teeth. "Think again."

He deliberately pulled her hand off him and wrapped his arms around her, taking hers with them and trapping them behind her.

With her big blue eyes looking up into his and her damp wheat strands framing her gorgeous farm-fresh face, he said, "I'm carrying as much guilt for the last two weeks as you seem to be carrying for walking away. What do you say to calling it even and starting fresh? You and me loving each other as the people we are now and leaving all the other shit behind?"

Her eyes turned smoky. She pulled one hand from his grip and reached between them, pulling her towel loose. It dropped to the floor, and the last twenty percent of Troy's blood rushed south.

"I'm on board," she said softly, sliding her free hand into his hair and pushing to her toes. "Make love to me, Troy."

The breath whooshed out of his lungs. There was no thought required in responding or fulfilling her request, simply letting go of all the restrictions he'd placed on himself and loving her the way he wanted to.

He groaned as he tilted his head and took her mouth. She opened immediately, warm and welcoming.

Home.

She was home.

Always had been. Always would be.

His ribs ached. His eyes burned. He needed her, all of her, and he needed her now. She wrapped her arms around his neck, taking the kiss deep, stroking her tongue into his mouth and circling, plunging, licking. Practiced, knowing, rhythmical, they kissed like long-time lovers, like they'd never been separated, like they fit perfectly, two puzzle pieces. The woman's mouth made him dizzy, but she was the one to sway toward him, pressing and rubbing that beautiful body against his in all the right places and in all the right ways.

"Baby…" he moaned between kisses. "Jesus."

He released her face, let his hands skim over her slender shoulders, down her smooth back. Traced the sleek indention of her spine, and let his hands ride over the curves of her ass. He squeezed the firm flesh and drew her against him, meeting the pressure with his hips and driving into her mouth with his tongue, simulating the thrust he would soon duplicate with his tongue, fingers, and finally his cock in her pussy.

She moaned into his mouth, her kiss so hungry, so passionate she made him spin. One curvy thigh hooked onto his hip, then the other. She locked her feet at his back and lifted her hips, rubbing against him like a cat, pushing his need from hot to urgent. Her hands combed through his hair, fisting the strands and shooting a delicious burn across his scalp, making him a little crazy.

His thoughts came in fragments. Counter was too high. Bed was too far. He stumbled a few steps to the breakfast area and kicked a chair away from the end of the farm-style solid wood table. With one arm stretched across her back, he leaned over and used the other to sweep everything to the floor—he didn't even remember what had been there, only heard the thump and clatter as it hit the kitchen tile.

Then he laid Giselle down, and he was free. Free to touch, taste, and ravage. He kissed every inch of her neck and throat. Cupped and squeezed one breast while licking and sucking the other. Her hips lifted beneath him, but he ignored them as he stroked a slow circle around and around one nipple, while mirroring the touch with his fingers on the other breast. Licking with his tongue and flicking with his fingertips. Sucking with his mouth and squeezing with his hand. Nipping with his teeth and pinching with his fingers. Then he switched hand and mouth and repeated.

He wanted to kiss every inch of her, but that would have to wait for another time. He didn't have the willpower to make her wait. He desperately needed to taste her. To feel her warmth on his tongue. To hear her cries of pleasure. Pleasure he'd brought her. And he took a direct route from her belly button to her sex, opening wide to cover her pussy with his hot mouth.

"Ah God." She came up in a half curl, fingers digging into his hair, thighs closing around his head, eyes heavy-lidded and dazed. "*God.* Yes."

Troy gripped the tops of her thighs and lifted his gaze to hers, watching the orgasm wash over her like waves on the beach as he worked her pussy beneath his tongue and lips. The muscles of her abdomen clenched and quivered. Her nipples remained puckered in tight buds.

Her mouth dropped open, her eyes closed, head dropped back, body curled tighter. "*Yes, yes, yes.* Please. God. *Yes.*"

Just when she was about to break, he relaxed all pressure and just breathed long and hot, bathing her wet pussy with warm, moist air. Her eyes opened, and a look of desperation crossed her face along with a high-pitched plea from her throat.

Lust struck Troy like lightning. He tugged her thighs wider, pressed his mouth fully over her sex, and sucked.

Giselle's body spasmed at the initial contact, then her hips immediately lunged to the rhythm of his mouth, her hands pulling his head into the rocking motion.

Her second orgasm hit instantly, a heat wave of muscle contraction so fierce, Troy was lost in the pressure of her thighs for long luscious moments. He waited patiently as wave after wave of pleasure washed through her, until she was panting, until she was lying flat on the table, one forearm flopped over her eyes. Then, with a wicked little thrill, he circled her clit with soft strokes of his tongue.

"Ah…" She wiggled her hips. "Mmm…" She rolled up to one elbow, reached for him. "Troy…"

He added a little pressure. When her breath caught, when her fingers tangled in his hair, when that look of pained pleasure crossed her face, he slipped one hand between her legs, separated her folds, and took her clit between his lips, and ever so gently, ever so slowly, almost not moving at all…he sucked.

She dropped back on the table, threw one arm out to the side and gripped the edge. She planted one foot on the table and pushed her hips into his mouth, then rolled up on one elbow to watch. And that was just too hot. Too fucking hot. He rewarded her with kisses and licks, only sucking her when she held herself there and ground against him.

"God…"

Her orgasm seemed to shake her to the core, twisting through her body like a demon of pleasure.

And nothing, *nothing*, thrilled Troy more than thrilling Giselle.

Giselle lay limp against the table, the wood hard against her back, but she was floating in bliss as Troy kissed his way back toward her mouth, then covered her mouth with all the lust he'd just released in her body still coiled in his.

A surge of need burned through her belly. Deeper than the sexual need he'd just satisfied.

She kissed him back and tasted herself on his tongue. A wild flash of eroticism spiked through her body. She grabbed his tank and dragged it over his head, then took his tongue again as she reached between them to work his pants open.

"Need you…" she panted, sitting up to shove his pants out of the way, "inside me."

"Need to be…" he echoed as he dragged his wallet from his back pocket, while his mouth kissed her everywhere he could reach, her jaw, her neck, her shoulder, "inside you."

She pushed his shorts and boxers over his hips but had to pull them over the muscle of his thighs to get them to the floor, and she let out a soft laugh between kisses, "Remember when…your pants would…fall right off?"

He tore a condom open with his teeth and rolled it over his length, something Giselle took over, stroking him as she went, making him growl.

He pressed his forehead to hers and gripped her hips, dragging her to the edge of the table, where he met her eyes. "And you loved me anyway."

She lifted one hand and laid it over his heart. "This is who you are. This is who I love." Then she smiled and slid one hand over the curved muscle of his shoulder. "But this is nice too."

A smile flickered over his lips, but when she brushed the head of his cock against her heat, intensity darkened his face.

"You're way too good for me," he rasped, rocking his hips. His wide head spread her entrance. Pressure radiated through her sex. "You know that, right?"

"Not true."

A growl rolled from his throat, and he cupped her face with one hand, lifting her eyes to his, holding her gaze as he rocked deeper.

"Ah God…" The words shivered out of her, half laugh, half sigh. "So good—"

His mouth covered hers, his kiss hungry but slow. He circled his tongue with hers in lazy circles and pulsed his hips just enough to allow the head of his cock to enter and exit her over and over and over. The stimulation created a wicked pressure wash through her whole pelvis, making her restless, making her writhe, making her lift into him to take him deeper.

She broke the kiss with a breathless "More..." pulling on his shoulder, lifting with her hips.

"Goddamn." He rasped the word before he thrust hard. Pressure pushed sensation through her sex, out through her pelvis, into her belly. "You kill me, El. Can't fuckin' say no to you."

He leaned forward, pressing his hands to the table at her hips, the muscles in his arms and shoulders taut. She wrapped her arms around his neck, whispered, "You never could. Love me, Troy." Then tilted her head and kissed him.

A low hum started in his throat, but as he gripped her hips and thrust home, the sound erupting from his throat transitioned into a low, primal sound of passion, one that rumbled through Giselle, raising her own pleasure.

With slow, deep, solid thrusts, he laid her back on the table, kissing her mouth, her neck, her shoulder. He hooked one arm behind her knee, pulled her thigh high and wide, and held her gaze as he drove deeper.

"Feel so good, Ellie." His eyes closed, and his forehead pressed to hers. "Missed you so much." He kissed her gently. "Love you so much."

The emotion behind those words, the twist of almost-pain in his expression cut at her heart, but her body continued to rise with pleasure, and she held on tight as his thrusts quickened and another orgasm rose to the surface.

"Mmm…Troy…"

"Let go, El," he rasped, kissing her lips, then pressing his forehead to her jaw. "I've got you."

The climax rocked her body off its axis. She bowed, screamed, and slammed a hand to the table for balance, curling her fingers around the edge as it crashed and rocked through her. Troy quickly followed, his hand covering hers, fingers threaded, head up and his gaze burning into hers as he broke.

The passion in his gaz just before they closed, the expression on his face as the orgasm slammed through him, was so very different from what she'd seen in the club or at the hotel.

This was her Troy. The real Troy. The Troy she loved. The Troy she wanted.

The climax finally ebbed, leaving him sweaty and weak. His arms shook, and he dropped his head to her chest, his quick, heavy breaths washing her skin with heat. "You fuckin' turn me inside out."

As she combed her fingers through his damp hair, Giselle closed her eyes and smiled at the pure sensation of joy filling her from the toes up.

For as long as she could remember, she'd been searching for a home. For a family. And she'd had it all along—in Troy.

Thirteen

Troy stood waist-deep in seawater off Malibu's shore, waiting for Giselle to paddle back to him, but she'd given up and collapsed against the surfboard, cheek pressed to the fiberglass, arms dangling over the side.

God, she was the cutest thing ever. "Come on, El," he yelled. "Get your fine ass back out here."

She turned her head and rested her chin on the board. "I'm dead. My arms have turned into noodles."

A wave slipped past him, splashing his chest while the sun warmed his face and shoulders. "You promised to keep trying until you rode one wave all the way in."

"That was before I found out it's a lot harder than it looks."

That was very true—surfing was way harder than it looked. And Troy was more than a little surprised she was in the water at all. This was the first time Giselle had ever stepped foot in the ocean, and all in all, she was handling it pretty well.

That devious part of him sparked to life, and he dove under the water, swimming below the surface until he reached the board, when he heard her calling out, "Troy, stop it."

He popped up beside her. "Boo!"

She screamed and dropped to the board laughing, making Troy laugh too. She was such a good sport.

"Would you stop?" She splashed him.

He sank down until his mouth was halfway underwater, then circled the board gurgling the *Jaws* theme song. "Da...da..." He started softly, slowly, building speed and volume as he moved. "Da, da...da, da...Dun, dun, dun, dun...dun, dun, dun, dun..."

"Stop it." She splashed him some more. "That's so creepy."

"Dun-dun-dun-dun. Dun-dun-dun-dun. *Dun-dun!*" He launched out of the water, landing on the other half of her board, and slid on his belly like a seal until his nose touched hers.

Her grin was bright and happy, filled with the kind of joy he remembered from their early years together when they were so in love and believed anything was possible.

And here they were again—in love, with all sorts of possibilities ahead of them. So many more, in fact, than there had been then.

"Well, hello there, beautiful." He tilted his head and kissed her. "Mmm." He tilted his head the other way and kissed her again. "Mmm." Then again.

She smiled. "What are you doing?"

"Deciding which way you taste best."

"How about this way?" She wrapped her hand around the back of his head and moved in for a hot, slow, open-mouthed kiss. Sliding her tongue against his, she sighed into his mouth, and Troy's head went light. Despite the cold water, his cock hardened. But what monopolized his attention was the deep twist in his heart.

When she pulled away, his eyes fluttered open. He caught her chin between his fingers, dropped a soft kiss on her lips, and met her eyes when he murmured, "I love you so fucking much, it hurts."

Her smile brightened, and her face beamed like the goddamned sun, which made Troy feel invincible. Then she rubbed his nose with the tip of hers, and he melted like butter. He was so fucking gone over her, it was pathetic. "I love you too."

He kissed her again, still unable to believe he was hearing those words from her mouth. They'd shared them a lot over the last two days together. Days filled with long, slow lovemaking sessions. Extended naps curled together on the sand under the sun. Laughing and teasing and tickling.

Definitely some of the best days of his life.

"I'll let you show me just how much as soon as you ride a wave." He slipped back and off the board, then dragged her out to sea.

She dropped her forehead to the board and groaned.

He turned her toward the beach. "Scoot up so you're ready to jump."

His attention turned out to sea as he gauged the waves while holding her board with one hand.

"Here you go, Ellie. This one's perfect. Get ready."

As the wave rose in a smooth swell of beautiful sea green about ten yards behind them, Troy kicked off the bottom, got up some momentum while watching the wave over his shoulder to time his send off, then shoved the board into the wave's path. "Go."

She paddled, gauging the wave's speed.

"Up, El," he yelled. "*Pop.*"

With her hands braced on the board, Giselle jumped, pulled her feet underneath her in a wide stance, knees bent.

"Yes," he murmured, watching her use her arms for balance as the board pitched beneath her feet. "That's it…You got it…"

And when the wave broke beneath her, and she was still standing, Troy's excitement exploded in applause and whistles. She pushed her fists overhead with a scream of triumph just before the surf tipped the board sideways and Giselle dropped into the water.

Troy swam toward shore, ready for a break from the sun. He stopped a few feet away from where she sat, waist-deep in the ocean on the mostly vacant, residents-only beach and shook his head like a wet dog.

"Troy…" Giselle complained.

He grabbed the board, hoisting it to his shoulder as he pushed to his feet. Then offered his hand and pulled her up, wrapping his arm around her waist for the walk to the porch. There he propped the board against the railing and stripped the surf skin from Giselle's top half, laying it over the rail to dry in the sun.

"Okay," she said. "That sport's fun versus work ratio is way out of whack."

He chuckled. "That's because it takes practice. For your first time in the ocean, I'm pretty damn impressed."

She gave him a sassy little grin. "Why, thank you, Mr. Jacobs. I had a fine instructor." She reached out and ran her fingers down the center of his chest. "And I do mean fine in *so many* different ways."

He grabbed her hand and kissed it. Life was perfect. He couldn't ask for anything more. At least nothing more than to keep Giselle in his life, because she was all his life was missing—a thought that brought their dwindling time together back to the forefront of his mind, and angst to the forefront of his heart.

He wrapped an arm low on her waist, cupped her jaw with the other, and looked directly into her eyes. "These have been some of the best days of my life, Ellie."

Her smile widened and softened. "I was just thinking the same thing."

He wanted to stay upbeat, stay positive, play the no-doubt-in-my-mind card, but he had so much of his heart riding on this, on her, on them. He ran his thumb across her soft cheek and searched her crystal-blue eyes. "Please tell me we can make this work."

Instead of fluffing him off with promises, instead of assuring him with all her heart, doubt and worry crept into her eyes, darkening them to twilight. "I guess we still have a lot to talk about."

His angst turned to fear and burned like a hot coal deep in his gut. He slid his hand around the base of her neck and held her gaze. "We've both been able to set everything else aside and put each other first for the last few days. I know we could find a way to mesh our personal lives with our professional ones. It won't be easy, I know that too. But I'm more than willing to do what it takes if it means more of this."

He dropped his head and kissed her with all the love, all the passion he'd had locked away for so long, leaving them both breathless. He pushed his hands into her wet hair and tipped her head back until her eyes met his. "Are you willing, Ellie?" he asked, half-terrified of the answer but still needing one. "Am I worth the work, the sacrifice, the trouble it will take to keep us together?"

"What kind of question is that?" she chastised with a frown. Then stroked his jaw, her expression softening. "Of course you're worth effort and sacrifice. And yes, I'm willing to make them. I love you. I just think you're oversimplifying our situation."

Frustration and fear tangled with all the love from the past, more love from the present, and created a messy knot of desperation around his heart. One that could turn dark if he let it. One that would turn dark if he lost her again.

"Baby, there's never been anything simple about you or me. Put us together and you can kiss simple good-bye. I've known that from day one. But none of it could make me turn away from you."

She stroked his cheek with cool fingers and searched his face with those beautiful eyes. "God. I wish I had half your strength. You're so amazing."

"Are you kidding? You're twice as strong as I ever was. And together, Ellie, we're unbeatable."

She smiled again. Nodded. "You're right about that. Together, I do think we're unbeatable."

Hope sparked in his heart. "That's my girl."

But something still felt off when they wandered into the kitchen and Giselle pulled open the fridge, staring into it but not actually looking for anything.

"Hey, have you seen my phone?" she asked, finally, drawing out two water bottles and turning to hand him one. "I should touch base with Chad. We've got a lot pending right now."

Troy's spark of hope flared into a lick of panic.

She scanned the kitchen counter, picked up a few things to look underneath, then checked the table and everything they'd pushed onto the floor a few days earlier before strolling into the living room.

"I can't remember the last time I had it," she said. "God, I hope I didn't lose it. All my contacts are in there."

He caught up with her in the living room as she straightened from rummaging around the coffee table, and slipped his arms around her waist, nuzzling her cheek.

"You promised me a week. It's only half over."

She turned in his arms with a soft smile. He leaned close, but instead of kissing her, ran his tongue over her lower lip. She responded the same way she always did— her body softened and her lips parted. It was so hot. So damn sexy to see and feel her respond to him like that. To feel her want him like that. An instant and powerful turn-on. He set his water on the coffee table and pressed his very cold open hand against her belly.

She gasped. "Oh God." She laughed and pulled at his wrist. "That's colder than the ocean."

"I know just how to warm it up." He slipped his fingers beneath the edge of her bikini bottoms and kept his eyes on hers as he pushed slowly over her mound and stretched his fingers over her sex with a long, low growl. He stroked back and forth a few times, and by the time his fingers were seated into her soft folds, her eyes were heavy-lidded.

"I love touching you," he said in a rough whisper, moving the tips of his fingers against her opening. "I love feeling every part of you."

She grabbed his bicep with one hand for balance. Her lids were heavy, her eyes sparking with lust. "God, that feels…"

She wriggled her hips a little, moving her body against his fingers, and her eyes rolled back in her head. Her teeth sank into her lower lip.

"Baby, that's so hot. Feeling you rub on me."

"Goddammit, Troy…" She lifted into his hand, and he met the rock and roll of her hips, spreading her wetness over her folds, pressing his palm against her clit. She moaned and dropped her head back, lips parting. "So good."

With his free hand, he pulled the ties on her top, and it fell away, leaving her almost naked. He pressed his hand to the middle of her back again, arching her spine to bring her breasts closer, then bent his head to stroke and tease her nipples with his tongue. One, then the other, then back to the first, while his fingers probed and stretched. teased between her legs.

Her sounds of pleasure soaked into him like tendrils of fire, snaking over his skin, invading his blood. He felt like he was burning from the inside out.

Lifting his mouth from her breast, he cupped the back of her neck, threaded his fingers into the hair at her nape, and mirrored the work of his hand with his mouth, stroking her lips with his tongue as he circled her opening, plunging into her mouth as he drove into her pussy.

He felt her orgasm building in the taut stretch of her muscles, the quickening rise of her hips to his hand. Heard it in her rapid breaths, in the rising pitch of her sexy sounds.

Troy relished the sensations, kept the steady build, holding back just enough to make her work for it, make the tease last a little too long, so her climax was that much harder, stronger, better. Wetter.

"I want you drenched when I slide into you, Ellie." He held her head at an angle where she had to look him in the eye. "I want you to come hard. Gush. Get all juicy for me."

"Mmm," she whimpered, rocking harder and faster, her brow tightening with that telltale sign of imminent release.

"Then I'll hammer home. Slide and drive. Slide and drive." He matched his words with his hand, stroking gently against her, then pushing hard between her legs. "You want that, El? You want me?"

"Yes."

"Are you ready to come?"

"Yes."

He kissed her, just little sips of her lips as he changed the position of his hand, putting more pressure, more motion on her clit.

"Ah God..." Her head dropped back, and plea-sure rolled from her throat just before her whole body tightened and she came, the orgasm jerking her muscles and washing her face with a blissful expression, filling Troy's heart with the same.

As she floated back to earth, he unfastened his swim trunks, pulled a condom from the pocket—he never went anywhere without one with Giselle around—and rolled it on. Then he slipped her bikini bottoms off and turned her toward the sofa.

She melted into the soft cushions and opened her thighs, the most beautiful, most welcoming sight he'd ever seen. Troy knelt between her legs and pushed deep on one thrust. Giselle bowed. A little sound ebbed from her throat. She crossed her feet at his back, stroked her hands up his arms, cradled his face and pulled him to her, where she kissed him and kissed him and kissed him while he made love to her just like he'd promised, in deep, passionate thrusts.

And when she was on the verge of another climax, Troy pulled back to watch the release wash over her face and haze her eyes, then let himself go. Let the ecstasy burst up his spine and out his limbs until his skin tingled with the perfection of it. The perfection of Giselle.

Giselle stretched and glanced over her shoulder and found Troy's eyes still closed. Smiling, she rolled over and ruffled his hair, snuggling close and absorbing his heat and scent. "Relaxing is tough work, huh, Renegade?"

"Mmm-hmm." His sleepy murmur made everything inside her warm and grow like a flower in rich soil.

Giselle's stomach growled, and she pulled her gaze from Troy's handsome face to check the time on the nightstand clock. Two p.m. They'd loved the morning away after her surfing lesson.

She rolled out from under Troy's arm and pushed to her feet. He didn't flutter an eyelash, didn't move a finger. She leaned over and kissed his forehead. "Want something to eat?"

He made a noise that could have been construed as just about anything.

"I'm going to take that as a yes, since we haven't eaten in hours." She couldn't stop smiling as she straightened and added a flare of drama when she added, "No, no, don't get up. I'll bring it to you."

His mouth curved in a sleepy smile, one that made her heart swell until she was sure it would burst.

Giselle pulled one of his T-shirts over her head and wandered through the house, squinting at the afternoon sun glistening off the ocean and spilling through the windows that looked out on the multimillion-dollar view. She felt loose and languid and loved to perfection. For the first time in longer than she could remember, she felt so completely and utterly happy and fulfilled and complete—as long as her mind stayed within the confines of this setting. Once it wandered outside these walls, outside this beach...

She sighed as she entered the kitchen. Not yet. She wasn't going to face those thoughts yet. There would be a lot to talk about. A lot to work out. And even though she believed they could do it, that together they could figure it out, a sliver of fear wound through all the dark places in her soul, pushing doubt to the surface.

Giselle stepped into the kitchen and forced the doubt back as she pulled open the fridge. With a little rummaging, she came up with enough food to put together a fruit-and-cheese plate. She added a bottle of chilled red zinfandel to the snack and called it perfect.

Gazing out at the ocean while she washed the berries and grapes, Giselle forced her thoughts to the details that made her life at this moment pretty damn fabulous. How amazing it looked moving forward with Troy in her future. He gave her life an entirely new dimension, one that added richness and light and fun and meaning.

But she couldn't look ahead without allowing her mind to wander outside this house, outside this beach, outside these stolen moments together. She tried to frame "meshing" their lives together in a positive light. But without knowing where her future lay, that was difficult. And when she thought of Troy's career with travel and hours just as crazy as hers, her angst intensified.

That thought turned her mind toward the sponsors she and Chad had been courting. Which made her wonder how things were going and if anything had happened over the last few days. She thought of Chad and Brook and felt guilty she wasn't there to help them carry the load.

She turned off the water while guilt and frustration battled beneath her ribs. She worked endlessly, suffered a near-death experience, and reunited with her only love. She deserved a few days off. Even the doctor had said so.

If only there was a pill to cure guilt. Or insecurities instilled in childhood.

Straightening, she turned and glanced around the kitchen again for her phone. Checking in with Chad was a double-edged sword, she knew. Knowing what was happening would give her a sense of control, but it would also give Chad the opportunity to drag her back in.

It was inevitable, though. She had to face it soon. Better to at least get an idea of what she'd be walking back into—if she could find her damn phone. "Where the hell did I leave that thing?"

She couldn't even call him on Troy's phone, because it had run out of battery two days ago, and he didn't have a charger with him. They'd been truly disconnected from the world—which had been heavenly, but it couldn't go on forever.

Her stomach cramped and rolled with a hellacious growl, so she gave up on it for now and tossed a strawberry into her mouth. She'd ask Troy to take her out later to pick up a new phone, or at least a charger for his. She had to ease herself back into the real world so she wasn't blindsided when it hit her full force.

She pulled two wineglasses from a cabinet, then went in search of a corkscrew. Drawer after drawer after drawer. "Come on," she muttered. "You've got wine. You've gotta have a—"

She tugged open the drawer at the far end of the island a little too hard, and all the contents came flying to the front. A flashlight, batteries, pens—

My phone?

She stared at it for a long moment, stunned, while a burgeoning sensation of dread balled up beneath her ribs. She couldn't seem to reach for the device, yet she couldn't take her eyes off it either. All she could do was stand there, frozen, while her mind scrambled to make sense of this.

But short of the phone accidentally getting swept into the drawer, she couldn't.

She reached for it, and as soon as she picked it up, her stomach dropped. The phone was too light. She flipped it over and found exactly what she already knew she'd find—the battery cover missing. The battery gone.

She rummaged in the drawer and uncovered both her battery and the cover. Her phone had definitely *not* ended up here by mistake.

Troy.

Her eyes narrowed. She shook her head in confusion. *Why?*

"You promised me a week."

Anger crawled across her shoulders.

She closed her eyes and clenched her teeth to tamp down the immediate resentment.

Don't snap. Put this in perspective.

Opening her eyes, she let her vision blur over the counter. He loved her. They'd been apart seven years, and he wanted a week alone. That wasn't too much to ask. Maybe the way he'd gone about it wasn't so perfect, but she had to admit she never would have given in willingly to being cut off from the world. And she also had to admit the time away had both changed her perspective and been good for her—mind, body, and soul.

The rationalization shaved off the sharpest edge of her anger. Exhaling, she stretched her neck right, then left, and replaced the battery, then the back, and switched on her phone.

She leaned her hip against the counter and felt her whole world shift as she waited for her phone to power up.

Back to reality.

She closed her eyes, her stomach tight and a little topsy-turvy. Man, this was going to be a rough transition.

The ding of her phone drew her eyes open. But what greeted her made them fly wide: twenty-two missed calls? Eighteen new voice messages? Thirty-five new text messages?

"What…?" Panic and dread blended to push her to the edge of an anxiety attack. Her heart raced as she tapped into the missed phone calls and scrolled through, finding the majority from Chad. "What the hell…?"

Troy told her he'd called Chad. That he'd explained…

Her mind snapped back to the way he wielded power over a film set. To the way he'd made sure she would get the best plastic surgeon for her stitches. It wasn't a stretch to imagine Troy spinning a tale to get her out of town.

She skimmED Chad's texts, but the messages stole her breath. She couldn't be reading that right: Offers from sponsors like Pepsi, Anheuser-Busch, and Bose had brought the big promotional guns AEG and Live Nation calling?

Holy shit.

Holy. Shit.

Her stomach floated into her chest. Her heart lifted to her throat. Giselle pressed a hand to her mouth to keep them both inside her body while she took little gasps for air. "Oh my God…"

She read the messages again, checking dates and times, hoping—praying—it wasn't too late to get back to them. These offers could be tenuous. Sponsors could be sensitive. If they weren't treated with the respect and deference they felt they deserved, they could easily turn their backs on an entertainer.

Her hand was shaking when Troy's voice broke into her thoughts from the other room.

"Ellie?" His tone carried alarm. Fear. And drained every ounce of excitement from her belly.

He knew. *He. Knew.*

Quick footsteps touched her ear just before Troy called again, "Ellie…" and came around the corner into the kitchen as if he were chasing her. But halted his forward momentum with a hand on the doorframe, and his gaze homed in on the phone in her hands.

And the look on his face—the oh-shit-what-have-I-done look on his face—told her everything. The phone was *not* in the drawer by accident. The phone had *not* lost its battery by accident. Troy had *not* disabled her phone so they could disconnect from the world together.

He'd done it *knowing* what the consequences would be for her.

A second of supreme, deafening silence stretched while Giselle quivered with tension, with hurt, with disbelief, praying he would blurt out some plausible reason—any plausible reason—for doing this.

But his eyes fell closed, his shoulders dropped, and his head lowered.

Everything from their past swirled in, combined with everything from their present, and cut into the possibility of their future.

"How did this happen?" she asked, holding out the very last thread of hope. "*Why* did this happen?"

He lifted his head and came forward with a look that implored her to understand while knowing she wouldn't. He'd pulled on only boxer briefs, and his hair was a tousled, sexy mess.

"His messages were getting more and more…crazy. I was afraid he'd trace your phone and I didn't want him coming here and creating any more stress for you."

"You read the messages."

He pressed a hand to the counter, standing so close, the afternoon light shone through his irises, turning them a beautiful and clear shade of brandy. "I…saw them."

She waited. Waited for him to pull some miraculous excuse out of the ether to make all the hurt inside vanish. But nothing more came.

"That's it? That's all you have to say?" Anger balled in her gut. "*You saw them?*"

He straightened and took a deep breath. One of those, oh-here-we-go-type breaths. "You promised me a week, El."

"Don't. Don't *even*. What you did here has absolutely nothing to do with any time limit, and you know it." She thought back over their time together, over the things he'd said. "You *knew* where my phone was when I asked.

You *knew* those messages were waiting. And you *knew* *exactly* how important they were."

She started past him toward the bedroom.

He caught her arm. "El—"

She jerked from his grasp. Pain throbbed beneath her ribs. "I can't believe you did this. I really can't."

"What can't you believe?" he barked. "That I love you and don't want to lose you to that damned career again?"

"No, Troy. I know I hurt you when I walked away. And I expected some insecurity. What I didn't expect is the way you minimized the importance of my career by hiding these messages from me." She held up her phone. "This is not *meshing* our careers. It's controlling and deceitful. It's *unacceptable*."

Turning away, she pushed her feet into the bedroom and grabbed clothes from a chair.

"Giselle," he said, following her. His use of her full name made her shoulders inch up around her ears. "Take a few minutes to calm down and put this into perspective."

Her mind felt like a messy, slippery knot of seaweed. Her heart felt like shattered shards of glass. She wouldn't calm down in his presence, and she wouldn't do it in a few minutes. Perspective in this situation would not come easily.

She jerked a skirt from the arm of a chair and pulled it on, then riffled through a pile of things on the dresser and found panties, dragging those on beneath the skirt.

"Pepsi, Bud, AEG, Live Nation?" She swung toward him, on the edge of hysteria. The more she thought about the magnitude of the offers on the table, the deeper his actions cut and the more panic-stricken she became. "We're talking promotion at the level of Kenny Chesney, Taylor Swift, Carrie Underwood, Luke Bryan... the Rolling-freaking-Stones, for God's sake. You *know this*. Seriously, Troy. *Seriously*. Step back for a minute and really *look at what you've done*."

She was yelling now, her emotions completely out of control as the enormity of the situation sank past the shock and the hurt. "You've made it look like I couldn't care less what offers are on the table. Like I don't have the time of day for the biggest opportunity the music world could offer. But what makes it even worse is that you did it *knowing* how long and how much I've sacrificed to get those very offers."

She pulled off his T-shirt, grabbed a bra, and fought to snap it into place with her fingers shaking.

"First of all, you shouldn't be yelling," he said, his tone measured but brimming with frustration. "It's not good for your head or your voice. And second of all, that's not true. Everyone knows what happened in the caves—it was front-page news. They know you were hurt. Chad and Brook will be covering you with explanations. No one but you—you and Chad—expect you to be at meetings now."

She finally got the bra clasped and reached for a blouse, desperate to get out, get space, find level ground. She had too many voices ricocheting around her head. Too many emotions twisting her heart. Too much pressure inside her gut. She felt like she was going to explode.

"And how much are you going to continue to sacrifice, El? At what point do you stop sacrificing? At what point should your career start giving back? After all you've given to it, what does it give you now? Stress, stress, and more stress?"

Fear and fury turned her vision red around the edges. "You've been back in my life two weeks, and you think you know what I want, what I need, how I feel?"

A familiar sense of claustrophobia settled in. The same type she'd experienced in the cave, where she couldn't think straight, couldn't breathe, just needed to get out.

Out, out, *out.*

She picked up her phone, opened her taxi app, and requested a cab to her location. "I can't fight about this now." She dropped her phone on the bed and looked around, trying to think what she needed to gather up for her trip back to Las Vegas. "I need to get this mess straightened out so I can think. So I have direction..."

But nothing here was hers. Even the clothes she'd come in were still in the washing machine.

"Don't go, Ellie." His words weren't a request or a plea. They weren't even a demand. They were a warning. A warning that lifted her hackles. "Yes, I hid your phone because I was being selfish and I wanted a few uninterrupted days with you. But I also did it because *you* needed it—for your health, for your sanity. No one knows you like I do, and I knew those messages would have you doing exactly what you're doing right now—jumping right back into the insanity too soon. You'll work yourself into the ground unless there's someone around to be your voice of reason."

"Voice of reason?" she said, her voice a harsh whisper. "You think *you're* my voice of *reason?*"

"Well, it sure as shit isn't Chad. Not when he's getting a portion of every dollar you're out there busting your ass to earn. And Brook, God, I think that girl would do anything you asked of her, which makes her a great friend but a lousy source of true reason, because all she wants to do is see you happy, so she's going to tell you whatever she thinks you want to hear."

"Stop. Twisting. *Everything.*" She picked up her phone and slid her credit cards and ID off the dresser, pushing them into the back of the case. "This is about *you deceiving me.*"

"Because *I love you,* Ellie."

His conviction vibrated inside her. Her heart reached for him. Her soul begged her to pull down the walls and let him in. Believe him. *Trust him.*

"I don't give a fuck about your money," he said. "I couldn't care less about your fame. I care about *you.* I care about your health and your happiness. And if you stopped long enough to really look at your life, you'd see you don't have either."

"*Excuse me?*" She pulled back, crossing her arms. "Who the hell are you to pass judgment on my life. On what I do or don't have in my life. Just because I've struggled, just because I've gone through a rough time does not mean..." She stopped and collected herself. "I'm not doing this. I'm not going to stand here and justify myself or my work or my lifestyle or my choices to you."

She cut a wide path around him and exited the bedroom.

"You've got a ton of money," he continued, so close behind her she could feel his breath on her neck, "which you don't even use. You've got the power of a celebrity, which you neither use nor want. You've got the hip and fast lifestyle of a musician on the road, which has done nothing but left you lonely and haggard."

That made her spin on him with rage boiling in her veins.

But he kept talking. "Have you ever sat down and even thought about what you really want from your singing?" His extremely direct question surprised her. Confused her. She lost her focus. Her direction. "Or have you been blindly following the path where it led the past seven years the way you did all the years before that?"

When he stopped talking, the silence seemed to smother her. "What…gives you the right…to judge me?"

He ground his teeth and dropped his gaze to the floor.

"What makes you think…you have the right… to make decisions for me?" She had to stop and draw air every few words. "Decisions that reflect poorly on me…both as a person and a professional? Without ever once…*talking to me about it first?*"

His gaze lifted from the floor, his eyes liquid, dark, filled with desperate emotions. "I love you, Ellie. *I love you,* heart and soul." He jabbed a finger at her. *"That's* what gives me *the right."*

A double honk outside cut into their fight and put a chill on the room. Troy's gaze flashed toward the window and hardened to rock. Giselle looked at the floor, searching her mind, her heart for the right solution. For the right thing to do.

"Goddammit, Ellie," he said, voice vibrating with tension and hurt. So much hurt it stabbed at her heart. "Don't you *dare* walk out that door."

Pull yourself together. Pull yourself together.

She met his eyes. "This is my career, Troy. This is what I've been working toward for as long as I can remember. You know this is what I was meant to do. You know how much it means to me. If you loved me, you wouldn't ask me to set it aside the same way I would never ask you to end your stunt career."

She couldn't take this torment another second. Yearned to cut herself free from the upsetting bonds of hurt, betrayal, distrust, and fear. Yet she found the act of turning away from him and forcing her feet to move excruciating. Found the door as heavy as cement as she pulled it open. Found the bitter, bitter taste of "Goodbye" lingering far longer than she'd imagined.

And found her drive to LAX as long as if she'd driven to Vegas itself.

Troy kept the side of his face pressed to the front window long after the taxi vanished from sight. Hoping against hope that she'd realize what she'd done and come back. That as soon as the anger cleared, understanding would set in and she'd come back. That as the hurt faded, their love would break through, and she'd come back.

Only…she never came back.

Not after he'd cried himself hollow. Not after he'd gutted himself with recrimination. Not after he'd smashed a dining room chair over the granite kitchen counter.

When he pried his wet face away from the glass, dusk was setting. He stumbled to the dining room and dropped into the lone mate of the broken chair and let his gaze blur over the hole he'd punched in the plaster wall—man, Rubi was gonna be pissed—thinking that he could draw a circle around the hole Giselle had left in his body, one encompassing his entire torso.

He'd promised her that if she'd given them a chance, he'd let her make her decision. That he would abide by that decision and let her move on. He'd done it because he'd believed that they belonged together. That their rough beginnings gave them a deeper understanding of each other. But it looked like he'd been wrong. Two fucked-up wrongs didn't make a right.

She'd made her choice.

She was gone.

He had to let her go.

But just how the fuck was he going to live without her now?

He didn't know how long he sat there staring at the hole in the wall. Only knew when the house's darkness and silence overwhelmed him. Until he couldn't stay in the house alone another minute.

He dragged himself into the bedroom, more zombie than human, dropped to a seat on the bed where he and Giselle had spent four beautiful nights together, and picked up the landline on the nightstand. He dialed, leaned on his knees, and rubbed his face as he listened to the phone ring at the other end of the line.

He felt gutted. Absolutely empty. Couldn't envision how this feeling would ever ease. Couldn't imagine going through every day feeling like this.

He pushed those dark thoughts aside as his boss answered. "Dude," Jax said, "you are on Ryker's shit list."

"Nothing new." Troy's voice came out gravelly, and he cleared his throat. "For Rachel's benefit, it would be good to warn him to stay away from me right now."

"Oooookay. Will do. No guarantee he'll listen."

"Never does. Look, I *really* need a job. Like *really bad.* And I *don't* want to be in Vegas. Know what I mean?"

A slight hesitation, then, "Ah, shit, man. I'm sorry." True compassion drenched his friend's voice and brought a fresh wave of tears to Troy's eyes. "Fuck, that bites." A heavy sigh filled the line, then a moment of silence as Troy imagined Jax thinking. "I just wrapped my work in San Diego. Other than Vegas, I've only got Wes breaking in the new guy on a skyscraper run downtown."

"Fine, great." He already planned on sinking into a bottle of Jamison to get through the night. "I'm pulling seniority. Stunt's mine. Tell me where to be in the morning."

"Actually, it's a night shoot. Gets started in about an hour."

"Even better." *Thank God.* "I'm there."

As Troy jotted down the address, he already knew this stunt would rock on screen, because right now he didn't give a flying fuck if he lived or died.

He was all in.

Fourteen

"Two hours?" Giselle tried not to whine, she really did. But when she was on the verge of dropping to her butt in the middle of the concourse, wrapping her arms around her knees and rocking herself like an asylum escapee, it was difficult. "Are you sure there's not another flight I can…?"

"I'm sorry, ma'am." The airline ticket agent said. "There's nothing sooner. We can only fix a broken plane so fast."

Giselle massaged her throbbing temple and accepted her lousy luck as she turned away from the gate attendant doling out details on the flight delay due to the plane's mechanical issues.

She'd managed to get through security and buy a ball cap without anyone recognizing her and even found a mostly empty seating area at another gate to sit down and listen to all the voice mails on her phone, holding herself together with slow, even breaths. But now, she needed a little liquid help.

She headed into the United member's lounge and ordered a glass of wine from the bar, then sank into a corner seat at the windows, pulled the brim of her ball cap low, and stared out at the night on the tarmac. Her mind veered toward the messages on her voice mail and Chad's attitude. She was so over it. Over him. His messages had transitioned from irate to apologetic to annoyed to irate again.

As soon as she got to Vegas, they'd be having a chat about that attitude. They'd also be having a very serious sit-down over the four other offers Giselle's agent, Gloria, had left messages about on her voice mail. Deals Chad *hadn't* passed on, including L'Oréal upping their already generous offer. If his attitude hadn't improved by the time she reached Vegas, she was cutting him loose.

Brook, Giselle's one true friend and a saint for putting up with all the woman had put up with over the last seven years, had left messages telling Giselle she missed her, hoped she was feeling better, and looked forward to having her back.

But that was it. Just her manager, her agent, and her assistant. Nothing from her band members or her backup singers. She had no friends—other than Brook— no family, no one close to her who cared.

She drank deep, wishing the wine would wash all her pain away—in her heart, in her head, in her throat. Yelling at Troy hadn't been smart.

"Bastard," she muttered around a fresh wave of tears. Why did he always have to be right? Why did he have to know her so well? Understand her so completely? While standing so adamantly in the way of what she was meant to do? Who she was meant to be?

She shook her head and forced him from her mind. With two hours to wait, she couldn't hold off talking to Chad until she got to Vegas like she'd planned.

Her fingers shook as she scrolled through her contacts and tapped his number. She took another long drink as she listened to his phone ring.

"Giselle?" Chad answered, guarded hope and shock in his voice. "Is that you?"

She swallowed. "Yeah, it's me."

"Oh, thank God. I was just about to send LAPD to track down Jax Chamberlin to locate Troy. Girl, don't do that to me again. You damn near gave me a heart attack. I thought something horrible had happened." As if he just realized he hadn't asked, he said, "You're okay, right?"

She couldn't even go there. "I'm sorry about the communication. Something went wrong with my phone, and I didn't realize it until today. Can you catch me up on what's going on?"

"Oh, Giselle, it's amazing. I wish you'd been here to experience it, what a rush." He rambled on and on about Pepsi influencing Bud, Bud influencing the smaller sponsors, and all the interest influencing the promoters to throw deal offers together. "...until it was like carte blanche. What does Giselle want? Where would Giselle like to see her career go? What can we do for Giselle?" His laugh was rich and satisfied. "Anyway, when all the dust settled...Are you sitting down?"

Her stomach clenched—but not in a good way. "Yes."

"Bud is partnering with AEG Live to offer you a head-lining tour throughout North America with a hundred and four stops all across America, including all the biggest venues. *One hundred and four*, Giselle."

Her mouth dropped open. She thought she'd been prepared for big, judging by his excitement in the messages, but this was *so* big. This was...unfathomable.

"Live Nation and Pepsi," Chad went on, "are partnering to offer you an overseas tour immediately after in eight countries, including stops at four military installations, for a total of sixty-three concerts.

"Both promotional companies have thrown out guest stars for various stops on the tours, names like Miranda Lambert, Jason Aldean, Gretchen Wilson, Luke Bryan, Sugarland. I can't even name them all. It still gives me goose bumps just thinking about it..."

He went on with details, but she was still grappling with the enormity of this breakthrough. This was that moment—the moment she'd always dreamed of. This was her break. This was her shattering the glass ceiling. This was her becoming a household name. This was her hitting the big time. This was...this was...

This was her biggest, deepest fantasy come true.

And she was sitting alone. In an airport bar. With a broken heart. And one friend. Miserable.

"How the hell did this happen?" She hadn't even realized she'd thought the words, let alone said them, until they were out of her mouth.

"Hard work," Chad answered, completely misunderstanding the meaning of her question. "Hard work, perseverance, talent, training, promotion, taking opportunities, and making opportunities. That's how this happened, Giselle. This throws you into a whole different sphere, honey. A whole different category of entertainment. You are a who's-who now. You're going to have more money than you ever dreamed of. There's *no limit* to where you can go, what you can do."

Chad kept talking—about ludicrous amounts of money, the things she could buy, the things she could have, the services she could employ, while the only thing rolling through Giselle's mind were Troy's words.

"You've got a ton of money, which you don't even use. You've got the power of a celebrity, which you neither use nor want. You've got the hip and fast lifestyle of a musician on the road, which has done nothing but left you lonely and haggard."

"Chad," she cut into his monologue.

"Yeah, yeah, sorry, I was getting a little long-winded."

"What kind of time frame are we looking at?" She already knew it was significant. That much travel and that number of concerts could only be done—

"I've got it mapped out on a two-year plan," he said. "It's a little tight in places, but doable. When are you going to get back? We can take a few days to go over the plan."

The throb in her head intensified and threatened to blow her skull apart. Her belly burned with anxiety, the kind that made her want to crawl out of her skin. Instead of laughing and jumping and clapping and ordering another drink—hell, ordering a round of drinks for the whole damn lounge—she inexplicably wanted to cry.

And she panicked over the bizarre reaction. "Um... you know...My head is still pretty bad. Did you get all my concerts at the Mirage covered to the end of my contract? Because…because…I'm really sorry, but I don't think I'm going to be able to finish them out."

Oh my God. Oh my God. Oh my God.

Had those words just come out of her mouth?

Her world was spinning on its axis.

Panic buzzed along every nerve, sizzling along her ribs, her spine, her neck…

"Oh, honey," Chad said. "I'm sorry. Here I am going on and on…I thought…Yes, absolutely. I've gotten all but the last three covered. I'll tell them you're out. It won't be a problem. Should I find a specialist for you there in LA? A neurologist?"

Maybe a psychiatrist.

Or a mental facility.

"Not…quite yet. Give me another few days. If it's not better then, I'll…"—*check myself into an asylum*—"go see someone. The ER doctor said concussions can take time." She paused, trying to gather her thoughts, her emotions. "On the…um…offers, can I get back to you? I need to sort some things out in my head."

A long, tense silence stretched taut over the line. "Get back to me? What in the hell is wrong?" He sounded genuinely worried. "Giselle, do you want me to fly out there? I can catch a plane and be there in a few hours."

She laughed and opened her eyes to the blurry image of the ticket to Vegas in her hand. "Thanks, but there's no need. I've got this. I just need a little bit of quiet to square up my brain."

She disconnected and sat there several long moments, staring at nothing. Then she pulled her legs beneath her, wrapped her arms around herself, and curled into a small package the way she had when she'd wanted to disappear as a kid.

There, she rested her head against her hand and cried silently. She didn't care who was watching. Didn't care if anyone recognized her. Didn't care how messed up she looked. Didn't even care how broken she really was. She only cared that at that moment, this was what she needed.

After half an hour of cleansing her soul with tears, Giselle dried her eyes on a bar napkin, picked up her phone, took a deep breath, and dialed Chad again.

Troy tightened the straps on his harness. The wind whipped at his hair, and at this height, after dark, with the fog rolling in off the ocean, there was nothing warm about this fucking city. Which was fine. It matched both his mood and the temperature of his heart.

He tightened his gloves. Opened and closed his hands. Took the clear glasses Ben, a crew member, handed him and slid them on. "Did you steal these from some kid's chemistry locker?"

"Right along with his collection of *Penthouse* rags, meth, and bubblegum," Tommy said.

Troy would have laughed if he'd been capable. He would have laughed and kept the banter going to reduce the anxiety of waiting to climb along the side of a building a thousand feet above the city, but his heart wasn't in it. His heart wasn't in anything but forgetting.

He looked down at himself, checking everything on his body—black tee and pants, both clinging like skin, black shoes. The makeup artist had gelled his hair back with what felt like cement and secured it at his nape with an elastic tie.

For a split second, Troy's mind slipped from his grip, and he pictured Giselle. Pain—knifing, how-will-I-ever-get-through-this agony—ripped him open. He squeezed his eyes shut and exhaled hard.

Go numb. He had to just let it eat at him until he went numb.

But that would take so long. So fucking long.

He opened his eyes to the night, the fog, and glanced over his shoulder at the crew. Wes was explaining different aspects of the stunt to the new guy they'd brought on board, Cameron, a successful actor following in Jax's shoes and jumping the fame-and-fortune ship, seeking a better overall quality of life in stunts.

And Troy thought of Giselle again, hating himself for not being able to convince her to do the same.

"Could really use some tunes right now," Troy yelled to the room at large. "Anyone got something to get my buzz going?"

Tommy dragged his phone from his back pocket and plugged it into some speakers nearby. While the camera and sound crew messed with technicalities and a chopper hovered outside, Troy walked to the open space in the side of the building where they'd removed a giant pane of glass from one of the skyscraper's top floors. He gripped a steel beam and gazed out over the city, his focus drawn to the airport and the constant, steady landing and takeoff of aircraft.

It made him realize just how quickly, how easily, Giselle had swept into his life, turned it upside down, and swept out again.

"Hey." Wes's voice drew Troy's attention and spiked alarm.

Without thought, he turned, gripped Wes's arm hard, and shoved him back and away from the opening. When they were both a safe distance, he said, "Dude, what the fuck? You don't have a harness on."

Wes's brow pulled in confusion. His gaze darted toward the window, then back. And when Troy's gaze followed, he realized Wes hadn't been as close to the opening as Troy had first thought.

"Do you know of some secret plot among the crew to pick me up and carry me close enough to the ledge to shove me to my death?" Wes asked easily. "'Cause I wasn't close enough to fall, even if I tripped over my own stupid feet, and yours, and Cam's, and Susie's, and John's, and—"

"Shut up." He cut Wes off before he named every member of the crew, but he breathed easier. "You don't know what you don't know. You know?"

"I think you missed your calling. You should have been a philosopher."

He glanced out over the open space again. "Maybe then I'd be able to figure out why life turns upside down on a dime sometimes."

Wes leaned against a bare steel beam of the unfinished commercial space and crossed his arms. He wore a T-shirt and jeans, and a headset hung around his neck. "Rubi says it's the universe giving us a kick in the ass. Says that most people get in a groove and keep living life one way because it's easy or familiar or whatever. And when the greater powers get sick and tired of waiting for us to take the next right step, it spins us like a top to get our attention. To make us think."

There was a lot of wisdom there. More than Troy had the ability to absorb in his current state of mind-fucked. "Rubi is one smart woman."

"Me," Wes continued in that easy way of his, "I just think it's karma giving us a kick in the ass."

Troy barked a laugh.

"Ready in five, Troy," the director called.

"Rubi told me things went south with Giselle?" Wes half asked, half stated.

Troy's head swung from the director to Wes. "It hasn't even been two hours. I haven't told anyone. How in the hell?"

"Ah, you know. You called Jax, Jax told Lexi, Lexi told Rubi—"

"Rubi told you. Criminy, you people."

"We care, bro. Could be worse. We could loosen the hooks on your harness, let you *splat* all over Wilshire Boulevard." He paused and sobered. "But seriously, I'm really sorry, man. Believe me, I know how crazy these women can make you. Took me and Rubi a long time, quite a few fights, and more than a few tears to find our groove." He paused, then added, "Even Rubi cried once."

Troy huffed a laugh past the pain expanding inside him until it felt like it filled every cell.

"But it's so worth it, brother," Wes said, slapping a hand to his shoulder. "*So* worth it."

In the distance, a 747 raced down the LAX runway before angling into the sky, and Troy wondered which plane Giselle was on. Wished he hadn't been so stubborn, so stupid, so set in his goddamned *groove* when she'd insisted on going back to Vegas.

He'd been wrong. He'd known it. Why hadn't he offered to go with her?

Whoa.

Good fucking question.

Why the hell hadn't he just offered to go with her?

"Goddamn." He bit out the word, unable to believe he'd been that stupid. Unable to believe the answer had been right there in front of him the whole time. "Could it be that simple?"

"I don't know what you're thinking," Wes said, "but my answer would be: probably not."

That telescoped Troy's mind out again, giving him a wider view, and Wes was right—it wasn't that simple. She could have done the same—simply asked him to come with her.

Yet neither of them had seen it as an option.

They were so busy pulling away from each other out of fear, they hadn't even seen the simple answers right in front of them. At least he hadn't. Maybe Giselle had, and she hadn't offered because she didn't want him with her.

But there was only one way to find out for sure. He hadn't gone after her the first time she'd walked away.

Hadn't been willing to be a target for her colleagues. Hadn't been willing to adjust to her new way of life. Hadn't been willing to be overshadowed by her career.

But he wasn't going to make that mistake again, because he wasn't that boy anymore.

And this was his chance to prove it.

"Troy," the director called. "We're ready."

He walked toward the opening but called over his shoulder to one of the production assistants. "Treena."

The redhead fluttered to the front of the crew. "Right here."

"I need a flight to Vegas. I want the first one you can get as soon as this is a wrap."

"Done."

At the window, now in a harness, Wes slapped Troy's shoulder. "Good call, bro."

Might be a good call, but it was based on a realization he should have made while Giselle had still been here. One he should have made seven years ago.

Troy climbed to the metal ledge of the skyscraper's open wall a mile above Los Angeles, ready to jump out, hoping this revelation wasn't too little, too late.

"Giselle Diamond," she told the man at the front desk in a breathless rush. "Jax Chamberlin called—"

"Right," the older man said, nodding. "Troy's girl. Dave will escort you up."

"Thank you."

At the elevator of the deserted lobby, another man in a navy blue security guard's uniform stood waiting for her, doors already open.

She stopped short and smiled up at the man. He was a little older than her, with a serious expression and close-cropped brown hair. "Oh, um…" She stared inside the elevator car. Wrung her hands. Licked her lips. "Can we take the stairs?"

"Mr. Jacobs is working on the sixty-second floor, ma'am."

"Sixty-second?" Okay, that would take a while, but… "I know this is going to sound crazy, but, could we still take the stairs?"

His are-you-serious? look quickly transitioned into the why-me eye roll. "Yes, ma'am, the sixty-second floor. We *could* take the stairs—all *twelve hundred and fifty-six* of them—but, depending on your athletic stamina, that could take anywhere from twenty minutes to…an hour or more."

That's what she thought. Not an option. She forced a tight smile for the security guard and held up a finger. "Just one second."

Lowering her gaze to the floor, she took a slow deep breath in through her nose, blew it out slowly through her mouth, and repeated that three times. She shook out her arms and stretched her fingers. Then cracked her neck both directions. Pushed her shoulders back. And stepped in.

Only to discover the ride to the floor where Troy was performing his stunt took several minutes.

Minutes that felt like hours.

A cold sweat prickled over her face and neck. She wiped her face with both hands while watching the numbers light up and go dark. She grew more light-headed with each floor they passed. By the thirties, she was leaning against the wall, gripping the handrail.

"Out of sixty-three floors, he's on the sixty-second. Go figure, huh?"

"The top two are the only unfinished floors in the building," he said. "Claustrophobic?"

"Ye*p*." She let the P pop from her lips, and massaged each finger in turn, microfocusing on the air moving in and out of her lungs, not on the crawl of her skin or the tightening of her throat or the roll of her stomach. "That obvious?"

"My wife's claustrophobic. Guess that makes it easier to spot."

Giselle was nauseous by the time they'd gotten through the forties. Ready to pass out by the time they'd cleared the fifties. Still standing by sheer will by the time the elevator finally came to a stop.

And as the doors slid open, a whole new kind of fear tangled with her existing anxiety. The fear of Troy's rejection. The fear of the bottom falling completely out of her life.

She kept a hand on some vertical surface as she stepped out of the elevator. The space was vast and open and cold. It felt like heaven to Giselle. Like falling in a cold pond on a hot summer day. Her head cleared. Her lungs filled. Her skin cooled. Her mind opened.

The space was indeed unfinished, and a familiar camera crew setup cluttered the commercial hull on the opposite side of the building, where—holy hell—a huge glass panel, a wall, really, had been removed, leaving nothing but about two feet of steel from the floor to the cavernous opening, where cold air blew through the floor's shell.

"Oh my God."

"Hey." A really great-looking blond approached with a casual smile, hand outstretched. "I'm Wes."

One of the Renegades. She was pretty sure Troy had told her he was their best stunt driver. He greeted her with a big, warm smile. "Great to see you, Ellie. I saw you briefly in the hospital, but you were sleeping. I was hoping Troy would bring you around, but he's pretty damned selfish. Hope you weren't here for him. He just left."

Her mouth dropped open. Her heart plummeted to her feet. "What...Where..."

A cute little redhead who seemed to bounce when she walked strolled up to the group, peeped out a "Hi" for the security guard and Giselle before offering a piece of paper to Wes. "Here's Troy's ticket. His flight leaves in two hours. It's changeable and refundable, so if he's not done here, I'll just, you know, fix-a-roo it."

Giselle's mind tangled again. Was Troy here or gone? If he was gone, where did he go? And why?

"Damn it, Treena," Wes said, a grin on his face. "You ruined my prank."

Her brows shot up, and she tapped the ticket twice with her pencil. "Then I guess you should plan better next time."

Then she bopped away.

"What's going on?" Giselle pressed a hand to her tripping heart.

"I was just messing with you. Gonna have to get used to it around here. Keep your guard up. I'll do better next time. Troy's out playing on the side of the building. He'll come in when he gets hungry or cold…or he finds out you're here. Until then, you can watch him on the monitors." He turned and put an arm around her shoulders. He walked Giselle toward a big flat screen, where a figure in black hung on the side of the building, lit up by spotlights. "Or, you can watch him out there."

Wes pointed toward the side of the building, where a circle of light cut through the night and illuminated Troy outside the building. Just…hanging there. His hair was trying to blow out of its restricted style, and his expression was serious, intense, focused.

A lick of panic made her grab a handful of Wes's tee. "What's he doing?" She didn't wait for an answer before she yanked his shirt, dragging them around to face each other, and demand, "*What…is he…doing?*"

Wes gripped her shoulders and met her gaze. "*His job.* This is what he does. This is who he is. If this isn't the man you want, if this isn't the man you can accept and love, go back to the airport, Ellie." His voice was direct, but level and compassionate. "No one should ever have to settle for being loved for less than his or her true self. That's the woman Troy loves in you. He deserves no less."

She held Wes's steady blue gaze. Around them, movement whipped up. The director and Troy spoke over the radio. "You called me…Ellie."

Wes's mouth tipped up in a confused smile. "Isn't that your name?"

The scope of her world shifted from telephoto to wide view. She saw Wes as just one of the people she would be accepting into her life by loving Troy. Her mind flickered through all the others whom he'd told her so much about—Jax and Lexi, Josh and Grace, Rubi, Rachel…it was such a big family that just kept growing. People who would welcome her into their circle based solely on her importance to Troy. The full realization of what Troy had been trying to give her—not just his love, but the love of a family, a community…

She'd come back for Troy, but she could clearly see she'd be getting so much more.

A smile broke out across her face. Tears filled her eyes. "Yeah."

"Oh Christ. Don't cry. If he thinks I made you cry, I'm going to lose some teeth." He turned, wrapped his arm around her shoulders again, and pulled her close to his side, walking her toward the set. "Come watch your man in action, El. This is gonna be great."

"All right, we're ready to go in here." The radio-roughened voice came over an open line on a speaker somewhere. "Troy?"

"I'm not feeling much like Cruise out here." His voice came over the radio sounding subdued. "Could use some *Mission Impossible* music."

"All right, everyone," Wes yelled. "On three. One, two, three—Dun, na-na…dun, na-na…dun, na-na… da-dun-na…"

Everyone joined in, and the room filled with the improvised *Mission Impossible* theme song. Giselle bubbled with laughter that rose up quickly and ended just as fast. She wanted to feel the same excitement, the same thrill filling everyone here, surely filling Troy. But she was still adjusting to the reality of him a thousand feet off the ground held up by nothing but cables. And as the crew rounded up their chorus with a vibrant finish and a round of applause, Troy's laugh sounded scratchy over the radio, but definitely less than exuberant. "I feel *clearer* already."

Troy's reference to Scientology made everyone in the crew roar with laughter.

The warmth filling the room, the way the crew came together to support each other, to support Troy, filled Giselle in a way she couldn't quite say she'd ever known. A way she may have experienced for a short time way back, when it was her and Troy and Nathan against the world. The joy that this filled Troy's daily life, the satisfaction, the sheer and deep gratitude swelling inside her, made it hard to breathe and choked off her words.

"Okay," Wes said, his smile soft, blue eyes warm. "I've got to get over to the window to drag his ass back in after this take. You hold this." He handed her the airline ticket. "Good thing Treena went for refundable. Doesn't look like he'll be needing it after all."

She caught Wes's arm, and when he looked back, she smiled, nodded. "Thank you."

"Always." He pulled his arm from her grasp until their hands met, and gave hers a squeeze. "*Always.*"

"Wes, get on deck." The director's voice pulled Wes away and drew Giselle's gaze to the window. To Troy, illuminated in the spotlight. "Let us know when you're set up, Troy."

Giselle glanced at the ticket and read the destination: Las Vegas. Her heart hicupped, but she couldn't get too excited. He'd been working there too. This didn't mean he'd been going after her. She curled the paper into her palm as, outside, Troy planted his feet against the glass, took one of the several ropes in his gloved hands, and said, "All right. Now or never."

Her heart tripped.

"Get ready to roll." The director's voice echoed over the speaker. "Here we go. And three…two…one…*action!*"

Giselle held her breath. She wanted to turn away from the window, but she couldn't. So she watched the chopper's light follow Troy as he pushed off the glass, flying away from the building in a smooth arc, only to touch down, several huge panes of glass away at a ninety-degree angle, then sprinted across the building.

Her mind couldn't comprehend how he did that. How they made that happen. Even standing on the set of the stunt, in the middle of the crew, with all the gadgets surrounding her, she couldn't fathom…

"*Cut.*" The director's voice jolted Giselle from her thoughts. "Nice, Troy. Wind's picking up. Let's call it a night."

"Roger that," Troy said, before he simply fell out of sight.

Giselle felt the floor open beneath her. She launched toward the last place she'd seen him. "Tro—"

Strong arms caught her, and the sudden stop knocked her scream from her lungs before it could reach its target.

"He's okay." The man's voice was new, but just as warm and confident as Wes's, and he was just as strong, holding her without effort as she struggled to twist from his grip, her gaze holding on the emptiness outside. On Wes, leaning out the opening but not returning with Troy. "He's fine."

"*How do you know?*" Her heart was in free fall. "He's... he's... *Where is he?*"

"It takes some time to reel in."

Her muscles gave in to exhaustion, and she slumped, but the man restraining her was there to keep her from hitting the floor. She was shaking, but the man slowly released her as she found her feet. And after what seemed like an excruciating amount of time—which in reality was probably more like a few minutes—Troy gradually rose into view. The crew broke into applause. Giselle almost hit the ground again.

The man nearby gripped her arms. "You're gonna have to grow a thicker skin if you plan on sticking around awhile."

She nodded, pressing a hand to her forehead, searching for a sliver of composure. "If he doesn't break my heart, he's going to give me a heart attack."

The man chuckled. "You steady?"

"Yes. Thank you." When he released her and stepped away, she finally looked up at his face. He was about Troy's size, sandy brown hair, greenish-gray eyes, rugged. She offered her hand. "I'm Giselle—"

"Diamond." His grin widened. "I know." He shrugged. "I'm a fan."

A smile broke over her face. "You're not my demographic. That makes you an extraspecial fan."

"And extra, *extra* special considering your guy totally bagged on my stunt."

"Uh…" She wasn't sure what he'd just said. "W-wha…?"

"Troy." He glanced toward the open door and the dark night beyond, lit up by the chopper's spotlight. "Just walked in and stole my stunt right out from under me, the prick. But…" He shrugged again. "I'm the new guy and all that." He offered his hand. "I'm Cameron. New Renegade."

"Nice to meet you." She shook his hand. "I'm not sure if I should apologize for Troy or not."

"*Pffft.*"

"Do you know…um…" She scraped her lip between her teeth. "Is he going back to work on the Vegas shoot?"

"No, he's done there. Keaton, Duke, and Z are tying it up." He leaned down to pick up a harness of some kind. "Guess I'm the cleanup crew. Catch you later."

"Thanks again."

As Cameron wandered away, Giselle's heart expanded with hope. Her eyes burned with tears. Excitement drew her gaze to the crew as Wes leaned out of the building, caught Troy's hand, and drew him in.

Wes said something that made Troy's head pop up, made his gaze sharpen on his friend's face. Then he was scanning the room, those pretty eyes wide and so filled with hope, the tears stinging her eyes slipped over her lashes. But she didn't breathe right until his feet touched solid ground. Her heart didn't beat right until he'd pushed through everyone and reached her. Even then, it rushed and skipped.

As soon as he was within reach, he cupped her face. "You're still here," he said, stroking her hair with one hand, scanning her face as if he hadn't seen her in months. "I was coming. Right after this. Right now. I was coming to you."

She nodded. "I know." She lifted the ticket and gave a little shrug. "They said it's refundable."

"I'm not refunding it." He wrapped her in his arms and kissed her. "Whenever I don't have to be working, I'll be with you." He kissed her again. "Wherever you are, whatever you're doing, it doesn't matter." He kissed her again, then pressed his forehead to hers. "I was stupid not to think of it before. And I was *really* stupid not to come after you seven years ago. I wasted that time when I could have been with you. I'm not doing that again."

Giselle's eyes closed, and tears spilled out. Tears of love, of joy, of gratitude…so many emotions.

"Baby, I'm *so* sorry—" he started, but Giselle lifted her fingers to his mouth and tipped her head back to look into his eyes.

"We agreed no more apologies." She let her hand slide from his lips and caress his jaw. "There won't be any need for them anymore, because I won't be walking away from you again. I will never, *ever* be putting my career before you again."

Confusion and a little worry crept into his eyes. "Did you talk to Chad?"

"I did."

"What did he say? What about the offers?" A sick look washed his features, and Giselle swore he paled two shades. "Holy shit. Did I...Did I *lose* those deals for you?" He grimaced as if he were in actual pain, then gripped her arms hard with a rock-solid determination. "You give me names and phone numbers, Giselle. I swear to God, I'll have those deals back within twenty-four hours."

"Troy—"

"I'm not the worthless boy you left. I know people now. Powerful people. People who like me. People who owe me. And since I *never* call in favors, I promise, there are a hell of a lot of huge ones hanging out there that I will pull on in a heartbeat for you." He gave her a little shake, and a lick of panic edged his eyes. "I can fix this, Ellie. Please, *please* let me fix this."

She took his face in both hands and held his gaze. "You were never worthless to me. *Not ever.* I deeply appreciate the offer, and maybe someday I'll use it, but not today. And not in the near future."

"Why *not?*"

"I don't need it. The offers were still waiting when I called Chad."

All his air exited his lungs. Relief washed over his face first, then anticipation and excitement. "So? What was the best final offer?"

"Oh, that," she said with a sigh and throwaway attitude, leaning into him and wrapping her arms around his waist. She glanced up at the ceiling for a second. "Let's see...Bud and AEG offered a headliner North American tour with over a hundred stops to be followed by a world tour in eight countries and another sixty concerts funded by Pepsi and Live Nation." She huffed a distracted laugh. The offers still felt surreal, but her decision about them didn't. That felt perfectly right. "I didn't even know there were that many countries in Europe big enough to care about me to have a concert."

He bent to meet her eyes, gripping her arms again. "Are you fucking kidding me?" Then louder. "Are you *fucking* kidding me?" He slipped his arms around her waist and spun her around. "Oh, baby, that's *amazing.*" He put her down, his face bright with true joy for her. "Where do you go first? When? You'll have to give me all the dates so I can work my schedule around them. Shit, we're going to rack up so many frequent flier miles—"

"Um, no," she said, a little nervous after his show of excitement. "We won't."

His smile dropped. Confusion clouded his expression. Dread crawled in. "Why not?"

"Because…" She bit the inside of her cheek. "I turned it down."

Oh God, hearing the words out loud shot a wave of sickness through her belly. But it cleared in three seconds flat, replaced by reassurance and strength and calm.

He straightened, dropped her arms, and put a hand to his forehead as if it was helping him think. "You… *what? No!* No, no, no!" He turned and paced away, swung around and paced back. "Call him. Call them." He yelled at the room. "Someone get me a phone." Then to Giselle. "You call whoever you need to call and tell them you've reconsidered. You can't turn this down.

This is your dream, El. You've worked your whole life for this. You've given up everything for this. Phone, someone, please!" He turned in a circle, raking both hands into this hair. "I think I'm going to puke."

Giselle fisted his tee and dragged him to face her. "Troy." She lifted her hands to his face and ignored the woman who stood uncertainly nearby with a phone in her hand. "Listen very closely to what I'm going to say. *I. Don't. Want. The. Deals.* And I'm relentless, remember? Nothing you can do or say is going to make me take them."

His hands flew out to the side. "Why the hell not?"

In her peripheral vision, she saw Wes herd the crew away from them, giving a small measure of privacy, which, while appreciated, wasn't required. Giselle would have stood on stage and said this in front of thousands.

"Because you were right," she said, smiling when his eyes squeezed closed. "About so many things. I *have* been letting my career just happen to me. I have been letting my career control my life instead of living my life and controlling my career. And I'm not happy.

"These crazy-ass tours require a two-year commitment. *Two years* of my life. Two years away from you. And I won't do it."

The air whooshed out of his lungs, and his expression registered pain and love and a handful of other emotions she couldn't define. "Oh my God, El. We can work it out. I promise, I—"

"Troy." She let her hands slide down his hard chest. "It's not what I want anymore. Maybe two weeks ago, but not now." She wrapped her arms around his waist, pressed her body against his, and looked up into those deep brown eyes. "Now, I want a home, a family, friends. I want more walks on the beach, more sunny days watching the ocean, more surfing lessons. And you know me. I wouldn't be standing here if it weren't true. I love *you*. I want *you*."

He enveloped her in his arms, kissed her hair, and whispered, "I love you so damn much." He pulled back just enough to kiss her lips, softly, slowly. Then he pressed her forehead to hers. "And when you decide what you want to do, no matter what it is, even if it's that crazy-ass two-year world tour, I'll be there. From here on out, I'm all in, all the time."

She smiled, with so much love in her heart it overflowed. "That makes two of us."

Epilogue

Troy jogged from the limo to the rear stage door, praying Giselle's show didn't end early. He hadn't seen her perform these new songs live yet, even though he'd heard her sing them a thousand times. Even though he could sing them all word for word himself.

He dragged out his wallet and flashed his ID for the security guard, then said, "Can you point me toward Brook Dempsey?"

The man gave him directions, and Troy wove his way backstage, passing the cast and crew, finding his way through the complex areas like the second home they'd become. When he spotted Brook monitoring the show from behind a pair of crimson velvet drapes, relief swept through Troy's body.

He pressed a hand to his heart as he slowed. And for the first time, his hearing seemed to come back online, and Giselle's gorgeous voice filled his ears, then his heart, then his soul.

When he reached Brook's side, he stopped, closed his eyes, and just listened to Giselle stretch her voice to the fullest, cleanest, most resonant deep belt he'd ever heard from her. From anyone. And even before he could fully appreciate the practice and skill she'd achieved to master that pitch, she utilized a lightning-quick melisma to traverse the registers, ending the song with her higher, brighter, lighter, more feminine voice, one that was crystal clear and airy, giving the song its cotton-candy, fantasy-inducing sparkle with an effort-less beauty that had kept the song at number one on Billboard's Top 100 chart for fourteen weeks running.

When the song ended and the audience exploded in applause, Troy reached for the nearest vertical struc-ture to steady himself.

Brook rushed over to him, her pretty face glowing with joy. "You're back in one piece. That always makes Giselle happy. How was Boston—? Whoa." Concern dragged her grin down a few watts. "Are you...okay?"

"She still takes my breath away. I can hear her sing in the shower, wander through the house humming, rehearse every damn day, but when she performs"— emotions welled up and tightened his throat—"she still steals my heart, every damn time."

Brook's grin returned. "Well, that's good." She set down the clipboard she was holding and dragged a small box from her pocket. "Because I got it."

"Oh God." Troy couldn't take the box. He just stared at it. "Are you sure it's the one?"

Brook gave an impatient sigh. "I'm sure. She dragged me around to two dozen different jewelry stores before she picked out half a dozen to take Nathan to. I *know* which ring stole *her* breath."

Giselle was performing another song from the soundtrack of *Shangri-La*, a Disney movie that hadn't even been released yet, but the music for which had nonetheless hit record sales and prompted a major pre-release promotional Disney on Ice tour. Music Giselle had both written and performed for the film.

She never had to work another day in her life if she didn't want to, and she would never have to compromise her standard of living either. Her decision to live her life and take control of her career had given Giselle more than she could ever have asked for out of life.

And Troy couldn't have been more grateful.

"Do you want to do this or not?" Brook's prod made Troy reach for the box.

"Did you clear it with Max?" he asked. Troy didn't want anything causing problems for Giselle's career or between Giselle and her amazing new manager, Max Collins.

"He's on board. Just told me to remind you this is a Disney theatre, so no sticking your tongue down her throat while the kids watch." Brook's grin turned a little whimsical. "She's dressed like a princess, so I'd suggest you go for something Prince Charming-ish."

Grinning, he glanced through the curtains and onto the ice, where Giselle sat atop a platform decorated like a castle, wearing a sparkling purple gown, her hair up in a mountain of curls, surrounded by a tiara. "She certainly is a princess." He opened the box, and his smile fell when he saw the single, simple diamond. "But...this doesn't look like a diamond fit for a princess. Maybe I've been in Hollywood too long, but isn't this kinda small?"

Brook laughed. "Giselle insists that it's not the ring you get but the man who gives it to you that's the real prize. She sees the ring as a sort of metaphor for marriage. Giselle believes that keeping the ring simple grounds a couple. You know, keeps them from getting caught up and distracted by all the flash. Helps them remember, when they look at the simplicity of the ring, the real reason they chose each other in the first place."

"Beautiful, talented, rich, *and* smart." He huffed a laugh and shook his head. "How *in the hell* did I get so damn lucky, Brook?"

Brook squeezed his arm. "Funny thing is, she thinks she's the lucky one."

Giselle couldn't stop smiling as she signed programs and hugged children and shook parents' hands around the ice rink's border. She was really going to have to learn to ice skate so she could get off this darn platform she always ended up stuck on and move freely.

She was exhausted, but in a good way. A great way. And as she reached for another chubby little hand and took in another toothless little grin, she knew she was exactly where she was meant to be. The only thing that could make her life perfect was having Troy with her.

But she'd talk to him when she reached the hotel. And see him in a few days when she flew back to Los Angeles from this leg of the tour in Miami.

"Attention, ladies and gentlemen." A familiar male voice filled the theatre and sent a sizzle down Giselle's spine. "We have a special announcement."

She turned and found Troy in the middle of the ice. Troy, holding a microphone and wearing ice skates. *Ice skates.* In fact, he wasn't only wearing them, he was skating in them. Gliding around the ice as smoothly as if he were walking around a movie set.

"Today is a special day here at Disney on Ice, and we hope you'll all share in our celebration."

"What are you doing here?" She turned on the platform to face him and lifted her hands. "You ice skate?"

He just chuckled as he glided by, but expertly managed the crowd, slowly leaking information about whatever he had up his sleeve, dragging the audience back from their exit strategies, gathering them around the rink again.

"Today is Miss Giselle Diamond's birthday."

A little gasp of excitement ran through the crowd, then light applause. As he traveled past, she said, "Aw. You remembered the date."

"Of course."

He took another lap while the rest of the cast and crew slowly ebbed from the background and circled the rink.

"To celebrate this very, *very* special day," Troy told the audience, "we would like you to share in some festivities—but first…" He came to a dramatic stop in front of her, spraying ice. "I have a few words and a little gift to share."

"Where did you learn to skate?" she asked, her voice echoing through the microphone and into the crowd.

"Let me think…" He bowed his head, put one finger to his chin, and with one skate secured in the ice, he made one slow, effortless circle. "It might have been... Oh no." Another slow circle to the audience's light laughter. "Oh, it must have been...No, no, that wasn't it." Another slow circle, more laughter. "Ah." Another dramatic stop. "I remember now. It was when I worked on the Disney movie *Power Play*." He turned to the audience. "Any hockey fans in here tonight?"

Applause erupted through the auditorium. Laughter tingled through her belly, and she delighted in seeing this confident, gregarious side of him.

"I thought so, I thought so," Troy said. "But I won't take this special night away from our true star."

He faced Giselle, growing quiet and serious. And as if the crowd could sense his mood, they also grew quiet. He met her eyes, and everyone else faded. Nothing mattered but the man in front of her and the way he filled her with happiness and laughter and love.

He picked up her hand and threaded their fingers, and while he never broke their gaze, he still spoke into the microphone, sharing this very intimate moment with everyone.

"It's no secret how much I love you, Ellie. Or how long I've loved you," he said, his voice smooth and rich and soft. "But some days just...*intensify*...that love. Like today."

Giselle reached for his free hand, and he held it, but only for a moment. Then he let go to reach into his pocket and pull out a small box, and watched himself turn it in his fingers. Her heart flipped with surprise, and the importance of his impromptu visit suddenly took root, spreading tingles through her whole body.

"And a little bird told me…that you believe in keeping love grounded in simplicity." Troy tucked the microphone beneath one arm and used both hands to hold the box. "I can't think of anything simpler than finding myself spending every free moment just thanking God for the day you were born. Or thanking God for the day you were brought into my life."

Her heart swelled until her ribs ached. Tears blurred her vision.

Then, as he held her gaze, he gracefully lowered to one knee, took her hand in his and offered her the box with the other. "I'd like to spend the rest of my life *thanking God* for the day you agreed to be my wife."

She gasped, and her mouth dropped open. Her tears spilled over. She heard a faint gasp around the edges of the room before everything drowned in the thud of her heartbeat.

Time slowed as she sat stunned, watching Troy scan her face, his expression open and vulnerable and so hopeful. Saw his mouth edge up with a grin. A warm, loving, I-can't-live-without-you grin.

She felt, more than heard, the words, "Yes, absolutely, there's nothing I want more" roll out of her mouth on a messy mix of laughter and tears, before she fell into his arms and kissed him to the applause of a thrilled crowd. To balloons and confetti falling from the rafters and littering the ice. To performers skating in circles around them, wrapping them in streamers as Troy slipped the ring on her finger.

She pulled back, brushing confetti from his hair, laughing. "God, I love you."

"Mmm, baby, I swear every day I couldn't love you more. Then I do."

He kissed her again, then picked her up, wrapped his arms around her, and skated around the rink with her while the cast and crew served cake and drinks to the audience.

At the first opportunity, he skated off the ice and ducked out of sight behind a stage curtain and pulled her in for a longer, deeper kiss, and she understood why he'd taken her off the ice.

He broke away to drag in air, his smile so wide, so joyful. "The ring isn't your birthday present."

She combed her fingers through his hair and pressed her mouth to his throat. She wanted to eat him. "No?"

"No. We leave for Turks and Caicos in an hour. A week of tropical bliss—that is your birthday present."

Giselle pulled back, grinning, dizzy and dreamy, unable to place the location—maybe somewhere near the Bahamas? Bermuda? "Turks and Caicos?"

"Turks and Caicos," he whispered, diving in for another kiss. "My angel deserves a little slice of heaven now and then."

She fisted his hair and kissed him hard, stroking his mouth with all the need built up over the days and nights they'd spent apart on the road, before pulling back and meeting his eyes deliberately. "Hmm. I bet we'll even find time to sneak in a little lick of hell into that slice of heaven. Devils need love too."

Her devil agreed with a laugh that mirrored the hot curve of his mouth and the burning kiss that followed.

Dear Reader,

Thanks for reading *Relentless*, book 4 in the Renegades series! This was an intensely emotional and sexy story to write, and I hope you enjoyed Troy and Ellie's story. Stay tuned for more Renegades! Sign up for my newsletter for notices of new releases, sales and other special deals and giveaways at: http://www.SkyeJordanAuthor.com/newsletter.

If you enjoyed *Relentless*, I would appreciate it if you would help others enjoy this book, too.

Recommend it. Please help other readers find this book by recommending it to friends, readers' groups and discussion boards.

Review it. Please tell other readers what you liked or didn't like about this book by reviewing it at one of the major retailers, review sites or your blog.

Until next time, happy reading!
Skye

CHECK OUT MORE OF JOAN'S & SKYE'S BOOKS

Phoenix Rising Series
(Romantic Suspense with paranormal
elements written as Joan Swan)
FEVER
BLAZE
RUSH
SHATTER

Covert Affairs Series
(Romantic Suspense written as Joan Swan)
INTIMATE ENEMIES
FIRST TEMPTATION
SINFULLY SCANDALOUS

Renegades Series
(Hot Contemporary Romance written as Skye Jordan)
RECKLESS
REBEL
RICOCHET
RUMOR
RELENTLESS

CONNECT ONLINE

Web
http://www.SkyeJordanAuthor.com

Facebook
https://www.facebook.com/SkyeJordanAuthor

Twitter
http://www.twitter.com/Skye_Jordan

Made in the USA
Lexington, KY
08 April 2017